How
We
Danced

Deborah Serravalle

CACTUS RAIN
PUBLISHING

Arizona USA

How We Danced

Published by Cactus Rain Publishing, LLC
San Tan Valley, Arizona, USA
www.CactusRainPublishing.com

ISBN 978-0-9962812-3-2

Proofreading by Certified Proofreader Anita Beery at AnitaBeery.com
Cover Design by Ali Purser Hie Communications
Brantford, Ontario Canada N3R 6A8

Published September 1, 2016
Published in the United States of America

Dedication

Twisted roots, strong branches and sweet fruit
For my big, messy, beautiful family.
Lang may yer lum reek!

Acknowledgments

It is often said that writing is a lonely endeavour. To some extent this is true. The most helpful tool in my writer's kit has been my family, friends, mentors, teachers and associates. If it wasn't for this support, I would not have completed one draft of this novel, never mind the gazillion versions that I did write. This writer has never felt alone. I thank God for each of you.

Another assumption about the publishing process is that it is painful, filled with angst and challenges. No doubt some authors have had a difficult experience. Thankfully for me, I landed with Cactus Rain Publishing. Nadine Laman has been a gem to work with. Her integrity, hard work, due diligence, combined with her obvious desire to ensure that I am happy, has made my publishing experience an exceedingly pleasant one.

It's often said one shouldn't judge a book by its cover. Still, it's important. I confess to having picked up and purchased novels because I felt drawn to the cover. For this reason, I am indebted to Ali Purser Hie, who designed the cover of *How We Danced*. I believe you captured the essence of the people and story contained within. Thank you!

The Great Canadian Book Club participants read a very early draft of this novel. Advice from readers is critical, and I certainly appreciated the passionate, honest feedback I received from Carol Ross, Alicia Snell, Jen Russell, Sue Hanna, Louise Johnston, Jennifer Scully, Maria Montini, Gabrielle Fredette, Lindsay Hanna-Brindle, Sarah McLoughlin, Barb Scully, and Norma Copeland. Perhaps we can reconvene to discuss the final version you helped produce.

The Writer Gals, Dawn Boshcoff, Michelle Morra-Carlisle, Grace Cherian and Sylvia May. Because of you, I not only write, I fiddle. I thank you, my neighbours may not. Your input was invaluable, and I hold dear our time together and continued friendship.

The Thursday Evening Writers' Group, Jim Bennett, Amy Corbin, Dr. Claire Carver Dias, Rory and Janice d'Eon, Steve Donnelly, Sylvia McNicoll, Jennifer Maruno, Chelsea Rainford and Gisela Sherman. Your feedback and friendship were crucial to the writing of this novel. Thank you for taking me in.

A special thank you to Jennifer Maruno, dear friend and mentor, who read the finished manuscript of *How We Danced*, and offered excellent advice on the structure. Gisela Sherman likewise read at least two versions of the story, each time giving helpful, critical reviews. Gisela also taught the novel writing course at McMaster University. Not only did

I learn the fundamentals of the form in her class, I made a lifelong friend. Thank you, McMaster!

Dr. Claire Carver Dias and I formed a writing partnership that saw me through a big chunk of major rewrites during my time with the Humber College Correspondence Program in Creative Writing. Claire's keen intellect and love of the written word saved me, and the novel. I am forever indebted to Claire and her kind tolerance of my crippling self-doubt.

My mentor at Humber College's Correspondence Program in Creative Writing, David Adams Richards, generously shared his knowledge of the craft with me. I am also indebted to The Writer's Trust of Canada for a scholarship which allowed me to participate in this program.

Award-winning Canadian author Gail Anderson-Dargatz offers writing camps and mentorship programs. Gail's exceedingly kind, honest criticism of my work, at the beginning of this process, was indispensable. Gail taught me what it means to rewrite, to embrace it, that writing is rewriting.

When it comes to writing programs, Brian Henry and his Quick Brown Fox Creative Writing Courses and Workshops are well-known in Southern Ontario. Brian teaches his students to never give up. I owe Brian a big "Thank You," for it was his voice I heard whenever I was discouraged.

Before sending the manuscript out into the world, it had a stopover with editor Allister Thompson for a substantive review. I am forever grateful to Allister for his affirmation and insightful comments. Small changes, big results. The only bit of advice I didn't accept from him was the suggestion I change the spelling of my character's name.

Having the love and support of friends has meant the world to me. Carol Ross listened while we ran and ran and ran and ran. Louise Johnston likewise listened as I prattled on about characters and storyline while we worked and worked. Emilia Doro Romano was always willing to run off a hard copy—or several—for me, even though she's not interested in "The Geller." Above and beyond, Josie Giovenco Robinson first believed in me. I have not forgotten.

Alicia Snell is the closest thing to a fairy godmother a writer could have. This woman has pushed, pulled, encouraged, threatened, subsidized, fund-raised, read, plotted (in a good way) and listened to me for years now. She's fed me, drank with me, cried with me and, most of all, laughed with me. Our connection goes beyond friendship. I am so grateful for your love and support. Words fail me. Imagine that!

When I asked my niece, Ali Purser Hie, for help revamping my website, I underestimated the extent of her graphic design skill and willingness to help. The opportunity to work together on the details of my brand has been an unexpected bonus. We are kindred spirits and I am grateful for your love and support. http://www.deborahserravalle.com

Life would not be worth living without my family. Many thanks go to my children and their spouses, Kyle and Lydia Mongiardi, and Jennifer and Rob Scully. You inspire and encourage me every day. To the Grands, Sean, Cohen, Andrew and Hailey, who think all Nana does is cook, Surprise! You guys are the frosting on top.

My deceased parents show up, in one form or another, throughout this story. Make no mistake, it is fiction. Still, I unabashedly stole some of their character traits, occupations, interests and expressions. That's what writers do. We're thieves and liars. Rest peacefully, Ron, Lucy and Mike. Thank you for it all. And for Laura, I'm glad you're here to read the final product.

Finally, a special and well-deserved thank you to my long-suffering husband, Eugene Serravalle, who doesn't read fiction but who has nonetheless loved, supported, encouraged and celebrated with me at every turn and in every way imaginable during the writing of *How We Danced*. Hold on dear, 'cause here we go again.

How
We
Danced

Deborah Serravalle

❀ ❀ ❀

CHAPTER 1

When Alastair arrived at the Legion for his weekly game of billiards, the hall was surrounded by squad cars and police tape. He braked at the parking entrance and sat for a moment wondering what had happened. The policeman waved him on. He had no choice but to drive away. That's when he spotted the guys on the corner, just outside the tape barrier behind a mound of grey, ploughed snow. They saw him, too, and pointed towards a parking lot across the street.

Car parked, he waited for a break in traffic, eventually crossing the street to reach his friends. He walked by the narrow divide between the Legion and the next building. A gust of air circled his feet, spiralled up his legs and torso. He cringed and turned his back on the dark chasm. Moments later he joined the guys.

"What's going on?" Alastair's breath rose like smoke. He rubbed his hands together and stomped his feet. These days he felt the cold more.

"Peter's dead. They found him out back of the hall, his head bashed in with some kind of pipe." Duffy sniffed and wiped his nose.

"Peter?" Confused, Alastair stared at Duffy.

"You know," Duffy sounded exasperated, "Peter, the faggot."

"Really?" Thinking perhaps this was Duffy's idea of a joke, Alastair looked to Steve and Gord, but they nodded in agreement with Duffy. This was no prank. Alastair rubbed his bum leg; it ached. He recalled the arc of the steel pipe and the crack of his shin bone breaking. Peter hadn't wielded the pipe, but it was still his doing. "What a horrible way to die." Suddenly dizzy, he closed his eyes.

"Steady, there." Steve grabbed hold of Alastair's elbow.

Alastair pulled away, managing a weak smile. "Thanks, Steve. I'm fine." Sweat broke out on Alastair's forehead. He wiped it off, and turned to Duffy. "How do you know all this?"

"We were already inside," Duffy said. "I was at the bar. You were late; we thought maybe you weren't coming, so Steve and Gord decided to set up. That's when the new manager, Wilson, came running up the back stairs hollering, and we went out."

Duffy shuddered. "I'm sorry that I did."

"Poor bugger." Gord shook his head back and forth.

Duffy shut his eyes. "I can still see him. What a mess, blood everywhere."

"What I don't get," Steve adjusted his glasses, "is who'd want to hurt poor old Peter, of all people."

"Are you kidding me?" Duffy screwed up his face. "For years we've laughed off his bullshit. Most men don't take kindly to having their arses groped. I'm surprised he lasted this long. He's lucky AIDS didn't carry off the likes of him years ago."

Alastair's stomach dropped. Before retirement, and their weekly round at the Legion, they used to stop after work at the King Eddie or The Red Lion for a beer. That's how they all met, although Peter had been on the fringe. Those landmarks were gone, now Peter was, too. Alastair wasn't sorry. Still, such a violent end seemed unfair. Even for Peter.

"That's uncalled for. Anyone can get AIDS," Gord said. "And Peter never groped any of us. You're exaggerating."

"Not much." Duffy looked at Alastair. "Right?"

Alastair glared at Duffy then looked away. "I'm going home."

"Don't you want to stay? Find out what happened?" Steve pulled his frayed toque lower on his head.

Alastair lifted a shoulder. "What for?"

"To get some answers," Duffy said. "It's not every day one of your friends gets murdered."

2

How We Danced

He struggled to keep his expression neutral. Peter wasn't his friend, nor had he been Duffy's.

A young blonde woman in tall leather boots came up beside them and stopped, phone to her ear. "Gotta go," she said, and then dropped the mobile into her handbag. "What's going on?" She looked from one man to the other.

As his three friends huddled around her, Alastair spotted a familiar young boy leaning against a building across the street by the parking lot. His head was cocked to one side, watching. Alastair wondered if this time he was real. Spotting a break in traffic, he decided to find out. But when he stepped forward, the intermittent pain that had sent him to the doctor returned.

"Where you going?" Duffy's loud voice followed him, fading like The Boy, when he reached the halfway point.

On the drive home, Alastair considered that at about the time Peter's head was being bashed in, his doctor was pronouncing Alastair good as dead. Eventually the pain would settle in, escalate; that was a concern, but the doctor had assured him there were drugs to help. The problem wasn't now, while he appeared well. Once cancer was announced, he'd be doomed. Shadowed smiles, furtive glances, brows curled with pity. He didn't want to be that man. He had time and he planned to spend it well.

Compared to Peter, Alastair supposed he was lucky. He could prepare his wife, put his affairs in order. When he thought of his daughter Jennifer, her husband Cameron and their two girls, his breath caught. He'd shield them as long as he could.

※ ※ ※

Lily sat across from Alastair as he watched TV. In healthier days, he'd filled the big recliner. Today he looked small, bordering on frail. No matter what she fed him, day by day a little more of him disappeared. The odd thing was, until he'd told her he was ill, other than a cough, he'd appeared well. But once he'd unburdened his secret, a floodgate had opened, letting loose his body's resistance.

In hindsight, perhaps there had been signs she'd missed. Or ignored. But now there was no denying it—her husband of fifty years was dying.

"Is it tea time?" Alastair interrupted her thoughts.

Lily got up, pleased he wanted something, even if it was only a cup of tea. "I've some nice chocolate digestives." She visualized the biscuits she'd bought earlier in the day, stacked in the cookie tin Jennifer had given them, a golden anniversary present.

Alastair turned back to the TV. She'd bring the biscuits, knowing full well he wouldn't eat them.

Waiting for the kettle to boil, she hummed the tune to the "Anniversary Song." They'd danced to it that night, maybe not as well as in the old days, but they'd done fine. She ran a hand over the cookie tin and sang part of the refrain.

At their party someone had asked them to reveal their secret of a long and happy marriage. She'd turned to Alastair, saw her confusion mirrored in his eyes. On impulse she'd said, "Commitment." He smiled and took the piece of cake Jennie handed him. Perhaps the answer came easily because she was on the spot. But once she said it, she knew it was true.

"What about love?" the neighbour's teenage granddaughter, Ali, asked.

Lily stood beside the young girl, a plate of cake extended, longing in her eyes. A memory. Not Alastair, David. Longing in his eyes, her hand on his chest, and the rhythm of his heart beneath her fingers.

With years of practice Lily pushed the image down and brought another forward. A telephone call, a final good-bye.

"Love," she answered, "without commitment means little."

Ali made a face. "That's not very romantic."

Lily smiled sadly and placed the plate of the cake in Ali's hand. Perhaps her answer had disappointed her daughter as well. Or perhaps she understood. Lily prayed that wasn't the case.

She threw two tea bags into the pot, poured in the boiling water and set it on the tray along with the cups, saucers and cookie tin. Alastair was waiting. She wouldn't let him down. He was always there for her. She pushed the kitchen door open with her bottom and walked down the hall towards the living room.

CHAPTER 2

Not wanting to disturb, Jennifer stood quietly inside the doorway of her parents' bedroom. Their dressers and occasional chairs had been shoved against the wall to make way for the changes. Closest to her stood an old Duncan Fyfe table with an incomplete jigsaw puzzle on it. As she watched her mother spoon broth into her father's mouth, she marvelled that her mother hadn't dismantled the puzzle. It was an odd thing for her to preserve.

But her parents' behaviour was no longer predictable. The malignant force of her father's illness had transformed them. They even looked different. Her mother's eyes, once burnished walnut, had lost their lustre. Sweatpants and fleece tops replaced the skirts and crisp cotton blouses she had always preferred.

The ruddy, freckled complexion that followed her father into his senior years had paled to an almost translucent grey—as had his fiery red hair. The proud aquiline nose on his sunken face now appeared hawkish. Birdlike, he roosted on a nest of pillows in the newly installed hospital bed, its metal railings and complex controls an austere contrast to the ornate mahogany dressers, bed tables and overstuffed chairs cluttering the room.

Observing them like this, she had gleaned snippets of their lives they had kept from her. And from each other. Though never enough to complete the picture, they were like the fractured puzzle; black gaps remained where key pieces should be. Determined to stay in control of her destiny, she'd once vowed never to marry.

Then Cameron came along and her resolve weakened. She loved him, and he seemed to need her. As it turned out, marriage suited her. She took the lead in their relationship, managing their careers and their lives. After Lindsay and Emma were born, Cameron suggested she give up teaching or at least go part-time, but the idea of losing her independence made her anxious. As did the prospect of too much down time.

She preferred supervising a whirlwind of schedules and activities. To do this, she broke the day into hours; the hours were halved and then quartered. Each slot was filled, accounted for. She used a checklist and marked off her progress throughout the day. She was good at being busy. Everyone said so. The days when she fretted about her parents were forgotten. Another life. Until now. But here she was again, right back at the beginning. Trying to fill the empty space and solve the puzzle.

Lily wiped Alastair's chin. "There we go."

Jennifer smiled. One constant was Mammy's accent. Daddy's, too. Even after many years in Canada, they sounded like they just stepped off the boat from Scotland. Like many couples after the war, they immigrated to Canada for a better life. No doubt much had changed for them, but not their accents. It was good to have that; a reminder of their roots, and hers.

Still, she was confused by the novel compassion between them. It seemed as incongruent as the rearranged furnishings. The enigma of her parents' bond twisted tighter, knotting her gut with doubt. That was why she'd resumed waiting and watching. She was looking for a crack in her mother's compassion, a tear in her father's tenderness.

Jennifer cleared her throat and walked into the room.

Lily turned around. A smile lit her face. "Oh Jennie, I never heard you come in. What a surprise! Shouldn't you be in class?"

"It's a Professional Development Day. I knew I was finishing early, so I decided to stop by for a quick visit." Jennifer bent to kiss her mother's cheek.

"It's nice to see you." Lily folded the tea towel on her lap.

Jennifer winked at her father. "Hey Daddy, how are you?"

"I'll do, lassie." Alastair eased further into his tower of pillows.

"Can I help?" Jennifer asked.

"No thanks, hen. We're done." Lily moved the tray to the side and stood. "Let's make you more comfortable." She lifted Alastair's head and removed a pillow from the mound.

He gazed at his wife as she performed this simple task, lifting a bony hand to caress her arm. Lily kissed his forehead and then straightened the bedclothes.

Jennifer looked away.

As her mother breezed past with the lunch tray, Jennifer approached her father. Eyes closed, a slight smile lifted the edges of his parched lips. From a nearby collection of towels and swabs and bottles and rubs, she took a washcloth and dipped a corner into the tumbler of water on the bedside table. She pressed the moistened cloth to his mouth. When his lips parted Jennifer thought he would speak, but his eyes remained closed. She wondered if he were already asleep.

"Come on, we'll let him rest for a bit," Lily called.

Jennifer started like a child caught stealing and dropped the cloth. She followed her mother to the kitchen. She took her place at the table while Lily cleared the lunch tray and wiped it.

Dirty pots, pans, plates and glasses were piled next to the sink, already overflowing with dishes. Bread, jars and cans cluttered the counter. This was not her mother's the tidy kitchen.

Jennifer tried to keep the alarm from her voice. "It looks as though a rest wouldn't hurt you, either." She stood, pushed up her sleeves and headed for the sink. "I'll do the dishes."

"Please don't, Jennie. I'd rather we just visit. I'll get to them later. All I need is a cup of tea to perk me up. Would you like one?" Lily put the kettle on the stove.

Jennifer sat down. "No, I'm fine. Thanks."

Lily opened the cupboard door that housed her collection of cups and saucers. Even at forty-two, the excitement Jennifer felt as a child stirred as the doors swung open and revealed the delicate jumble of china. It was the same collection they used for tea parties. Back then they sipped milky tea from the delicate cups while Jennifer posed her dolls at the table. But it was never as much fun as she hoped. Between her mother's prolonged sighs and distracted glances at the clock, Jennifer had gagged down a lunch of gelatinous scrambled eggs or slimy sardine sandwiches that her mother prepared for the occasion.

Lily set the floral cups and saucers on the table.

"Why didn't you let me know you needed help? And groceries, I could have picked up a few things and dropped them off," Jennifer said.

"You have enough to do. I think your father and I can survive a couple of days."

Jennifer brushed stray crumbs into her palm, avoiding a nick in the plastic tablecloth as she swept and scooped. *Why is she always so stubborn*, Jennifer thought as she got up and put the crumbs into the crammed garbage bin. "You can't go on like this. You need help."

Lily sat and poured her tea. "I have help. The home care lady comes every week."

"It's not enough. Look at this place." Jennifer returned to the table. "It's a 24-hour job to care for someone who's dying."

Lily flinched and took a sip from the steaming cup before answering. "He doesn't want to go to hospital."

"What Daddy wants and what's needed are two different things." Jennifer leaned forward. "How could you make such a promise?"

Lily's teacup clacked against the saucer. She refilled it and added a little milk.

Jennifer slid back and ran a hand through her hair. "I'm only looking out for your best interests, and Daddy's."

"I suppose." Lily kept her eyes lowered.

"What does that mean? What other possible motive could I have for suggesting you admit Daddy to hospital?" A frisson of guilt lifted the fine hairs on Jennifer's arms.

Lily slumped back in her chair, closed her eyes and took a long gulp of the hot tea.

"Look at you. You're exhausted. And it's only going to get worse."

"I know."

"Why do you always do that?" Jennifer's cheeks flushed.

"What?" Lily frowned.

"You don't listen to me."

"Of course I do …"

"No, Mammy, you don't. Whenever there's a problem, no matter what I say, you nod and agree and then do what you like."

"Jennie, don't be angry with me." Lily's voice cracked and her face crumpled.

Jennifer rushed to her mother's side and crouched down. "Please don't cry. I didn't mean to hurt your feelings. It's just that I'm frustrated."

Jennifer wanted to make things right. A bit frantic, she looked about for inspiration. Again she noticed the mound of unclean dishes. Only this time the pile appeared higher, more cluttered and a lot dirtier. Bits of dried food clung to the surfaces; forks and knives stuck out at odd angles. No wonder her mother was touchy. Anyone would be near tears in this mess.

"I'll tell you what." Jennifer stood up. "If I clean up, you'll feel better." In two strides she was at the sink, running water and firing dish soap onto the heap. "After I finish, maybe we could go talk to Daddy. Explain. I'm sure he doesn't want you collapsing."

CHAPTER 3

Alastair pulled himself up in bed and looked around the room. Lily and Jennifer were gone, but he could hear them talking in the kitchen.

Without them the room was empty. He wished they hadn't left. Even if he didn't participate, he enjoyed listening. For a moment he considered filling the silence with the TV, but reached for the newspaper instead.

On the front page, near the bottom, a small headline caught his eye: *Two Charged in Legion Beating Death.* Alastair's mouth went dry, and he quickly scanned the article. *Two local men have been charged with second degree murder in the death of Peter Maynard, 68, in December of last year.*

Good, he thought. Someone needed to pay. Alastair was surprised, both by his outrage at Peter's murder and his relief that the killers had been apprehended, especially since he had never liked Peter.

Alastair went back to the article, read it thoroughly this time. It contained comments from a local group speaking out about violence against gay people. The police chief was quoted, "You have our full support. This type of violence against innocent citizens will not be tolerated. Not on my watch."

Alastair threw the paper aside.

How We Danced

Years ago now, during a series of police raids, gay men were entrapped and publicly humiliated. Alastair remembered reading the articles about the trials. At the time he'd felt a strange mixture of relief—thank God he wasn't involved—and pity for one particular family guy. Innocent or guilt-ridden, the wretched sucker had pulled over on the highway and shot himself. The chief might have been a rookie then. He could have set up the camera or watched the surveillance tapes. Alastair wondered if anyone on the existing Force ever gave that man a second thought.

It was around the time of those raids that Alastair first met Peter. He often turned up at the King Eddie where Alastair went after work. He found Peter's flamboyance obnoxious and did his best to avoid him. Unfortunately, one evening Peter went too far.

He had sidled up to Alastair at the bar and, in a loud voice, started offering personal information Alastair had no interest in knowing. Then Peter began asking him questions and making embarrassing comments. "Where do you work? I've seen you around. I'm always here, if you need company."

A picture of a humiliated man Alastair had read about in the paper flashed across his mind. One of eighteen arrested for sex offences whose names were published in the newspaper; the man, alone and defeated, committed suicide in his car. Alastair couldn't shake the thought of him.

Agitated, he turned his back on Peter and sipped his draught. Someone nearby sniggered. Another joined in. Whispers. Kissing sounds. Alastair imagined the men nudging each other, laughing at him. He glanced over his shoulder. Peter was still there, hand on his hip, waiting. Alastair's embarrassment flared to anger.

He spun around. "Piss off!"

Peter turned a bright shade of red. The men around them chuckled and then went back to their beers.

Alastair had stared Peter down for a few seconds, but looked away when he saw tears filling Peter's eyes. Ashamed, Alastair had turned back to the bar, downed his beer.

"You'll be sorry," Peter had said.

And he'd been right. Alastair had been sorry, many times since.

Breathing heavily, Alastair reached for his newspaper. He folded it over, rolled it up and smashed the wall. The sound was dull, impotent. Unsatisfied, he whacked the wall harder and harder. Gasping for air, he lifted the paper higher and higher, hitting the wall again and again and again.

※ ※ ※

"Wait—" Jennifer turned towards the door. "Is that Daddy calling?"

Both she and her mother stopped to listen.

"Lily?" Her father's voice was choked.

An electric chill surged through Jennifer's chest. Lily made a dash for the bedroom. Jennifer followed. When she reached the door, the rancid smell of vomit hit her like a slap and she took a step back.

Within seconds Lily had the top sheet and blanket stripped off the bed and piled on the floor. Helping Alastair sit up, Lily swung his legs around until he was perched at the edge of the bed. His pyjama top was soiled. Lily removed it and threw it onto the growing heap of dirty laundry.

"I'm sorry," Alastair moaned.

"Nonsense, it can't be helped." Lily pulled Alastair's undershirt over his head. "Jennie," she called out as she worked, "get a warm facecloth."

"Oh—of course." Jennifer headed to the bathroom, berating herself for acting like a paralysed voyeur. Waiting for the water to run hot, she inhaled a deep, cleansing breath. The high-pitched whine of plumbing pipes accompanied the soft rhythmic cadence of water on porcelain. Water soaked the facecloth and pulsed over her wrists and hands, flowing off the tips of her fingers, where it finally spiralled down the drain. Face upturned, Jennifer swallowed tears and imagined her father's cancer funnelling away with the water.

Jennifer returned to her parents' room, her father was nestled on a stack of pillows, hands folded over a freshly turned top sheet. At the bottom of the bed, a clean pyjama top was laid out. When she looked at her father, he stared back with an expression as shattered as his complexion. He opened his mouth to speak. Jennifer waited. Alastair swallowed and cleared his throat. Another few seconds passed. Finally, he spoke.

"Your mother's taken the laundry downstairs."

"Oh, okay. I thought—" She paused and let out the breath she'd been holding. "Never mind." Straightening her back, she stepped forward. "Here you go. I brought a warm facecloth." She held it out at arm's length.

Alastair closed his eyes and turned away.

Sitting on the edge of the bed, she placed a hand on her father's shoulder. Surfacing bones jabbed her palm, their message sharp and urgent.

Alastair turned to face her.

Jennifer pressed the heated facecloth onto his brow and then smoothed his cheeks and chin. His eyes closed. As she cleaned crusty debris from the edges of his mouth and then wiped his chest, she pretended not to see the tears sliding down the side of his face and onto the pillow.

She didn't hear her mother come up beside her and started when Lily placed a hand on her back. "Thanks, Jennifer."

She got up and passed the cloth to her mother, who took her place at the bedside. Then she walked over to the desk and grabbed a pen and note pad. She wrote swiftly, digging the pen into the page.

"Jennie?" Alastair was trying to sit up.

"Lie down," Lily said. She rearranged the blankets. "She's just at the desk writing out a grocery list."

Hearing the tone in her mother's voice, Jennifer looked up from scribbling her list and saw Lily's stern expression. Anxious for her father, Jennifer couldn't focus on what more to include on the list, or leave off. She felt like a kid again, a Daddy's girl, as her mother had called her. When Jennifer was about eight, she realised what that meant.

Daddy had taken her under his tool belt and introduced her to woodworking. She could still see him back then, healthy and vigorous with that wide leather contraption strapped around his waist; metal box in hand, full of nuts, bolts, screws and washers. From the outset, she had loved the dusty workroom, with his tacky collection of nautical prints plastered on every wall.

Together they'd made a small table, a birdhouse and a decorative mirror. Daddy had included her in regular household repairs: the screen door, the garden fence and shed. Because of their projects she'd learned how to paint, stain and sand; how to wield a screwdriver, a hammer and chisel. She'd planed wood, loving the curlicues that fluttered to the ground and the sweet, smoky smell of cedar. When she was old enough, he'd admitted her to the screaming society of power tools: the jigsaw, miter saw, router and drill with interchangeable bits that she called stingers. They'd yell and laugh above the racket, and when the noise became too much, her mother would flash the basement light. Throughout this process they'd fashioned a strong relationship. Even as a youngster she had known it was special.

But she learned that it came with a price. One afternoon, when she and Daddy were puttering away in the workshop, she turned to find her mother standing at the door, a basket of laundry held at her waist. Her expression was blank, yet her eyes were filled with a sadness that alarmed Jennifer. Before she could speak, her mother had turned and walked up the basement stairs.

Unable to say why, Jennifer hadn't pursued her. But she had felt sorry for her mother. Worried too; that she had done something wrong and that Mammy was angry. After her mother went upstairs, Jennifer went to the laundry tub and, following an urge she didn't understand, washed her hands over and over and over, until her father had called her back to help him.

After that, every now and then, she'd catch a glimpse of Mammy watching them at work. On her mother's face was that same, silent, sad yearning. Then she'd disappear. It seemed the closer she got to her father, the farther she was from her mother. She hadn't wanted Mammy to be left out. But neither had she known how to fix it. Or if anything was indeed broken.

"Right then, I'm off to the grocery store," Jennifer addressed Lily, her tone cheerful.

From Alastair's bedside, Lily nodded.

"Bye, Daddy."

Alastair opened his eyes. "Kiss those lassies of yours for their old granddad."

The sudden stab of grief was so intense, Jennifer opened her mouth to respond. After a moment she only said, "I'll be back."

How We Danced

"We'll be here." Lily sat down, her back to Jennifer.

❋ ❋ ❋

Lily got up from Alastair's bedside, went to the window, and drew the curtain. She heard the front door close, and saw Jennifer on the porch fumbling with her car keys. She wasn't looking where she was going as she jogged towards the stairs. How many times had Lily asked her not to run down those stairs, to pay attention to where she was going? The risers were steep, and the space between the slats of the tread was too wide. Lily glanced at Jennifer's high heels. If she caught one, she'd go flying. Jennifer knew that. A tumble down those stairs had ruined her grade eight graduation dance and her summer.

Jennifer had been so excited that afternoon. Ceremonies over, summer vacation underway, with high school to look forward to in September, she had been heading out to a party; her friends were waiting in a car.

"Bye, Mammy!" Jennifer called as she ran out onto the porch.

Lily went to the door, caught the screen before it slammed. "Jennifer, wait—"

There was nothing Lily could do, no time to even call out a warning. She stood helpless, watching as Jennifer charged down the first couple of steps, stumbled, tumbled, and landed in a heap on the stone walkway below. Lily had known the moment she'd seen Jennifer's twisted arm that it was broken.

Now Jennifer was running down the same stairs. All Lily could do was watch and wait, brace herself for whatever happened. Lily pulled her cardigan tighter and then returned to her place beside Alastair.

CHAPTER 4

Jennifer's heels tapped her escape down the stairs like a frantic message. Hopping into the sanctuary of her car, she put the key in the ignition. She sat back and took several measured breaths before turning it. The sixties Turtles tune blasted the space, *So happy together* ... She reached over and silenced it. *I don't think so*. Throwing the car into reverse, she backed out of her parents' driveway.

At the corner, she waited for a break in traffic. As cars whizzed by, she tapped her foot, brushed dust from the dashboard, fiddled with the button on the gear shifter—anything to keep from bursting into tears. When traffic still didn't break, she sought distraction out the window. The street was huddled beneath the escarpment that ran the breadth of Hamilton. All about, winter-stripped trees were capped in the green pledge of summertime. Encouraged by this idyllic springtime vignette, she exhaled and joined the flow of traffic as if all was well in the world.

The light ahead turned red and she applied the brakes. An old woman pulling a shopping cart entered the crosswalk, and she recalled her mother's inability to get to the grocery store. If she'd realised how dire their situation had become, she would have insisted on helping sooner. Why hadn't her mother asked for help?

How We Danced

When the light changed, she moved forward. She wanted to turn the car around and tell her mother she was sorry for the way she'd acted; sorry for not noticing sooner they'd needed help.

That pitiful cry! Her father's strangled voice echoed in her mind, followed by a flashback of her mother throwing down the sheet and pyjamas reeking of vomit and God knew what else. Seized by a violent shudder, she attempted to purge the terrible picture and imagine something else—anything at all. But nothing worked. All she could think of was her parents.

The grocery store was just past the next intersection. With tears streaming down her face, she pulled into the lot. Instead of parking near the entrance doors, she drove in between the building and fence that lined the street and turned off the engine. Her parents needed her. And if she was going to be of any use to them, she had to get a grip on herself. She yanked out some tissues from a dusty box stuffed in the door cubby, sat back and blotted her cheeks. Enough. From this point forward, she'd step up and do her part. First thing tomorrow, she would talk to her jerk-of-a-department head and let him know what's going on and that she'd be leaving every day as soon as the bell rang. He would just have to deal with it. *Check.* Then she'd ask her assistant coach, Trish, to take over the soccer team; no problems there. *Check.* Tonight she'd make after-school arrangements for Lindsay and Emma so a few times a week she could go straight to her parents' place after work. *Check.* This evening she'd talk to Cam; fill him in on her plans, let him know how he could help. *Check.* There. She sat back and relaxed a bit, grateful for her lists. She loved them: Itemization, categorization, elimination. You could count on them. They put life in perspective, kept you in control.

Looking in the rear view mirror, she dried her eyes and blew her nose. Reflected there, beyond the fence, was her old school. Jennifer twisted around. She'd played on this lot as a kid. Was the slight hollow in the asphalt still here, where the ice slide appeared in winter? Craning her neck to get a better view, she was surprised to see the dip remained. Kids had lined up by the dozens, taking turns to skid its meagre length. Most times she hadn't been willing to stand out in the cold long enough to take a few turns. But one day, when she had been forced to stay late for detention, she had the slide all to herself.

Darlene and her gang had been waiting for her at the front doors when she was finally dismissed from school. Jennifer was hoping the freezing temperature and blowing snow would discourage them. No such luck. She knew they wouldn't believe she hadn't told on them about the smokes. But she hadn't. If she was going to do that, she would have answered truthfully when the teacher wanted to know where she *claimed* to have found the cigarettes, and not served the detention for having them on her. She wished she hadn't agreed to hold onto them for that idiot Darlene in the first place. Miss Coughlin said she was going to call and tell her parents, too.

To avoid Darlene and the girls, Jennifer ran from the front doors where she was supposed to exit after detention, to the side entrance, where she routinely left. Silently, she slipped out and bolted across the street, through the break in the fence and onto the grocery store parking lot. After a quick peek back to make sure she'd lost them.

Jennifer started walking across the snow-sprinkled asphalt. Her breath came in short puffs, forming smoky patches that disappeared behind her. Already her fingertips nipped from the cold. After taking off her mitts, she huffed warm breath into her cupped hands. It was then she slipped. Getting up, Jennifer brushed the snow from her hands. Then she scuffed her feet about, clearing the snow from the ice. With each step the icy patch grew longer. When the ice ran out she looked up. The strip was about fifteen feet long and three wide. Taking a few steps back, she launched herself down the stretch. At the end she turned around and did the same. It was exhilarating. Back and forth she went. But then she started to calculate how far back she needed to be to get the longest slide or the fastest. Eventually she figured out how to control the slide: knees slightly bent, sometimes crouched down. Every so often she scanned the lot to make sure Darlene wasn't there. It was starting to get dark, and she told herself she wouldn't stay much longer. But with each slide, the ice was getting smoother, shinier and more slippery. And it was so much fun without anyone else about.

How We Danced

Hot and sweaty, she took a break to pull off her hat and mitts and stick them in her pockets. That's when she noticed the car parked in the far corner. Behind the car a street lamp flickered on. Snowflakes shimmered in the stream of light, showering the roof and hood. There was someone in the driver's seat. Although Jennifer couldn't see a face, she knew it was a man, because he wore a wide-brimmed hat like her dad. Jennifer resumed her sliding, but with the stranger watching, it wasn't as much fun. Her mother was terrified of strangers. So much so that Jennifer had only disobeyed the *Never Talk to Strangers Rule* once. And that was when she had been too little to understand. Even still, every day when she left the house, her mother warned her not to talk to them. Sometimes Jennifer felt they lurked behind corners or shrubs, ready to lunge. Those were the days she walked rapidly to school.

It was getting late, she should go home. Besides, she imagined the car speeding over and the stranger's arm reaching out of the window and scooping her up and away. She pulled out her hat and mitts and put them on. As she did, the car started up and drove towards her. Heart pounding, a scream hovered at the back of her throat as the car approached but then turned towards the exit. The car was dark inside and she couldn't see the driver's face, only his profile. Turning quickly, and slipping only once, she left the parking lot the way she entered, through the fence and ran, ran, ran home.

Jennifer looked to see if, after all these years, the big gap in the fence was still there. It wasn't. The chain link had been repaired or replaced. Why was she wasting time recalling that ridiculous girl Darlene and a few stolen moments on an ice patch when she was a kid? Reaching into her purse, she got out her make-up bag, or what her girls called "the repair kit." From a travel-sized pouch, she pulled out a baby wipe and cleaned her mascara-streaked face. Then she removed the other items one by one and laid them on the console: foundation, blush, eyeliner, mascara, lip liner and lipstick. After she applied each product, she returned it to the make-up bag. With a final, satisfied glance in the mirror, she tucked the bag in her purse and got out the grocery list.

Driving the car closer to store entrance, Jennifer parked next to an SUV. Beside her was a young mother unloading a large, clumsy stroller. Careful not to hit her, Jennifer opened the car door. With envy, she noted the tenderness with which the woman lifted and then strapped in the sleeping child who woke just long enough to smile at her mother. Jennifer hoped the child would remember this moment. The mother looked up; she straightened and frowned. Jennifer realised only then she had stopped and was staring. How pathetic she must appear.

"Make sure she's strapped in good and tight," she said. "This lot is bumpy."

Red-faced, she turned back to her car, locked the door and headed into the grocery store.

❁ ❁ ❁

Light from the street lamp created its usual halo around the darkened blinds. The ticking of the clock in the hallway and Lily's gentle snoring were punctuated by the occasional whoosh of tires on wet pavement. Alastair had dozed earlier, as he did most afternoons, and now, during the night when he wanted to sleep, he couldn't. His senses were on high alert. Day and night, like his life, had been turned upside down.

Repositioning himself yet again, his hand grazed something trapped between the mattress and the wall. With an easy tug he pulled out the day's newspaper. He remembered the afternoon's drama when Jennifer was here, him throwing up after reading the article that Peter's killers had been arrested and charged. What a horrible day that had been, first his cancer diagnosis and then arriving at the Legion and learning they'd found Peter out back, beaten to death.

Alastair is walking away from the guys, crossing the street, The Boy is on the other side, watching, waiting, fading.

Why had The Boy shown up that day? For the most part, Alastair had come to accept the child's mysterious presence in his life. But his turning up then rankled. Wasn't his illness and a man's death enough to deal with? At this point, a reminder that his life wasn't what it should be seemed unnecessary, and futile.

Alastair's stomach clenched at the sudden memory of another boy. He pulled himself up against the headboard. Good

God, he hadn't thought of wee Andy in years. Why was he remembering him now?

He'd gone over it hundreds of times. There was nothing he could have done. His mammy had reassured him, as had Andy's. He was only a lad himself, and there had been too many of them, all bigger.

"Hey there, Nancy-boys!" Jock's raucous call had been unmistakable.

Alastair stopped and went rigid with anger.

"Don't turn around," Andy pleaded, "just keep walking."

Alastair and Andy, who was a year younger, had lived in the same Glasgow tenement their whole lives, their mothers went back and forth for tea. As long as Alastair could remember he'd looked out for Andy. No one had told him to, he just felt it was right.

He thought it unfair the way the other lads picked on Andy. After all, it wasn't his fault he had weak lungs. His mammy said it was because he'd been born before his time. Whatever the reason, Andy couldn't run farther than the front door without getting winded. Football with the rest of the boys was out of the question. Instead, Andy played house and dolls with the lassies who doted on him. He sang in the church choir, read books by the dozen, was the teacher's pet. Alastair took a few more steps, face flushed, his fists squeezed so tight his knuckles burned. He glanced sideways at Andy who looked ghost-like, all colour drained from his face, eyes wide with terror.

"You hard of hearing, Nancy-boys? Or just scairt?" Jock laughed.

Other lads joined in. Jock was never alone.

Something inside Alastair exploded. He stopped and spun around.

"No, no," Andy pulled at his arm.

"Come here, Jock McNally," Alastair said, "and I'll show you just how much of a Nancy-boy I am."

Sneering, Jock left the group of lads and walked forward until he was nose to nose with Alastair. The other boys, Alastair figured there were eight, formed a circle around them. He was aware of Andy pressed against his back.

"Here I am." Jock smiled and looked around the circle. He showed too much gum over a row of tiny, decayed teeth. He reminded Alastair of the rats that often found their way into the midden.

Jock was still smiling and looking about at his cronies when Alastair brought his fist back and jabbed the gummy grin off his face. Stunned, Jock took a step back. Blood oozed from his cut lip. All the boys were quiet as Jock put a hand to his mouth, wiped it and then looked at his bloodied fingers.

"Get him, lads," Jock hissed.

At his command, the boys woke from their reverie, rushed forward and grabbed Alastair by the arms and chest.

"We've got him!" someone yelled, as Alastair struggled to free himself.

Jock walked up to Alastair and spit in his face.

As the wet glob rolled down his cheek, Alastair spat back at Jock, who dodged the wet missile.

"Coward!" Alastair yelled.

Jock sucker-punched him in the belly. All the wind was driven from Alastair's lungs. For a long moment he couldn't draw a breath.

Smiling, Jock looked around and spied Andy gasping and crying. "Come here, you wee bufter."

When he was able to breathe, Alastair called out to Andy, "Run!"

Andy hesitated and Jock pounced. In seconds he had Andy by the scruff of his threadbare coat, his feet dangling mid-air.
"Pick on someone your own size," Alastair said. "Let him go. Fight me."

Ignoring Alastair, Jock brought Andy's face closer. The boy's eyes were squeezed shut and he was whimpering. Jock held him higher in the air and shook him. There was a tearing sound as Andy's coat ripped. When the front of Andy's trousers darkened, Alastair's heart sank in shame and sympathy.

Jock dropped Andy like a hot stone. "He's pissed himself," he laughed. "The shitebag's actually pissed himself."

Alastair struggled, but he couldn't break free from the band of jeering boys clutching him.

Andy curled himself into a ball. His sobs were barely audible over the hoots and hollers of the boys surrounding Alastair.

Jock prodded Andy with a foot. He flinched but didn't look up.

"Disgusting," Jock said as he brought his foot back and kicked Andy in the head.

The boys let out a collective gasp and Alastair broke free with a roar.

"Run!" one of the boys said. "He's kilt him."

Alastair rushed to Andy, saying, "Oh my God, oh my God." He rolled the boy onto his back, terrified of what he'd find. Andy's lashes fluttered and he came round. And then, as comprehension dawned, his eyes flew wide open, he shot up and frantically looked around.

"It's all right," Alastair had said. Cradling Andy, he'd sat back on his haunches and glanced about to make certain Jock and his gang of ruffians had left. "Let's get you home."

In the dim light, Alastair looked at the rolled newspaper he was still holding. He tried to unfurl it, but it wouldn't cooperate, the sheets curled inward. He wondered if Andy was still alive. They'd lost touch years ago. But the last Alastair heard, Andy had done well for himself; he worked at the bank and still sang in the choir. He married a nice lassie from the tenement row across the way, and they'd had three children. Alastair opened the newspaper, rolled the sheets in the opposite direction and forced them to lay flat. He folded the paper in half, quarters. Alastair sighed, tossed the newspaper aside and slid back down under the sheets. At least wee Andy had shown the bullying naysayers—he was no Nancy-boy.

❀ ❀ ❀

"Lily," Alastair rasped.

Hearing her name, she ascended from a sleep jumbled with people and places from the past. In dreams she was her younger self. Waking, she knew something was amiss.

Propped on an elbow, Alastair reached out and grasped her hand. "You were talking in your sleep."

"I was?" She blinked. When her vision cleared, she raised the recliner which was pressed beside his hospital bed. "I must have dozed off. What time is it?" She lifted the alarm clock and squinted.

"It's morning." He jerked his chin in the direction of the sunlit shade, grimaced and then lay back down. "Why aren't you in bed?"

She glanced across the room at the abandoned bed they'd shared for years. "I'm not the only one who talks in my sleep. You had a bad night."

"Oh."

"You don't remember?"

"Bits and pieces." He shielded his eyes with a forearm.

"Who's Erin?"

"Erin?" He uncovered his eyes and turned to her.

"You were mumbling. And then you asked for Erin. At least that's what it sounded like. It was then I grabbed a blanket and came over here." Lily had felt only curious when she'd asked the question. But she knew he wasn't telling the truth, and his feigned ignorance pushed her to the cusp of anger. Pressing her lips together, she slid forward and eased herself up. "Ow!" She stumbled.

"What's wrong?"

"Nothing." She rubbed her knee and did her best to suppress her irritation. The man was ill. She could hardly badger him about a name she *thought* she'd heard him cry out. "Do you have to go to the bathroom?"

"I do." He plucked at the bedspread.

"Would you like the urinal?" Lily wondered if she was mistaken about the name. Why would he lie to her? Especially now. Perhaps he'd said something else all together.

"No."

"It sure sounded as if this Erin was someone you knew." She sat on the bed. "Here, lean on me."

"I'm fine."

"You're not fine! You'll wind up on the floor and then what'll I do? Lean on me."

Alastair relented and placed his arm across her shoulders. Together they stood.

As she put her arm around his waist and steadied herself, she noted how easily she bore his weight. Until recently, he'd been the stronger one. She glanced down at his bare feet in sad disbelief; the skin was now tinged a worrisome grey hue. Although he was a big man, he'd always moved with grace. Just this past January they'd gone to a Robbie Burns Dinner and Dance. While other couples their age had shuffled around the dance floor, she and Alastair had effortlessly fallen into step with one another. During a beautiful waltz Lily had closed her eyes, and as Alastair whirled her round the floor, she pretended they were in their twenties again. She still found it difficult to believe, that in four months, their lives had gone from that to this.

"Much better. Now, can you step into your slippers?" She pointed with a toe. "They're right there."

For years they'd stood like this, arms wound around one another, poised to take the dance floor. Now it was she who led Alastair as they scuttled across the room and down the short hall towards the bathroom. He stopped and pressed his free hand against the wall.

"That's right, just take your time."

He nodded and then moved forward.

When they reached the bathroom she helped him onto the toilet. "Just call me when you're done." She left the door ajar.

She wanted a cup of tea, but instead opted to take advantage of Alastair being out of bed. With one ear listening, she fluffed his pillows, tucked in the sheets and folded back the bedspread. She decided that this would be the perfect time to give him a sponge bath. Lily pictured herself stripping him down, bit by bit, washing, rinsing, drying and dressing him in clean underclothes and pyjamas. How familiar she was with Alastair's body. And he with hers.

Gathering up an armful of towels from the linen closet, she thought about her life with Alastair and concluded that marriage, even one that lacked proper intimacy like theirs, at least allowed for practical understanding. Knowledge without knowing. She listened at the bathroom door. When she heard the toilet flush, she knocked. "Can I come in?"

"What do you want?"

She pushed the door open. Alastair was slumped over on the toilet, head on crossed arms resting on his knees. "For goodness' sakes! What's wrong with you this morning? You're not the only one who had a bad night." He sat up but turned his face away.

"Come on now." She tried to sound more encouraging than she felt. When he didn't move she placed the pile of towels on the counter. "Do you need help getting up?"

"It's a bad bloody day when your wife has to help you off the toilet."

"It could be worse. Think of all the poor folk that have no one." She moved in and assisted him to a standing position with one hand and, with a skill borne from child rearing, pulled his pyjama bottoms up with the other. They stood face to face.

"I don't want to die, Lily."

Stunned, she stared back at him. "Well you're not dead yet, and you're not dying today. Let's get you back to the room. I've freshened up the bed. We'll give you a sponge bath and change your pyjamas." Remembering the towels, she decided they were too much to manage, she'd come back for them.

She moved beside him and he put his arm around her shoulders. They made their way back into the hall.

About midway to the room Alastair stopped. "I'm sick of pyjamas."

"Fair enough. What would you like to wear?"

"My Rangers football jersey."

She laughed and risked a sideways glance at him. "With track pants?"

"That'll do."

CHAPTER 5

Jennifer swallowed the tea—her second cup this morning—and stared out her kitchen window. She needed to talk to Cameron, let him know what was going on with her parents. That's what she'd planned to do last night, once the kids were in bed. But he'd called to say he had to take a client out for a late dinner. She'd started to tell him then, but he seemed distracted by laughter in the background. "We can talk later," she'd said, when he asked her to repeat herself a second time.

"You okay, Mom?" Lindsay had asked.

She had been poised with her left index finger on the disconnect button; the handset dangled from her right palm.

"Of course," she'd smiled at her daughter and lifted the phone to her ear. "Daddy's working late. Go tell Emma we're ordering pizza."

The rest of the evening had been quiet. Tired, she'd gone to bed not long after the girls and flipped on the TV. Within minutes she'd drifted into a deep, dreamless sleep. She hadn't even heard Cam turn off the TV and slip in bed beside her.

Jennifer took a big gulp of tea. It was cold and bitter. She made a face and poured the remainder down the drain. The coffee she'd made for Cameron was ready. She listened for the sound of running water. Nothing. Assuming he was out of the shower, she poured two mugs and carried them upstairs, hoping this was a better time to talk.

From the landing she called out to the girls, "Get a move on, ladies. Cereal and milk's on the table."

Emma stepped into the hall. "You're not having breakfast with us?"

Jennifer looked at Emma, hand to hip; the image of her father. She glanced at the mugs. This might be her only chance to talk to Cam today. "Tell Lindz I said to get off the computer, please."

Jennifer nudged the bedroom door with her foot. As she entered the room, Cameron walked out of the closet with a tie slung around his neck and headed for the dresser.

"Hey, babe. Double-fisting the java this morning?"

She smiled. "Very funny."

The steam from the shower had drifted from the en suite into the bedroom, fogging up the mirror. Jennifer could see Cam's reflection, but she wasn't sure he could see her. He'd cleared only a small section for himself. She handed him a coffee.

"Thanks." He stopped knotting his tie and took a swig. "Ah, that's good." He put the mug down on the dresser, undid the partial knot and started again.

Jennifer recalled a time when Cameron would have shuddered at the thought of putting a tie on every day to join the corporate rat race.

"What happened to our dreams of opening our own business and working side by side?" Jennifer asked.

Cameron stopped struggling with his tie for a moment. "What brought this on?" He smiled and threw the thinner end of the tie over his shoulder.

Jennifer shrugged. "I don't know. Life's short and we had such dreams—"

"I understand, babe. And believe me, I'd like nothing more. But then we bought this house and had the girls. Speaking of which, why aren't you having breakfast with them?"

She moved his mug onto the coaster and set their forgotten dreams aside. "I need to talk to you about my parents."

"Shoot." He undid his tie and started again.

How We Danced

Jennifer splayed her fingers and tried to resist the urge to yank the tie from around his neck. "Turn around, I'll do it."

"It's fine," he continued tying the knot, "tell me what's going on." He glanced at the clock.

She looked at the reflection in the mirror; saw her own face peering over his shoulder, ashamed at the needy woman who was staring back. "If you're in a hurry—"

"I'm not." He turned to face her. "A meeting in the West End. Same crew as last night. That's all, but it can wait." He reached out and pulled her close. "Tell me about Lily and Alastair."

He was looking at her, ready to listen.

"Wait," he said. "Before you begin, I don't want to forget to tell you I'll be late again tonight." He smiled. "Okay, your turn."

Jennifer tried to form the words, but she was unable to concentrate. She did her best to ignore the asymmetrical knot, the misshapen tie.

"Jennifer?" Cameron bent his face to hers.

She knew she should just look up at him. "Please let me redo your tie. It's crooked."

"Fine." He shrugged and loosened the knot.

She spoke rapidly as she pulled, crossed and tucked the tie. She told him about the surprise visit she'd made to her parents' home the day before, the condition she'd found them and their home in, and how she planned to help. When she was finished, she patted the perfect Windsor knot. "As far as school goes, I'm speaking to my department head today. But some days I'll need your help with the girls—picking up and dropping off."

"Of course." He stuck a finger inside his collar and moved his head from side-to-side. "Just let me know— whatever, whenever. I'll help if I'm able."

"Okay." She wished she could say something meaningful. A word of thanks. But he was already walking away.

"Oh God, look at the time." He grabbed his suit jacket off the bedpost. Stopping at the door, he turned around.

In that moment she thought he was going to come back, take her in his arms and tell her what she needed to hear; that everything would be okay, they'd get through this together. And she'd tell him how grateful she was for him, for their family.

"We're done, right?"

"Yes."

Jennifer sat on their unmade bed and listened to him charge down the stairs. She heard him yell, "Bye, girls," and the front door open and close.

Rooted to the mattress, she thought about his promise, *I'll help if I'm able*, and questioned if it was a proper commitment or the doublespeak he offered clients. The dampness from the towel he'd thrown onto the bed leached through her pants. She jumped up, twisting round to assess the damage. Now she'd have to change. Angry, she walked into the en suite and flung the towel onto the heated drying rack. Then she snatched a fresh washcloth from the linen closet. After spraying disinfectant into the sink, she blasted the hot water and scrubbed it down until all the black specks of shaved stubble that reminded her of roach shit were gone.

❋ ❋ ❋

Alastair adjusted the sleeve cuff of his football jersey and glanced down at his sweatpants. Still comfortable, these clothes were a step up from pyjamas. The thought of never wearing anything but flannel again was depressing. The feel of it conjured the scent of hospital disinfectant and lumpy porridge. Come what may, the day was easier to face in sweats and a jersey. He hunkered down in his chair and switched on the TV and, out of habit, tuned it to the 24-hour news channel.

They were reporting that a young soldier had been killed in Afghanistan by a roadside bomb. Photos of the slain soldier with his wife and young son, in happier times, flashed on the screen. In one, his wife laughed while the little boy clung to his father's back like a monkey. Alastair was heartsick knowing the tyke would grow up without his old man. Another photo came on the screen, this time just father and son, the two of them kicking around a soccer ball, the child a bit older. Alastair leaned forward in his chair, squinted at the screen in disbelief. The child bore an uncanny resemblance to Johnny Stoneham!

Alastair turned to the window. He hadn't thought of Johnny or his family in years. The house they'd lived in was across the street, he could see it now, its outline softened through sheers. Poor Johnny had lost his father, too.

How We Danced

Johnny's parents, Big John and Diane, moved in about the same time as he and Lily. They hadn't been close; it was more a good morning wave or the occasional beer after mowing the front lawn.

All that changed when Big John died. Then he and Lily had stepped up to do what they could, even if it was only a sympathetic shoulder for Diane to cry on, someone to talk to.

Alastair recalled the first time they visited after Big John's passing. Lily was pregnant with Jennifer at the time, and Alastair felt protective. He'd gone mostly because he didn't want her, in that condition, to face Diane alone. He'd planned to offer his condolences and make a quick retreat once the ladies were settled, until he saw Johnny standing behind his mother looking bewildered and forlorn. Walking off and leaving the boy to listen to the women talk and cry just didn't seem right.

Alastair knew from their beers together that Big John, who had played football in his youth, had been a diehard Tiger-Cat fan. Maybe Johnny was, too.

Alastair smiled at the boy. "Do you own a ball?" he asked.

Johnny nodded.

"Go get it. We'll go to the park, leave the ladies to talk."

The edges of Johnny's mouth curved up, only a fraction, but enough that Alastair knew he'd done the right thing.

When Johnny came back downstairs with a ball that was meant more for the beach than the football field, Alastair didn't comment. Instead, he asked Johnny to cross the street with him and wait on the porch while he ran in to get his soccer ball.

At the park, they started with simple passes, back and forth, close enough to carry on a conversation.

"My dad didn't like soccer; he said it was for sissies."

Alastair shrugged. "He was a big man, your dad, better suited to football."

"He was a linebacker. Got hurt before he married my mom and had to quit. He said it was his one regret."

Johnny lifted his foot to kick the ball and missed.

Alastair smiled. It was obvious the child was parroting something Big John had said. Judging from the boy's slim build and manner, he favoured his mother. His comments left little doubt that he measured himself against his father's brawn. A tough spot for a boy.

"Try making contact with the side of your foot, not the toe. That's right."

The ball lifted, landing neatly at Alastair's feet.

"Well done."

Johnny face split into a grin.

"The trick is to find *your* game, what you're good at. Your dad was big and strong, perfect for a football linebacker where the strategy is to stop your opponent. Soccer, on the other hand, is a thinking man's game," Alastair tapped the side of his head, "and you need to be as nimble with your mind as you are with your feet."

"So you think soccer might be my game?"

"Could be." Alastair smiled, delighted at the upswing in Johnny's downcast demeanour. He knew firsthand how difficult life was for a boy deprived of a father's love and encouragement. If he was able to help, he would. "But as I said, it's a game of skill."

"Would you teach me, Mr. MacAulay? Then maybe I could try out for the school team."

Johnny's trust and faith in him were touching; Alastair agreed without hesitation.

"He scores!" Alastair shouted, the first time Johnny managed to deke by him and make it to the net.

When the boy charged over and threw his arms around him, Alastair was surprised. He patted the boy's slim back. "Your dad would be proud; well done, son."

Johnny stepped back, smile gone, and shrugged.

Alastair assumed bringing up Big John had shaken the boy. "I'm sorry if mentioning your dad upset you, Johnny."

Johnny kicked a bald spot in the grass. "I don't care." He kicked harder at the patch of dirt. Bits of earth flew.

Alastair put a hand on Johnny's shoulder. The smell of churned earth lay between them, heavy and pungent.

The boy stopped toeing the ground but kept his head down. "It's not that."

"Not what?" Alastair asked.

"I'm not sad because you brought up my dad."

"Okay." He waited.

Alastair had said upset, not sad; that was Johnny's interpretation. If Alastair was patient, the boy might explain. Or not. Alastair didn't want to push.

Johnny looked him in the eye. "I'm glad he's gone."

Alastair had not expected that. He tried to keep his expression neutral, his tone even, but he needed to clarify before the conversation went any further. "You're glad your father is gone?"

Tears welled in the child's eyes. "That's right. I don't miss him at all. Not even a little bit."

Alastair let out a sigh. "I see." He had asked for clarification. Now that he had it, what was he to say? "Let's go sit down, have a drink of water." He put his arm around the boy's shoulders and led him to the bench where they'd left their jackets.

They'd just sat down when Johnny started to sob. "I didn't want him to die, just leave me alone."

Alastair stiffened. He prayed the boy hadn't been beaten, or worse. He pulled a handkerchief from his back pocket and handed it to Johnny. "What do you mean, leave you alone?"

"My dad wasn't proud of me—ever. And he wouldn't be happy I was trying to play soccer, or get on the school team. Nothing I did was ever good enough."

Relieved Johnny hadn't been physically abused, Alastair relaxed somewhat. Still, the child's comments were disturbing. He hadn't known Big John that well, but he was sure the guy loved his family. He'd sung Johnny's praises on more than one occasion, said he was proud the kid had more brains than his old man, that Johnny was going places.

Alastair thought of the baby Lily was carrying, how much he already loved him or her. He hated to think his son or daughter might one day be in Johnny's shoes. Or that as a father, he'd be judged as harshly as Big John was right now.

Alastair put his arm around Johnny. "I can imagine how you feel, but you're wrong about your father. You weren't a disappointment. Quite the contrary. He told me time and again how proud he was of you. Your dad thought you were brilliant, and that's the truth. He was so proud of your good grades at school."

"Really?" Johnny sniffed, wiped his nose.

"Really. It's just that sometimes dads expect a lot—maybe too much—from their boys. Not because they don't care, but because they do. If your dad was tough on you at times, it was because it was his job to get you ready for the world."

Brow furrowed, Johnny nodded but said nothing.

❀ ❀ ❀

Johnny's ball skills continued to improve throughout the summer. Even after Lily had stopped going to see Diane as regularly, he and Johnny continued with their practices at the park. Alastair looked forward to these breaks, the feel of the ball at his feet, the boy, eager to learn from him, smiling, increasingly confident. Diane thanked him over and over again, claimed it was helping Johnny deal with Big John's death. Alastair never shared with Diane the things that Johnny had told him, simply said he was glad to help.

When the snow flew that year, Johnny and Diane moved away. She had rented out the house and left with little notice. Alastair fretted that somehow it was his fault, that perhaps his relationship with Johnny had alarmed her. Even though Alastair realised the idea was ludicrous, he couldn't keep the thought at bay.

One day after a melt, thinking the exercise might help, Alastair grabbed the ball and went to the park alone. It was deserted, and the long stretch of grass where he and Johnny had practised was covered in a white film of frost. The frozen grass crunched beneath his feet as he dribbled the ball towards a dense clump of trees, their leafless branches entwined and twisted like barbed wire. The ground beneath them was carpeted with the dried remnants of their discarded foliage.

When he was about halfway there, The Boy stepped out from behind a sturdy trunk. Alastair stopped. Panting from the run, his breath rose in white wisps, and then disappeared. He hadn't seen The Boy in some time. Why was he here now? Alastair would find out, put an end to this nonsense. Head up, he dribbled the ball forward to where The Boy stood. As Alastair drew near, The Boy vanished. Alastair had been watching him the whole time, never took his eyes off the child, yet he never saw him leave. The Boy was simply there one second, and gone the next.

Alastair bellowed and kicked the ball into the trees. It landed with a thump, followed by the crunch and spray of dried leaves. Then all was quiet. He stood stock-still for several minutes, staring at the copse, looking and listening for any movement. In the distance, a church bell rang, car engines droned, a dog barked, but there was no movement or sound, save the gentle rustle of wind from the thicket.

Alastair ran in amongst the trees. "Who are you? What do you want?" he called out. He peered behind every naked shrub, searched around the tree trunks. The Boy wasn't there, never had been. Sweat ran from Alastair's brow into his eyes. He had wiped it off and walked away without retrieving his ball. It wasn't until he'd reached home that he'd realised the ball hadn't been in the thicket. It, too, had disappeared, along with The Boy.

Alastair turned from the muted view of Johnny's old house back to the TV. A dapper young man was slashing lines and arrows across a map of North America. A nasty weather front was heading towards them at an alarming rate. With a heavy grunt, Alastair pushed out of his chair, hobbled over to the window and closed the drapes against the certain storm.

CHAPTER 6

The clock chimed half ten. It felt closer to noon. Lily eased into her chair and put her feet up on the ottoman. She took a gulp of hot tea and closed her eyes. Bright morning sunshine filtered through maple leaves, danced about the living room. Their cheerful shadows against her closed lids seemed to say to her, *Life goes on.* She took another swallow of tea and considered the day ahead.

She'd throw on a load of laundry and then sort out what to make for lunch and dinner. When it came to making meals, the decision was always half the battle. Drumming her fingers on the arm of the chair, she stared out the window. Not that meals or laundry or—she glanced down at the dusty window ledge—the housecleaning routine mattered much anymore. Her gaze followed the stream of sunlight that, only moments before, had seemed so cheerful. It was full of dust motes and disease. She imagined Alastair breathing in the fine, sharp particles, their microscopic edges ravaging his lungs. If she'd been a better housekeeper or a better wife, perhaps Alastair wouldn't be ill. All she could do now was keep him comfortable.

She drained the last of her tea and ran a finger around the cup's delicate, gold-rimmed edge. Seeing the dainty spray of heather etched on the inside, her expression softened. So fine was the bone china, the tiny lavender buds glowed from the light that shone through it. Her mother had sent the single cup and saucer from Scotland years ago—a rare gift. And one that must have cost her a fair penny. A yearning for her long-dead mother seized hold. If she could live her life over, she'd write home more often. Maybe she wouldn't leave at all. She'd be a better daughter, like her own.

Thank goodness for Jennifer's support. Especially now. How grateful she was for another pair of hands to help—and to hold. The mere thought of Jennifer coming lightened the weight of her burden. Lifted her spirits. A sign that perhaps God hadn't forgotten them after all.

She'd better tell Alastair that Jennie would be coming after school a few times a week. He was asleep when she'd telephoned yesterday evening, and Lily hadn't bothered to wake him. Considering how the rest of the night had turned out, it was a good thing.

Alastair was sleeping now and that was a relief. The pain was one thing, the nightmares another. They were getting worse. A consequence of the morphine, no doubt. At one point during the night, he didn't even know her. When he'd cried out in his sleep and thrashed about, Lily had gone to his bedside.

"Alastair," she'd whispered. And then laying a hand on his shoulder, she gently prodded him. "Wake up."

"Erin?" He'd looked at her with unseeing eyes. "Is that you?"

"It's me, Lily," she'd said and peered closer trying to track his gaze. But he had only grumbled something she couldn't make out, rolled over, and had gone back to sleep.

Again Lily wondered, who was Erin? When she'd asked, Alastair had seemed truly unaware. Had she misunderstood? His words were garbled. And she couldn't think of anyone they knew by that name. Unless she was someone he had kept secret. Over the years she'd wondered if there was anyone else. But until now, there was nothing that would lead her to believe he'd been unfaithful.

Except for the void.

Despite all their years together, she was still unsure why their love had never blossomed. From the outset there was a problem.

On their wedding night, Lily had put on her pretty peignoir set, hopped into bed with her legs stretch out, her back against the headboard. Alastair surprised her by walking into the room with a bottle of fizzy cider and two glasses. They'd toasted their new life together. Each silent, they'd sipped their drinks. The pink tips of Alastair's ears betrayed his nervousness and made her feel tender towards him.

"I love you," she said, laying a hand on his warm cheek. Putting her glass on the night table, she took off her dressing gown and slid beneath the cool sheets.

"I'm cold, Alastair. Come warm me up." She whispered the command, doing her best to sound sultry.

Smiling, he set his glass aside and began to undress.

Despite her outward confidence, she was shy. To avoid looking at him, she stared at the print on the opposite wall; a table draped in a red tartan; across it, a hewn walking stick, a silver pot; and at the centre, a clock, hands poised to strike the hour. Lily smiled. Her time, too, had arrived.

When Alastair lifted the bedding to join her, the outdoor smell of clean sheets wafted up, along with the thought of wash days spent with her mother and sisters; how they'd laugh and carry on as they hung out the laundry.

Wee Ellen, barely ten, was forever cocooning herself inside the dry sheets, her voice muffled as she called out, "Ooo, they smell lovely!" Now here she was, alone with her husband. He was her family now. When she followed him to Canada she would leave her mother and sisters behind. Would she ever see them again?

Her confidence waned. Lying beside this man while wearing nothing but a flimsy nightgown felt odd. Her heart quickened, her mouth went dry and her palms were sweaty. And if all that wasn't enough, Alastair was now staring at her. Could he sense her discomfort? To avoid his gaze, she dried her sweaty hands on the blankets as she pulled them to her body and waited, unsure of what to do, what to say. The desire to bolt from the bed and the room came into her head, but she pushed it aside.

"It's okay," he said and drew her close.

She managed a weak smile. And then reminded herself that this was Alastair, the man she'd known for years, and now her husband.

How We Danced

He kissed her then, and she closed her eyes and tried to focus on the sensation of his soft lips, the familiar scent of his skin and tang of cologne. As his kisses deepened, her body warmed, softened and unfolded. Her curiosity was aroused. What did he look like under the covers? She thought about reaching down to touch him, but still felt too shy. When he cupped a breast through the slippery fabric of her gown and his fingertips brushed her nipple, she drew a quick breath at the jolt of pleasure. As his caresses continued down the length of her back, she wondered if it was the cider or his touch that was heating her cheeks, flushing her neck. There was also a need building inside her, an unsettling urge that left her breathless and fidgety as he continued to kiss her.

With these feelings came the desire to show Alastair that she was ready to be his wife. Inspired, she flung off the bed sheet. He pulled back a bit, frowning as though confused. When he took her in his arms again, she felt a corrective tension in his embrace.

"Slow down," he said.

Although the words were whispered, Lily heard the authority in his voice. Perhaps if she followed his lead, like on the dance floor, he would be happy with her. He'd often said she was the best partner he'd ever had, claiming she wasn't clumsy or pushy like some of the other girls. The last thing she wanted was to seem forward or fast tonight.

Kissing her again, his hands wandered down her back, to her thighs and up again. His touch was gentle at first and then became more intense. At one point, he pressed his hips against hers while his hands kneaded her bottom. After several minutes of this attention she became breathless again, warmer still and once more full of strange energy. Surely now he would want her to somehow respond to his lead. She wanted to be a good wife.

Unable to remain lifeless and still a moment longer, she stroked his back and slipped her hand between their bodies to stroke his belly. She wondered what it would feel like to touch him lower. Lily had never laid eyes on a naked man. And she'd never touched one. Her sister Dolly said she let her boyfriend rub against her when they kissed. Lily asked what it felt like. Dolly laughed and asked about Alastair. When she told Dolly that Alastair never behaved that coarsely with her, her sister had sniffed and refused to answer any more questions. When Lily persisted, she told her to figure it out herself and left the room.

Now as Lily's fingers crept lower on Alastair's abdomen, she hoped he would show her what to do. He grabbed her wrist. With a firm grip, he brought her closed hand to his chest and held it there. Breathless, she waited for his next move. To the steady beat of Alastair's heart, she waited. Seconds passed. Confused when he still didn't move, she tried to pull free.

"Not yet," he said.

Lily heard the frustration in his voice and wondered why. Was there something she didn't know? Her sister had offered little information about men, her mother nothing. She was doing something wrong, and to fix it she needed to know how.

Regardless, she felt claustrophobic. "Let me go." She wriggled her hand.

He released her and rolled onto his back.

"Tell me what's wrong." She ran a fingertip around the rim of his ear.

"Nothing is *wrong*." Alastair stared at the ceiling. "Why would you ask me that?"

"Because you sound angry. Did I do something? If I did, I'm sorry. I didn't mean to." Lily tried to swallow the lump of sadness forming in her throat.

Alastair shook his head. After a moment he turned to her. "It's not you. There. Is that what you needed to hear?"

But maybe it was. She'd always worried about her small breasts. Teeth chattering, she glanced down at her chest and gathered the warm blankets close. But they were poor protection from the chilling self-doubt that had crystallized around her heart, tightening its icy grip with each beat.

"Please, Alastair—" Unsure of what else to say, she let her words fall away.

He shifted further to his side of the bed, creating a barrier she was afraid to cross. "You always expect too much of me."

In the back of her mind she knew this was wrong, but she said nothing. He rolled onto his side and lay silent.

How We Danced

In the weeks after their honeymoon and before he left for Canada, Alastair never touched her. Even when she'd snuggled close in bed and kissed his back.

Once he'd found a job and rented a place for them to live, she'd followed him abroad, where she'd hoped for a fresh start with a different conclusion. But she'd been disappointed.

The mantel clock chimed the hour. Lily shook her head and returned to the present. *Eleven already!* Gathering up her tea tray, she considered what to serve Alastair for lunch and prayed he'd have an appetite. But the past lingered. She stomped into the kitchen. Of course she hadn't expected too much of him. In hindsight, she should have been *more* demanding, not less. But most of all, she wished she'd listened to her instincts and insisted on answers.

CHAPTER 7

Jennifer walked into the Phys. Ed. office, placed her lunch into the fridge, and then dropped her book bag onto the table at her work station.

Trish wheeled her chair back from her desk.

Without saying a word, Jennifer sat down, took out her laptop, and opened her class schedule and lesson plans.

"You all right?" Trish asked.

"Yeah." As she spoke, Jennifer removed notebooks from her bag and arranged them on her desk. "I have a favour to ask, and then I was going to catch Woody before the bell rings. Do you know if he's in his office?"

"He is." Trish pulled her long, dark hair into a ponytail. "What's the favour?"

"You know my Dad's sick?"

"Uh-huh." Trish wheeled her chair closer.

Jennifer closed her empty bag and stowed it under the desk. Then she turned to face Trish. "I need to start helping. Which means something's gotta give. I was hoping you'd take over the soccer team and maybe get someone to fill in as assistant—I thought Taz might do it. Talk to her."

"Not a problem," Trish said.

"Great." Jennifer looked in the direction of the athletic director's office. "I'll go talk to Woody."

How We Danced

Jennifer muted her phone before she knocked on Woody's office door. A big man, he sat hunched over his keyboard. As much as she disliked him, she had to admit he was aging well. His thick hair showed no signs of thinning and few greys. He'd kept the chiselled good looks women loved. At least *most* women. He was a little too beefy for her liking. But she'd heard that he'd been quite an athlete when he was young. Unfortunately, he'd traded in his basketball jersey for teaching, and his six-pack for a beer belly.

Woody looked up from his computer, but waited a moment before he motioned her in. She closed the door, refusing to give him the pleasure of asking her to do so.

"What's up?" he said, not bothering to look at her again until he'd wheeled his chair back from the screen. He cracked his gum and straightened the sign at the front of his desk, *L. Woodworth, Athletic Director.*

As much as Jennifer hated sharing her personal life with him, she had little choice. "My father is ill, and my mother is caring for him at home."

"I'm sorry to hear that."

"Yes, well, thank you." The genuine look of concern on his face threw her off. "They need my help. Most days I'll head to their place right after school's dismissed. Trish has agreed to step in as coach for the soccer team. And she's going to see if Taz will assist."

"Hey, you gotta do what you gotta do."

Sensing he wasn't through, Jennifer remained quiet.

"I'll tell you what—I admire you. It's a tough row to hoe, looking after elderly parents and kids to boot. And your husband, Cameron, right? He's a big-time exec, isn't he? There's no way he could cut out early in the business world. That's what's great about teaching, isn't it?" He leaned forward and lowered his voice. "Is it the big C?"

"If you're asking if my father has cancer, the answer is yes, he does."

He shook his head back and forth. "Terrible disease. Terrible. My dad died of it a few years back. I'll tell you what. You're in for a rough ride. All chemo this and radiation that. Be prepared. It near wore my sister out. And she's one tough cookie. The old man withered away to eighty pounds. Nothing but skin and bone." He shuddered. "Gawd! It was awful."

Jennifer started to get up.

Woody stood. "Remember, as your department head and the athletic director," his eyes darted to the embossed nameplate, "I'm here to help. Just keep me informed of what's going on."

"Right."

He walked around to the front of the desk and crossed his arms. "I want you to know that I'll do my best to make sure you keep your classes."

"Pardon?"

"Relax." He held up his hands and moved closer. "I just mean if your situation continues into the new school year. If you're not able to coach, I may be forced to reassign some of your Phys. Ed. classes. Now don't look like that. I'll make sure you end up with a decent schedule. Besides, you wouldn't want to let the students or the players down, now would you? We're a team." He put his arm around her. "We pull together."

Jennifer's face burned and she pulled away. "Thanks."

"Sure." He stepped forward and held the door open. "That's what I'm here for."

❀ ❀ ❀

Alastair settled into his recliner and turned on the TV. The Rangers-Celtic match would start shortly. He looked down at his royal blue football jersey, a gift from Jennifer. The lettering was worn, the hem frayed. Maybe he'd ask for a new one at Christmas.

Christmas? Not likely. I'll be dead by then.

He pushed this thought down, away and turned up the volume on the TV. The commentators were engaged in their usual pre-game banter. Their guest was a retired player, good in his day. Even better than his father, a striker whom Alastair had known well.

The commentator's discussion ended, and Alastair heard the referee's whistle signal the start, but he wasn't watching the game on TV. Another game played out in his mind. Once again he was running up the middle of the pitch, the ball at his feet, Danny, as always, matching his stride, just ahead on the right.

How We Danced

The opposing defender charged, Alastair faked to the left, back right, and continued forward. Halfway to the net, he checked to see which striker he'd pass to. Danny's defender had stepped forward, placing Danny offside. Too late to pass. The defender on Alastair was challenging him for the ball. Alastair deked around him. A surge of energy charged his limbs. The net was almost within striking distance. Decision time. Dougal was in a perfect position to score, but the big defender was getting the better of him. No pass. The risk outweighed the advantage.

The match was tied. With only seconds left on the clock, a goal now would end the game and secure the championship. Alastair pushed the thought aside, focussed on the ball. Having figured out his defender's tactic, Danny was onside. Their eyes met. The exchange was brief, but Alastair understood not to pass. He brought his foot back and forward. The ball's arc was perfect. It sailed through the air, over the heads of the players. The goalkeeper's feet left the ground as he dove right, towards the ball. For a millisecond Alastair feared the ball would hit the top of the goalpost. But it didn't. Entering at the top right corner, it missed the goalpost by a hair's width and crashed into the back of the net. The beaten goalie was sprawled on the ground, paralysed by defeat. The referee's whistle blew.

A cheer went up. They'd won. The lads on the bench rushed onto the pitch, and Alastair was swarmed by his teammates.

It was Danny's voice Alastair heard above the rest. "You did it, MacAulay!"

Danny and Dougal hefted Alastair onto their shoulders; others helped keep him aloft as they paraded over to the fans. He looked into the stand of supporters, on their feet, whooping and cheering his name and the club's.

After the coach had said his piece and everyone had showered and changed, the team headed to the pub.

Colin, a good-natured midfielder, shook his head back and forth. "I couldn't believe my eyes," he said. "That big lug was on Dougal. But Danny was in the clear. I thought you'd pass to him—it would have made sense—but then, BOOM!"

Alastair looked at Danny, beside him, smiling.

"I can't explain it, Colin." Alastair shrugged. "I just knew."

"I can," Coach Murphy said. "I've seen it before. It's rare, mind you. But it happens—between brothers and sisters, husbands and wives and, when a coach is lucky, players. The one always seems to know what the other's going to do even before he does it." Coach Murphy looked at Alastair and Danny. "You two are like that."

"Well, here's to my partner, Alastair!" Danny raised his glass. The others followed suit with a cry of, "Hear, hear!"

Alastair was treated to pint after pint. His stomach roiled. When his teammate Sandy got around to buying, Alastair knew he couldn't drink another drop.

"Thanks, Sandy, but I'm done." Alastair raised his hands in protest.

"Are you sure?" Sandy asked.

"I am, mate, but thanks." Alastair smiled.

"Right then," Sandy glanced at the clock and stood. "I should be heading home."

Dougal followed suit; Colin and Coach Murphy not long after. Soon Alastair and Danny were the only ones left.

The waitress was clearing up at the table beside their booth. Danny and Alastair simultaneously raised a hand to signal her.

"I'm going to order some fish and chips," Danny said.

Alastair laughed, "Me as well."

After the waitress took their order, Alastair stretched out his legs. Danny followed suit.

"Quite a game, eh?" Danny said.

Alastair snorted. "That it was."

Danny sipped his ale and then set it down. "Do you think it's true what Coach Murphy said, about us, I mean?"

Alastair shrugged. "I dunno. I suppose. Maybe."

Danny stared into his ale, nodding.

Their fish and chips arrived within minutes. Famished, Alastair dug in. The battered haddock was crispy on the outside, moist, hot and delicious within. Alastair salted his chips and reached for the vinegar just as Danny tried to grab the HP Sauce. Fingers entwined, Alastair looked at Danny, who was staring at him. Danny's lips were slightly parted, and Alastair heard him draw a quick breath. Neither moved. Alastair had the sudden urge to draw Danny closer. The feeling confused and disturbed him, and yet made perfect sense. It was as though the world, always slightly off-kilter, shifted into place.

"Are you lads in need of a refill?" the waitress asked.

Alastair jerked his hand away and fumbled the vinegar. The bottle fell onto the floor with a crash. Shards of glass scattered. Alastair scanned the room. Conversations had stopped mid-sentence, forks were held halfway between plate and mouth, and all eyes were on him and Danny. The choking reek of vinegar was everywhere.

Coughing, Alastair had slid out of the booth and tossed money onto the table. "I'm sorry," he'd said. "My fault."

Danny had followed. "No, wait—"

Alastair blinked. The TV screen came into focus, along with the current Rangers-Celtic match, now well underway. He sat back, determined to enjoy it. But the tang of vinegar lingered, souring his mood.

❋ ❋ ❋

Lily squeezed between a chair and the Duncan Fyfe table just inside the bedroom entrance. "Lunch time," she called to Alastair.

"We'd better get those things downstairs before you fall and break your neck." He pushed himself up on the pillows.

"I'll get to it later." Lily held out the lunch tray. "I've brought your favourite: beef with barley soup and a cheese sandwich."

"I don't think I can eat right now." He shrugged. "I'm sorry."

"If you don't want the soup, please try the sandwich. Just a bite," she urged. "It's made with the aged cheddar you love."

Alastair laid a hand on her wrist. "I'm sorry, hen. I haven't the appetite for it. Maybe later."

"What about your tea? Do you at least want that?"

"Not now." He squeezed his eyes shut and grimaced. "I'll just rest for a bit. And then maybe we can see to that furniture."

"Hmph." Lily put the tray down. She peered into his face. A sheen of sweat covered his creased brow, streaked his upper lip. "Are you in pain?"

"A bit." His eyes remained closed, but he gave her a weak smile. "Go. Have your own lunch or go out into your garden for a bit. It'll pass."

Deborah Serravalle

Lily chewed her lip and nodded. With a sigh, she picked up the untouched tray and turned to go. Halfway to the door she glanced back. The furrows on Alastair's brow had eased somewhat and his lips were parted. With a quick prayer that sleep would bring him relief, she continued on. Lifting the tray higher, once more she eased between the furniture at the doorway. Alastair was right. These pieces needed to be stored away. Rearranging the room to house the hospital bed had created clutter. Nothing was where it should be. It pained her to see their valuables scattered hither and yon about the room. But lately nothing was where it should be. Their lives were coming apart at the seams. What she needed was to create order out of this chaos, and then she'd feel better.

While Alastair slept, she'd carry this stuff down the basement. If she didn't do it now, he would insist on helping when he woke. She could manage. The pieces were awkward, not heavy.

But the lunch tray she was holding *was* getting heavy. Reaching the door, she tried to readjust her grip, but her hand slipped. The teapot slid, tottered and the lid clattered onto the tray.

"Ah!" Alastair yelled.

"What's wrong!" As Lily swung round, she lost her hold on the tray. Swaying this way and that, she tried to regain her grip, but instead she hooked her foot on the leg of the chair. There was a loud popping sound as though someone had snapped an elastic band. She yelped as searing pain zipped up her leg like a rocket. Still gripping the tray, she crashed and tumbled into the Duncan Fyfe table. Before her head hit the floor and the wave of darkness swept her off, she wondered if the "pop" was the sound of her leg breaking.

CHAPTER 8

By the time her lunch period rolled around, Jennifer was starving. It had been hours since she'd gulped down a bowl of Cheerios. There was no one in the Phys. Ed. office when she returned. No students loitering about, waiting to ask a question or a favour. Happy for a bit of solitude, she took her lunch out of the fridge. After putting her leftover pizza in the microwave, she sat down at the communal table, opened her water bottle, took a long pull and looked around the room. At some point, solitude could be overwhelming; slip into isolation. It happened to the infirm and elderly. She thought of her parents. Setting the water bottle down, she spread her hands on the table top. The backs already showed the effects of sun damage. Age spots. Her time was coming.

The microwave buzzer sounded. She got up and slid the hot pizza onto the aluminum foil she'd brought. Halfway back to the table, the phone rang. She could tell from the ring it was the front office. She put her pizza down and picked up the receiver.

"Roberts speaking."

"Line two for you, Jen. A woman. Says she's your neighbour."

Jennifer looked at the flashing light. The Martins were away right now, so it couldn't be Annabelle. That left Isla Lafferty. Jennifer cringed. She couldn't imagine why Isla would be calling. Unless there was a problem at the house—fire? Flooding?

Alarmed, Jennifer thanked the secretary and pushed the flashing button.

It wasn't Isla after all, but Tina Albanese, her parents' neighbour.

"What's wrong?" Jennifer asked.

Tina explained that she was staying with Alastair; that Lily had fallen, that she was likely now at the hospital since the ambulance had arrived about an hour ago. And no, she didn't have any more information than that.

"I don't understand, Tina. Why didn't you call my cell? My dad knows the number."

"I left four messages," Tina said.

Jennifer pulled her phone from her pocket. She'd put it on mute when she'd gone in to talk to Woody.

"Can I speak to my dad?"

"If you like," Tina hesitated, "but he was pretty upset. I just got him settled—"

"Never mind then. I'll talk to him later."

After thanking Tina and saying goodbye, she stood for a moment. *Fallen* could mean anything from a twisted ankle to a fractured skull. She tried to recall the name of the actress who had bumped her head skiing in Quebec, seemed fine and then died a few hours later of an undiagnosed brain injury. She probably never said goodbye to her kids and husband. No doubt she and her family had gone to bed that night assuming there would be a tomorrow to say what needed to be said, to do what needed to be done. Pursued by the fear that this would happen to her family, she fell into the expected motions: calling the office to get her classes covered, insisting to the secretary she was okay; tossing her lunch in the trash; wrapping up her laptop cord, round and round and fastening it tight. When she passed by a group of sullen-looking goths near the school exit, she felt a tear roll down her cheek. Poised in their black coats and ashen faces, they stared. Gloomy harbingers of death.

When Jennifer asked after her mother at the Emergency Triage Station, a young doctor glanced up from his writing. Startled by his perfect smile and tanned good looks, she thought he appeared better suited to the ski slopes than a hospital ward.

How We Danced

He came around the desk. She stepped back, adjusted the handbag slung across her shoulder.

"You must be Mrs. MacAulay's daughter. Your mom said you'd be coming."

"I am." She held her hand out. "Jennifer Roberts." Mouth dry, she swallowed. "How is she?"

"She'll be fine," he said. "Dr. Shekter." His grip was firm, his skin soft. "Come on. I'll walk you to her and fill you in."

Acutely aware of the warm hand he laid on her back, her fear eased. "Does she have to stay?"

"Only for observation. So we can keep her right here in ER."

He turned and smiled at her as they walked the corridor.

"Mrs. Roberts?" He stopped and waited.

"This way." Dr. Shekter motioned for her to turn right. "Your mom took quite a tumble. From what your dad told the paramedics, she tripped on some furniture. We took an X-ray—no break or fracture. But she did tear the anterior talofibular ligament which connects the front part of the fibula to the talus bone on the front-outer part of the ankle joint. It's the most commonly injured ligament. Hurts like hell to bear weight. It'll take some time to mend."

"I suppose it could have been worse."

"Definitely. But she does have a concussion. That's why I want to observe her for twenty-four to forty-eight hours. Just to make sure nothing more serious develops. Besides, I can't send her home until we've sorted out her circumstances."

"Circumstances?"

"Your mom's living arrangements. No doubt her mobility is going to be an issue. Also, she tells me your dad is ill, and she's his primary caregiver."

He was right. Who would take care of Daddy if Mammy couldn't? For that matter, who would take care of Mammy? It would have to be her. There was no one else. No brothers or sisters to share the burden of ill and aging parents.

As a child, Jennifer had begged her mother for a baby sister. Perhaps if her mother had answered one way or the other, Jennifer would have let it be. But because the question had been avoided, Jennifer had become frustrated.

51

Deborah Serravalle

"Why won't you answer me?" Jennifer stomped her foot. "It's not fair. I want a sister. Why can't I have one?"

"Jennifer, please—"

Her mother threw the coloured pile of dirty clothes into a laundry basket and headed for the basement stairs. Jennifer followed.

"Fayne's mother is having a baby. Soon Fayne will have a little sister or brother. I have no one." Jennifer jumped from the second-to-last step onto the concrete floor.

"Jennifer. Please stop." Lily didn't look up as she stuffed clothes into the washer. "You have your father and me."

"But it's not enough!" Jennifer huffed and crossed her arms.

When she had said this, her mother was reaching for the soap on the shelf above the machine. Arm outstretched, Jennifer still recalled the way she froze and then after a moment turned around to face her, eyes brimming.

At first too shocked for words, Jennifer had thrown her arms around her mother's waist and buried her face against the cushion of her breast. When her mother silently sobbed and her body shook, Jennifer screwed her eyes shut and said, "It's okay, Mammy. Please don't. I changed my mind. You're right, it's better that it's just us. A baby would ruin everything."

From then on, whenever Jennifer had felt the desire for a sister, she remembered her mother's quivering sobs and repeated *a baby would ruin everything*. She did that so often, she eventually came to believe it and revelled in her only-child status. A brother or sister would be great right now, she thought.

❀ ❀ ❀

"Mrs. Roberts?" The doctor's hand was on her arm. "Is someone with your dad now?"

"Pardon? Oh—yes, a neighbour."

"Your mother can't go back to caring for your dad right away. They'll need help."

"I see."

He winked at a pert young nurse. "Hey Amanda."

"Hi, Dr. Shekter." A rosy blush stained her cheeks.

As they continued along the corridor, Jennifer felt confidence vibrating off him like heat. She hoped that self-assuredness translated into excellent care.

How We Danced

"Just around the corner, here we go." Privacy curtains separated the beds. The one at her mother's bed was open.

Turned towards the window, her mother worried the edge of the blankets. She looked tiny and frail. Diminished.

When Dr. Shekter said, "Knock, knock," her mother turned. "Oh, Jennie, thank goodness." She sat up. "Can I go home now, doctor? My daughter will help me." She threw off her covers. A couple of ice packs fell to the floor.

She went to her mother's side. "Mammy, wait—"

"Get that foot back up on the bed, Mrs. MacAulay. And keep it elevated." Dr. Shekter bent down and retrieved the ice packs.

Jennifer stepped back and allowed him to take charge.

Lily wriggled up the mattress, dragging her leg back onto the bed.

"That's good. Here, let's get that foot up on the pillow." After securing the packs around Lily's ankle, Dr. Shekter pulled the covers across her legs. "Now, don't put your daughter on the spot. I already explained that you're not going anywhere today. Everything at home is under control, correct?" He looked at Jennifer.

She moved closer to the bed again. "That's right."

"But what about the girls?" Lily asked.

"They're fine. My friend is picking them up after school."

"Your daughter will sort everything out so that you can get home as soon as possible. Your job is to rest. You don't want to make things worse by putting any undue stress on that ankle."

"Jennifer, your father can't be alone."

"He won't be." Jennifer sat down on the bed. "I'll go spend the night. Cam can pick up the girls at Trish's. It'll be fine."

"Assuming all goes well, you'll be up and using crutches tomorrow," Dr. Shekter added.

"I've made a fine mess of things." Lily hung her head and sobbed.

"Mammy, please don't cry." She took her mother's hands in hers. "Look at me." She waited. "That's better. Now listen. We'll get through this."

"But how? Your father needs me. If you'd just let me try, I'm sure I can walk." Once again, Lily folded back the bed sheets.

"Mrs. MacAulay, I can't chain you to the bed. But I can tell you this: if you put any weight on that foot, you may do serious harm that could land you in here for a long time. The choice is yours." Dr. Shekter threw up his hands and waited.

"Please, Mammy—"

Lily sighed and pulled the covers back on.

"That's better." Dr. Shekter drew a chair up to the bed and sat down. "Now, if you're no longer able to care for your husband, there are other options."

Lily sniffed. "Like what?"

"There are services available that will allow you and your husband to remain at home—"

"Oh no—" Lily moaned.

"Mammy," Jennifer squeezed her mother's hands, "isn't that what you wanted?"

Lily's grip tightened as she addressed Dr. Shekter. "I don't want strangers invading our home. My daughter can help me." She turned to Jennifer with pleading eyes. "Isn't that right?"

Jennifer looked from her mother to the doctor. "Well, yes, I was planning to go most days after work. But is that enough?"

"No, I'm afraid it isn't." Dr. Shekter softened his voice. "Mrs. MacAulay, you'll heal, but you're in rough shape right now. You need assistance just getting around. Bearing that in mind, how do you propose to care for your husband? And you told me your daughter has a full-time job and her own family." He pivoted around to face Jennifer.

"That's true." She drew the words out; tried to think, to decide. All the while she could feel her mother's eyes boring into her, begging. What about school? Woody would whine, maybe try to take away her best classes. To hell with him. But her students—she'd be letting them down. Mitch, a young basketball player who counted on her, flitted across her mind. He was so much like Cameron when he was young. Oh God, Cameron—the girls. She suppressed the temptation to lift them up like a shield. Instead she drew them closer. "But family comes first. And it's nearing the end of the school year. I'll apply for a leave of absence. In the meantime, I have accumulated sick days."

How We Danced

Dr. Shekter stood up. "When do you plan to move into your mother's?"

"As soon as possible, I suppose." As the words tumbled out, Jennifer knew she'd made the right decision.

"No rush." Shekter stuck his hands in his pant pockets. "But, if you planned on going over tomorrow, I could sign the release papers in the morning," he raised his brows at Lily, "*after* we get you up and running on crutches."

Jennifer cleared her throat to push down the myriad of obligations that threatened to choke her ... *I'll have to visit HR and get the paperwork going ... Woody ... Oh God, I can't think of that idiot right now ... Mitch ... I'll talk to Trish. She'll help ... Cameron ... he'll be swamped ... poor little Emma ... Lindsay ...* "Al-all right," she stammered, "that should work."

❀ ❀ ❀

Scorching pain roused Alastair as he turned. Grasping a fistful of bedding, he winced and waited to see if it would escalate or subside. The pain eased and after a bit he settled, grateful for the respite. Sleep gripped him again, and as he began the familiar descent into oblivion, the Westminster Quarters chimed.

> *Oh Lord our God,*
> *Thy children call.*
> *Grant us Thy peace,*
> *And bless us all.*

Now a different bell jangled. Alastair walked out of his shop. The air smelled sweet compared to the cocktail of chemicals he used to clean and repair typewriters. The alcove was shaded and cooler than the street, so he stayed while pondering which direction to turn. Retrieving his wristwatch from his trousers, he strapped it on and checked the time—1:05 p.m.

Unlike the other fellows, he liked to work Saturdays. It was just half the day, and the extra money came in handy. Besides, the shop was quieter. It moved to a different rhythm and so did he. More relaxed, more focussed. When possible, he saved his difficult, intricate repairs for Saturdays.

He took a pack of Black Cats out of his shirt pocket and lit one. He could go home, but then he remembered Lily was at work. Or did she say she was off to the shops? No matter, she wouldn't be home. Lily. If only he could lead her in the bedroom like he did on the dance floor. There, she read his every move, responded so willingly. For a moment he could sense her in his arms, her back arched and eyes closed, waiting for his next move. He could almost feel the fabric of her gown slide between his fingers. With a deft flick he tossed the extinguished match to the curb. He stepped down from the shop's alcove and onto the sidewalk.

Casting a glance north on John Street, he reconsidered, turned left towards King and fell in line with the crowd of Saturday shoppers. If he went home, he could help Kevin work on the basement project. If Alastair's skill was on the dance floor, Kevin's was in the tool shop—the hum of a table saw and the burnt smell of sawdust replaced the orchestra and the heady scent of Evening in Paris. Alastair envisioned Kevin's biceps straining with effort, the tang of male sweat that made his nostrils flare and breath quicken. Yet today he felt restless, and the idea of working with Kevin on the project held none of its usual appeal.

Throwing his smoke away, he picked up his pace. As he came to the bus stop in front of Kresge's, he hesitated. A tall man, with a petite brunette who reminded him of Lily, rounded the corner on Hughson and disappeared from sight. It was only a fleeting glance, but something in the man's posture, the protective way he led his woman, saddened Alastair.

Instead of heading home, he'd walk to the Red Lion for a beer. Just one wouldn't hurt. Who was he kidding? There was no such thing. One led to two, three or more, which awakened urges best left sleeping. His stomach grumbled and he turned around. He saw Kresge's lunch counter through the double glass doors. A hot roast beef sandwich and a slice of pie couldn't hurt.

When Alastair pushed open the door to Kresge's, two laughing young lads ran under his arm and out to the street. One of the boys stopped, turned and smiled at Alastair before rushing off. Alastair thought he knew his face, but before he could be certain, the child was gone, and he had to make way for a harried woman carrying a little girl—presumably the boys' mother—who rushed outside after them.

"Tommy, how many times have I told you not to run ahead of me!" she yelled.

One son, then. The other a figment of Alastair's imagination.

Despite the admonishment, he detected a hint of pride in the mother's voice. No doubt the boys' confident energy was a result of the nurturing only a good mother could offer. For a moment he imagined himself laughing with the boys; giving and taking good-natured shoves; the mother taking him in tow; giving him a telling and then roughing his hair. Within seconds the woman and her son were swallowed by the swarm of shoppers. Alastair released the door and stepped to the side to make way for other customers.

Beads of sweat had formed on his brow from the brisk walk. He ran his hands through his hair, shoving back a damp hank. He took a breath. On this hot day, the air-conditioned atmosphere in the store felt nice. He closed his eyes for a second and enjoyed the sensation. Then he got a whiff of the grill and his stomach grumbled, reminding him why he'd come.

The two horseshoe bars of the restaurant were joined in the middle. The grill was at the back, along the wall, and ran the width of both sections. On Saturday afternoons the place was packed. And today was no different. Alastair wondered if he'd even find a stool. Then he spotted an empty space at the far side and made his way around.

Because he often stopped in for coffee and a slice of pie, Alastair knew most of the waitresses. They all wore the standard uniform. But some looked better than others in the little white cap and apron. Most were all business, a couple were friendly. His favourite was the Hungarian woman, Aranka. He got a kick out of the stilted, formal way she spoke. Like him, Aranka was an immigrant and married. But unlike her , he hadn't had to struggle with a new language or deal with three young children. Although Aranka didn't say much about her family, Alastair sensed she was a supportive wife, a loving mother. Aranka's family was lucky to have her. With his own parents gone, it was up to him to create a new life and a family. Lily always said, *Blood is thicker than water.*

Alastair was pleased when he saw Aranka coming to his section, balancing several plates down the length of her arm.

Aranka lifted her chin and smiled at him, "I'll be right with you."

Alastair returned her smile. He imagined lying abed on a Sunday; Aranka calling out from the kitchen that she'd be right there; moments later arriving with a breakfast tray of all his favourites; knowing, without him asking, that he'd prefer fried bread to toast. "Here you are," she'd say, each word enunciated with her Hungarian accent.

"Alastair?" Aranka stood there smiling. She pulled out a pencil from behind her ear, her pad of guest checks from her apron. "What may I serve you?"

"Coffee and a hot roast beef sandwich."

"With your roast beef, mashed, yes?"

Alastair smiled. Often he'd leave out a detail, see if he could catch her up. But no, Aranka always got it right. He was certain she was like that with her husband, that she always anticipated his needs.

From under the counter Aranka produced a cup and saucer. She grabbed the coffee pot from the centre island, filled his cup and set down a couple of creamers. Then she made her way to the grill, stopping here and there to stack an increasing amount of plates, cups and cutlery on one arm. The lunch rush was over.

People were laying down their cash and leaving. Nearby was a young couple with a toddler between them. Holding his parents' hands, the boy giggled and kicked his legs in the air. "Again!" he said. Before swinging him into the air, the parents exchanged a loving glance. One day soon, Alastair thought, he'd toss his own son in the air, and Lily would look across the boy's head to him with respect and love in her eyes.

Alastair turned his attention to the coffee before him. He poured in two creamers and one and one-half teaspoons of sugar. He put the spoon aside and lit a Black Cat. Closing his eyes, he exhaled the smoke and pent-up energy that pestered him all morning. He took a sip. It was perfect, not too sweet with just the right amount of cream. Alastair wished the rest of life was as simple to orchestrate as a good cup of coffee. Still, everything was going as planned—a fresh start in a new country with a beautiful wife, a good job, and a respectable number of friends. He took a swallow of his coffee and saw Aranka coming with his order. She set the steaming plate in front of him, along with a knife and fork wrapped in a napkin. "Enjoy."

As Alastair dug into his roast beef, Aranka went to the pedestal pie stand and lifted the glass top. She cut a thick wedge of lemon meringue and gave it to a man sitting opposite. His hair was jet black, peppered grey at the temples, his skin swarthy. Alastair wondered if he was Italian. The man stopped eating and met his gaze. Somehow feeling guilty, Alastair looked away. As he gathered up a forkful of potatoes, his eyes wandered back to the man. Running his middle finger around the edge of the pie, he raised it; a fat glob of lemon custard hung from the tip. The man delicately licked and then sucked his finger. With a tender smack, the digit was released, along with a sigh of pleasure from the gentleman.

Alastair bent his head and shielded his eyes with a hand. He massaged his lids, rubbing harder and harder as he tried to erase the image of the man. What was he doing here? Someone like him had no right.

Lily. He'd think of Lily … on their wedding day … the beautiful suit she wore, the perfect shade of pale blue that contrasted with her dark hair … *the man's hair is dark, thick* … But Kevin's hair was a rich brown, auburn, really. Much nicer, a true friend. Like his mother, God rest her soul. She had been good to him, loving him like no other. Alastair conjured his mother's image; she was telling him how proud she was, that he was so brave to leave his homeland for a better life … his mother pulled him close … *it was the man now, pulling him closer, closer … off the stool … leading him back to that other life.* Alastair squeezed his eyes shut tighter.

How could this be happening to him again? He had been so confident those times were behind him, left in Scotland along with the rain and dampness. He was a different man now. He had a wife. Mind over matter, Lily would say. He could do this, would do this. For her, for them. More in control, more confident, he opened his eyes and sat up.

Aranka had her back to him; she was clearing dishes, collecting cheques and money. The dark-haired man was scraping the last bits of meringue and lemon custard from his plate with such earnestness that for an instant Alastair wondered if he'd imagined the encounter. Then, as the gentleman set his money down and started to get up, their eyes met. Alastair reached for his cup, sloshing coffee onto the saucer. A slow smile stretched across the man's face. Turning from the lunch counter, he walked in the direction of the exit. Alastair took a five-dollar bill out of his wallet and put it down. Without finishing his lunch or saying goodbye to Aranka, he slid off the stool. Keeping the man in sight, Alastair followed him through the door.

❀ ❀ ❀

Alastair's eyes fluttered as Jennifer helped him to a sitting position. After a moment, he muttered, "Nightmare," pulled his knees to chest and lowered his head. The distant past slipped back into place, and the previous day's events whirled round, then settled—Lily taking away his lunch tray, the table by the door, her tripping. The crash—hers, his.

Alastair's backside hurt. He'd spent too many hours in bed. He looked up at the mattress. By the tangled bedding hanging down, somehow he must have tumbled onto the floor. If he'd fallen outright, he'd likely have broken something. Lucky him.

Jennifer got behind and squatted down between him and the bed. "Let me get you back where you belong."

He pressed his lips together, forming a grim line. Although he realised he needed to be there, that sick bed was the last place he *belonged*.

Jennifer tried to hook her arms through his. He looked up at her. Tears of pride pricked his eyes. When he was gone, she'd remain. Cameron, the girls. Lily. His family; his legacy.

"Come on now, Daddy," Jennifer said.

Unsteady, he shoved his elbow back, hitting the hard edge of the bedside table with a hollow thump. "Uh," he cried out as a jolt of pain skittered to his wrist, numbing his fingers.

"Daddy, don't be like that. You can't very well just sit here on the floor."

He rocked back and forth. The pain and numbness in his arm, jagged. Speaking was impossible. He pasted his arms to his sides and shook his head.

She stood. "All righty then. Let me know when you're ready."

This was said in a sing-song voice that reminded Alastair of a nursery rhyme. His temper flared. He was sick, yes, and injured for the moment; in large part due to her manhandling. But he wasn't a child. Nor had he lost control of his faculties. When the pain eased a bit, he turned around to tell her not to speak to him that way. But before he had a chance, she said, "Good," and scurried back into position.

"On the count of three …" She hoisted him up.

"Sit at the bottom of the bed while I fix it. That's perfect, near the edge." She picked up the pillows that had fallen to the floor and untwisted the blankets and sheets. "There we go." She stepped back, hands on hips. "Now lie down."

He wanted to tell her he would do this part himself while he was still able. And that he wasn't tired. He'd slept. And that he'd prefer to sit up for a bit. Maybe watch some TV. Forget the past, escape the present. But he changed his mind when he saw her standing at the ready, raring to help. Instead of speaking up, he stretched out and stared at the ceiling as she pulled the blankets up, folding them uncomfortably, just beneath his chin.

When Jennifer was young, Alastair had sometimes tucked her in at night. One evening, when Lily had looked tired but Jennifer was bright-eyed, he'd offered to put her to bed. Playfully setting the covers up and under her chin, he had teased that if she didn't go to sleep, the Sandman would come for them. Later, Lily went in to check on the child. When she didn't return, Alastair followed her. From the doorway he heard Jennifer's stuttered sob, "I have to go sleep or the Sandman will get us." He took one step into the room. Lily looked up, glaring. Stiff and sniffling beside her mother, Jennifer had turned a tear-streaked face to him. Unsure of what to say, fearing he'd make things worse, he'd backed away, returned to the living room and with unseeing eyes watched TV.

Jennifer was halfway between the bed and the door when she turned back. "Call me if you need anything. Promise?"

Sad at the prospect of being alone yet keen to have her gone, he forced a smile and nodded. He'd still promise anything for her.

Minutes later, when he heard her banging about in the kitchen, he kicked off the covers, sat up. Then he turned on the TV, muted the sound and stared at the voiceless people on the screen.

❀ ❀ ❀

Although only seconds earlier Lily had checked to see if Alastair was asleep, she glanced across his way once more before opening the tiny box she'd smuggled into their room. If he stirred, she planned to stuff it the already-open drawer of her end table. It was risky bringing her treasures out from their hiding place in the clock and into the open. They hadn't seen the light of day in years. She sat for a moment and marvelled at her daring. It was so unlike her. And that wasn't the only change. She spent much of her time now daydreaming about days gone by. She supposed it was Alastair's illness, the knowledge that he'd soon be gone. Perhaps it was natural to go back and remember.

Lily shrugged and with a soft sigh held up a miniature gift card. Even after all these years, it looked like it had been written yesterday. *When you're 'In the Mood,' wear them and think of me.* She traced the initials that followed, *DM.* She set the note aside and lifted the tattered square of cotton batting covering her treasures. A final glimpse Alastair's way and she raised a pearl earring to eye level. The teardrop pendant swayed and sparkled in the stolen light. Her hand folded around the perfect jewel that had come to symbolize her broken heart. The other earring lay in the box, incomplete without its mate. Ironic, since this set had been meant to replace another damaged pair. She closed her eyes, relaxed her shoulders, and took a deep breath in, then out.

Smiling, she visualized her younger self, swaying on the Wondergrove's dance floor under the stars, the huge Spanish fireplace off to the far end. The orchestra emerged in her mind's eye. She heard the sweet melody of "Begin the Beguine." Once again she was in Alastair's arms gliding across the crowded floor, her cheeks flushed with pride as he led her with confidence and grace around the other couples. A final flourish and the music ended.

"I'm going to the little boy's room. I'll meet you at our table." Alastair strode off without a backward glance.

As couples danced around her, Lily remained on the floor. It would have been nice if he'd at least offered to escort her back. Within seconds he disappeared, engulfed by the crowd. Arms crossed, she watched and waited for him to emerge at the other side. Rather than go to the men's room, he walked to the bar. On tiptoes now, she saw the bartender set a shot glass in front of him. A bosomy blonde with lips so red they'd stop a bus, leaned toward him holding a cigarette. Lily's stomach clenched; her cheeks burned. The woman was only asking for a light, she reasoned. But another voice questioned why her husband had detoured to the bar when he'd abandoned her to go to the bathroom. Was this a planned rendezvous? Alastair smiled, and reaching into his pocket, pulled out his cigarettes and matches, lighting the woman's first before taking one for himself. Head tilted back, the blonde blew smoke into the night air. Alastair stared, one brow raised seductively. Cigarette held high, the blonde moved closer. Was she handing him a note? Lily imagined the woman's curly script inviting Alastair to call her. He laughed and shoved whatever she'd given him into his pocket. Afterwards he slammed back his drink and headed for the bathroom.

He seemed so ... Lily searched her mind for the right word ... captivated. What did that woman have that she didn't? Maybe she'd ask him. But as soon as the thought had formed, Lily knew she'd never say a word. Why borrow trouble?

The music started again. "In the Mood." Everyone swarmed the floor as though Glenn Miller himself had taken the stage. Couples wove in and around as Lily made her lone expedition to the fringe. With a silent curse, she wondered why she was always going against the flow.

A couple whirled by and bumped into her. "Sorry," they called out, and continued their dance.

Something slid down her neck and off her collarbone. She raised a hand, brushing her unadorned lobe. "My earring!"

Deborah Serravalle

Her skirt billowed around her like a parachute as she crouched to retrieve the earring before someone two-stepped over and squashed it. Spotting it a couple of feet forward, she duck-walked to where it lay and scooped it up. But as she rose, her heel caught the hem of her skirt. Balancing herself on one bouncing leg, she tried to extricate her high heel from the dress.

"That's an interesting step!"

Lily hopped around to face the man who had spoken. The new couple, David and Catherine, who'd joined their group, stood before her. Lily's friend Jean had said David was nice enough, but Catherine was "old Hamilton money" and stuck up. Judging by Catherine's down-turned lips and crossed arms, Lily thought maybe Jean was right. Catherine glanced at Lily's face, to her legs and back again. Lily opened her mouth to explain but once more lost her balance.

David grabbed hold of her elbow. "I've got you!"

She tipped over into his arms as the heel of her shoe came free. They both laughed and then, for a split second, Lily thought they'd fall, but Catherine, straight-faced, managed to steady them.

With two feet planted on the floor, Lily examined her hem for damage—a slight tear. She smoothed her skirt, taking the moment to subdue her mirth.

"Are you all right, Lily?" David asked, chuckling.

Lily smiled at him, surprised he'd remembered her name.

As was his wife. Catherine's head turned so fast in his direction that her own dangling earrings were still swinging when Lily looked at her.

"I'm fine—just clumsy, that's all. Got my earring, though! See?" She held out the offending bauble, now bent and scratched. "Oh, darn. I was too late."

"Still, that was an impressive piece of reconnaissance." David smiled and turned to his wife. "Wasn't it, Catherine?"

Catherine cleared her throat. "At least it wasn't valuable."

David ignored his wife's comment. "Come on, we'll walk you back to your table."

"Oh, I'm fine, really. You two go finish your dance."

How We Danced

David hesitated, but Catherine found her tongue. "You heard her." She took his arm. "Lily is a most capable woman." Her voice was sharp and sweet.

It was then that Alastair appeared, back from the men's room. "Everything okay?"

Lily thought his colour looked high, his eyes too bright. When he put his arm about her shoulders she pulled away.

"Fine. My earring fell. I stumbled trying to pick it up."

Catherine moved closer to David, red lips stretched across white teeth. "The Wondergrove's cocktails pack a punch."

Lily blushed but kept her voice steady. "I wouldn't know."

David looked down and adjusted a cufflink. Catherine narrowed her eyes.

"We'll see you back at the table."

Lily politely nodded and walked off. Within seconds Alastair was at her side. "Where's the fire?"

That summer David and Catherine invited everyone to Catherine's family cottage, Falconview, on Lake Joseph for a week in July. Lily would have preferred to keep her distance from Catherine and David.

Lily dropped the earring she'd been holding onto her lap and lifted another treasure from the box: a matchbook from a diner in Muskoka. She and Alastair, and the rest of the gang, had stopped there en route to Catherine's cottage, when David scribbled his telephone number and slipped the matches into her hand. Lily shook her head and handed back the matchbook. She wasn't that kind of woman. And she told him so.

However inappropriate, she hadn't blamed David for the gesture. Over the course of that week, she witnessed Catherine call out to him in a shrill voice, "David, don't do anything stupid," as he ventured out to split wood for the fire, or replace a torn panel on the screened porch. On several occasions, she mentioned his position at the company where he worked, which her father owned. Otherwise, Catherine ignored David.

Lily felt bad for him and did what little she could to be pleasant whenever their paths crossed. She had her own worries with Alastair. The life of the party, he started every day with a beer and tomato juice. By late evening he was drunk. Several times Lily discovered him on the bed, fully clothed, and snoring. But the nights he passed out were better than the ones when he picked an argument she couldn't win.

Near the end of their stay in Muskoka, David ran up the stairs and met her as she made her way down to the dock. Trapped between the house and the beach, with their friends in full view at either end, he begged her, "Call me," and, pretending he was only politely touching her as he passed by, he once more slipped a book of matches into her hand.

"I can't," she murmured, but this time tucked the matchbook into the side of her beach bag.

"Please, it's safe, my private line." His bare arm was against hers; breathless, she inhaled the scent of him—his musky perspiration mingled with sand and cedar. For a brief second she allowed herself to imagine what it would be like to lie naked beside him, the length of their bodies touching. When she looked up she saw he knew her thoughts. Feeling exposed and then angry, she said that she meant it; she wouldn't call. She pushed past him and ran down the steps.

When she returned home, she threw the matchbook in the trash. That evening the power went out. Alastair usually looked after such things, but he wasn't home. He'd worked late, and, judging from the time, he stopped for a beer. She managed to find candles, but no matches. Irritated, she began a blind search for a lighter or matches. That's when she remembered the matchbook in the trash. After the lights came back on, she put the matchbook in the false bottom of hall clock. She told herself she was keeping them there for safe measure.

A few days after the power failure, Lily went to get the mail and, along with several bills, found a small package wrapped in plain blue paper. There were no postage marks, only her first name written in silver block letters. Her birthday wasn't for another week. She smiled. Wasn't it nice of Alastair to surprise her early. She sat at the kitchen table and carefully unwrapped the package. Inside was a Birks' jewellery box, and taped to the lid was a miniature gift card. Lily unfolded the card and read: *When you're 'In the Mood,' wear them and think of me.* Not Alastair. Her heart beat faster as images of David came to mind

How We Danced

... at the dance hall, laughing ... at the cottage, helping her into a boat, his hand around her waist ... eyes pleading, call me; the matchbook ... his phone number. Lily lifted the lid, then a layer of cotton batting. A pair of pearl earrings, far more beautiful than the set that had been damaged, lay inside.

Each day of the week that followed, she had gone to the clock, flipped open the false bottom where she'd stored the earrings and matchbook. She willed herself not to call the phone number David had promised was safe. She didn't want to encourage him. Yet not calling seemed rude, especially when he'd been so thoughtful.

By the end of the following week, Lily paced the sidewalk of a downtown corner waiting for David. In the end, she had decided that it was best to call to say thank you for the earrings. And to explain, that although it was a lovely gesture, she could not accept his gift. But somehow she'd agreed to meet him. Now that she was there, she wanted to run away. But leaving at this point would complicate the situation further. She laid a hand on her purse that contained the earrings in their tiny gift box. She'd better stay, but only to return the present. Afterwards, she'd go shopping, as she had told Alastair.

To take her mind off the fluttering in her belly, she walked over to a shop window and examined the display of posed mannequins in the latest fashion. When she looked up, her reflection materialized in the glass. Lily smiled. She loved her own new dress. Twirling slightly, she watched the skirt move with her. There was no way she could resist buying it when it had come on sale a few days before. It was bolder than what she usually wore. The large, blue hydrangeas splashed over the white cotton and were so vivid she could almost smell them. She hoped David would admire it when she returned the package.

"Waiting for anyone in particular?"

Warm breath, delicate as a feather, tickled her neck and disappeared down the back of her dress.

Lily spun round. "Oh! I thought you were going to drive up. You were supposed to stop there," she pointed.

"I parked down the street. Come on, we'll walk." David extended his elbow.

67

Lily took his arm, but fear surged and she remained as immobile as the storefront mannequins. "Walk where?"

David turned to face her. "I'd like to walk you up and down every street in Hamilton to show off how gorgeous you are, especially in that dress. Considering our present circumstance, I think it best we walk to the car and then go for a drive."

Lily couldn't speak. She felt breathless and a little dizzy. Her heart pounded in her ears. It was crazy, but she wondered if David could hear it. Fearful thoughts bombarded her as she tried to slow her breath. If she fainted, what would happen? How would he explain who she was to those passing by? Still paralyzed, she stared at him and continued to say nothing.

David reached out and cupped her bare shoulder. Desire smothered fear; need replaced resolve.

"It'll be okay," he said.

She had believed him. That touch had been her undoing.

Even the memory gave her gooseflesh. She crossed her arms, running her hands up and down their length, the matchbook and earrings strewn across her lap along with the faded box and tattered batting. The hall clock chimed the hour. Lily packed away the tiny mementos. Reaching out, she tucked the box into the drawer of her bedside table. She'd return it to the clock's hidden compartment afterwards.

Relaxing back into her chair, she let out a long, slow breath and, closing her eyes, visualized her younger self … David behind her; his hands circling her tiny waist; his fingertips tracing the outline of her flat tummy, hips and thighs … A flutter of kisses running the length of her neck. *I love you.*

CHAPTER 9

After lying awake in her childhood bed for several minutes, Jennifer got up and straightened the fitted sheet, pulled up the top one and folded back the edge. Then she shook out the duvet and parachuted it onto the mattress. It took three tries, but it finally fell evenly. Fluffing each pillow, she set them on the bed angled against the headboard.

Warmed from the effort, she walked over to the window and flung opened the drapes. There was a burst of sound and light as the curtain rings scraped the rod, and the day's first sun filled the room. She cranked the window fully open. Fresh air gushed in. Leaning on the sill, she took a long, cleansing breath and looked at the front garden. The leaves of the maple had started to unfurl. From one of its boughs, the old rope swing with the weathered wooden seat swayed in the breeze. She pressed her fingertips against the cool screen. Goodness knows she spent many happy hours playing there. How easily she'd amused herself as a child. Just as well. Those were the days when her mother's eyes often had a faraway look. She'd sit for what seemed like hours to Jennifer, saying nothing. Her temper flared if Jennifer asked a question or was too noisy. On those days, her mother sent her to the front lawn to play, always with strict instructions not to talk to strangers. Jennifer would nod and run off. Only once did she break her mother's rule.

It had seemed so natural at the time. He'd appeared from nowhere. Veering off the pathway towards the porch, he walked up to her while she sat on the swing, eating a ripe plum. He knelt down and kept his blue eyes level with hers. Jennifer liked that. Most adults towered above her, and when they spoke, she was forced to look up into their hairy nostrils.

Reaching into his back pocket, he pulled out a handkerchief. "That looks like a juicy one." He laughed and passed the hankie to her.

The handkerchief smelled good. Like Daddy after he shaved in the morning. And like Daddy, this man didn't mind if she made a mess. Mouth full, she wiped her face and searched his bright, blue eyes.

"Your mommy's name is Lily, right?" he said.

The way he asked made her feel special. She passed back the gooey handkerchief and played along, "How'd you know?"

Without taking his eyes from hers, he folded the hankie and slipped it back into his pocket. "I'm a friend of your mom and dad's."

Jennifer considered that for a moment. His face looked the same age as her parents, but his hair was white, like Mr. Albanese's next door. Mr. Albanese was old. Jennifer decided she didn't care. Even though she'd just met the man, she liked him. He made her feel happy. Like Daddy.

"I bet I know how old you are," he said.

Jennifer waited, her plum held mid-air, now convinced that he could read her mind.

"Five. Am I right?"

She nodded. Feeling the need to please him, she said, "I can swing really high. Wanna see?"

But as he opened his mouth to answer, the screen door slammed. The man stood up. Dried leaves clung to his knees, and he brushed them off while staring towards the house.

Bang, bang, bang ...

Jennifer turned to see her mother charging down the wooden stairs, high heels pounding the steps like gun fire. Jennifer hopped off the swing and covered her ears.

"Get in the house." Her mother glared at the man, but Jennifer knew the command was for her.

"But Mammy ..."

Jennifer wanted to tell her that it was okay, the man wasn't a stranger.

Her mother thrust her palm forward like the stop sign the crossing guard used.

"Do as I say." Without shifting her gaze, she pointed a sharp finger to the porch.

Jennifer looked at the man. Still smiling, he winked and with the quick tilt of his chin, motioned for her to go.

As she ran to the porch she heard him say, "Sweetheart, please don't be angry." At the steps, she glanced back. Her mother had moved closer to the man. Spine rigid, she now pointed away from the house, towards the street. "Never come back here again."

The suppressed rage in her mother's voice frightened her, and she turned and ran into the house.

Afterwards, her mother came into her room where she was sitting at the edge of her bed. She looked away, but felt the mattress give as her mother sat beside her. In a quiet voice Mammy asked her to promise never to talk to strangers again. Jennifer didn't want to give her word. Mammy was always taking things away from her. It wasn't fair. The man wasn't a stranger, and he'd been nice. She liked him. Jennifer picked at the hem of her skirt and told herself not to give in. *Don't do it, don't do it.*

"Look at me," her mother said.

Don't do it, don't do it. Jennifer refused to look at her mother. In silence she tugged at a loose thread on her skirt's hem; she continued to pick at it, not wanting it to break, fearing if she did, something terrible would happen.

"Your father will be disappointed by your behaviour today. But," her mother had paused and laid a gentle hand on Jennifer's shoulder, "*if* you promise not to talk to strangers again, I won't tell him. It'll be our secret."

Jennifer had tucked the unbroken thread back into her hem and nodded.

Stepping back from the window, she shrugged on her bathrobe. Her mother's anger had been so charged with emotion that day. Yet the expression on the man's face when her mother appeared had been so tender. "Sweetheart …"

Jennifer turned back to the bed she'd just made and admired how neatly the comforter's edges were aligned. She had an urge to make other things right and decided this would be a good time to have a go at the rest of the house. Rather than disturb her parents, she opted to check out the old spot in the basement for the stash of cleaning products. Minutes later, Jennifer stood on the bottom step of the cellar stairs with an armful of bottles, brushes and towels. She looked up, wondering if she could make it to the top without dropping anything. Framed in the doorway was her mother. After a furtive glance up and down the hall, she clopped back into her room and closed the door.

Jennifer slumped down onto the step; spray bottles, polishing creams and dusters jumbled around her. Secrets. It seemed too much like old times.

❀ ❀ ❀

Alastair was having a good spell, and he wanted to make the most of it. He'd enjoyed the mince and tatties Lily and Jennifer made for dinner. But it had just been he and Lily who'd eaten. Jennie had gone home to visit her man and the girls.

From the confines of his chair, he watched Lily as she cleared away their dinner trays. Although her ankle was still sore, according to the doctor, it was healing well. The crutches were gone, replaced by a cane that allowed her to move with a bit more ease. When Lily headed for the kitchen, he reached for the remote, turned on the television and, heedless of the program, raised the volume.

What he wanted now was a cigarette.

He glanced at the table drawer where he'd stashed a couple of Rothmans and a lighter. Seconds later, he'd lit up and tentatively inhaled. Then he took a proper drag, closed his eyes and exhaled. Cramped hands relaxed; arms and legs tingled in the rush of nicotine. As he raised the cigarette to his lips again, he wheezed and the coughing started. *It'll stop in a moment. Stay calm. It never lasts. Stay calm.* Like every other time, the jag ended with a forceful hack.

The sound of running water from the kitchen stopped. "You okay?" Lily called out.

He croaked, "Fine."

The rush of water resumed.

How We Danced

Trembling, he dipped the lit end in his water glass and then returned the butt to the drawer. His breathing resumed its shallow, irregular rhythm.

He tugged out the cushion Lily had tucked behind him and tossed it. The corner clipped a rock she kept on the end table. It fell to the floor with a clunk near his chair.

Alastair leaned over and picked up the quartz stone, rolled it around in his hand. Veins of pink and pewter shimmered. Most of the knick-knacks Lily displayed were more refined. As he recalled, she'd found this particular one many years ago on a trip north and kept it as a memento. That trip had been special to both of them, at least at the outset.

With little money, it had been a rare treat to get away to the Muskokas. None of their gang would have gone had it not been for David and Catherine. Alastair's mouth curled in resentment at the memory of David Mallory. Alastair had never liked him much, nor his wife. Catherine's family had money, and Alastair suspected that's why Mallory had married her. Yet he acted like Lord of the Manor, especially around the women. Alastair rolled the rock in his palm and rubbed a thumb along a rough edge.

Alastair remembered a conversation he'd had with Catherine during that time, in the Great Room of Falconview. Lily had been off doing God-knows-what with the other women. He was up late that morning, hungover. Catherine, looking bedraggled as well, grunted something to that effect when he asked where everyone else was. Uncomfortable, he tried to make small talk and asked if there actually were any falcons in the vicinity. She suggested he find out for himself. Within seconds he had binoculars slung around his neck and was out the door.

The sun was already high and hot. The glare of it bounced off the pinkish rock and clear water, blinding him as he walked down the steep steps to the dock. Having lived in the honk and screech of the city all his life, Alastair marvelled at the soft sound of lapping water; the breeze in the branches and the tang of pine and cedar that became more pungent with each step.

Beneath the wooden stairs there was the scurry of feet, and he smiled. He figured it was one of the chipmunks he'd seen gathering peanuts Catherine had scattered on the deck.

Midway down, a lone cloud covered the sun. Lifting the binoculars, he searched the horizon. Nothing. The cloud passed and he continued. In the distance he saw a small rocky island. On it stood a towering pine; the perfect roost for a hunting bird. Adjusting his binoculars, he peered at the tiny island. Sure enough, a large bird swept out of the tree. He admired the bird's free flight as it circled the treetops and into the scrub below. As Alastair followed its descent, the glint of something metallic caught his eye. Since he'd lost sight of the hawk, he focussed the binoculars on the shiny object. It appeared to be the prow of a small boat; perhaps a couple of fishermen trying their luck from the craggy shore. Lifting the binoculars again, he searched for the bird. There it was, perched on the thick bough of the tall tree pulling flesh from a small furry creature. Alastair made a mental note of the hawk's light-coloured belly, streaked brown. Sweat from his brow ran into his eyes. He removed the binoculars and rubbed his eyes. When he looked again, the bird was gone.

Giving up on the raptor, Alastair turned the binoculars back to the boat. Two people were seated, Kevin and Carol. Both were looking up at another couple, just emerging from the bush. Alastair re-focused the binoculars. He was rewarded with a clear view of David helping Lily into the bobbing boat—the tender way he steadied her; clasping her hand, holding her waist. That simple gesture made his heart skip like a stone over the still lake. She scanned the shoreline and then up to where Alastair stood on the landing. Of course she couldn't see him. Yet her delighted expression filled the lens. Alastair let the binoculars drop to his chest. He ran up the steps and into the house.

Later, around the campfire, David shared how Catherine's grandfather had acquired the land and built Falconview.

Alastair sucked back the last of his beer and interrupted, "About the falcons," he began. He told everyone about scanning the island and spying the raptor. He was pleased when the focus shifted. The questions came in rapid succession: *What did it look like? What was it doing? Colour? Markings? Wing span?*

"This was the bird perched in the big pine?" David asked.

All eyes turned from David to Alastair. He nodded.

"That wasn't a falcon. It was a red-tailed hawk," David added.

Kevin said, "Red-tailed hawks aren't that big. Alastair claimed his had a wing span of three feet." He spoke to Alastair, "Right, buddy?"

"Actually," Catherine said, "the female hawks *are* that large. They're bigger and more threatening than the males." She smirked at Kevin and then Alastair.

"Maybe I saw a different bird." Alastair rubbed his knuckles. "I'm sure it was a falcon."

David smiled. "It's an easy mistake."

"You couldn't have seen the bird I did. Not from where you were." Alastair flushed. "What I mean is, I had a better view from the landing, through my binoculars."

David got up and stoked the fire and added a log.

Kevin cleared his throat. "Anyone for a beer?" He leaned over and opened the cooler.

Catherine stretched, lifted her arms high above her head and yawned.

Alastair wished Lily would say something that would let him know she took his part. He risked a sidelong glimpse. Her body was turned towards David. From the blanket covering her knees, she rolled a twist of the fringe between her fingers.

That's when Alastair realised he must make love to his bride or risk losing her. A woman less kind, less tolerant would have left months ago.

The next evening, Alastair suggested to Lily they forget the campfire and turn in early. All day he imagined their evening together. He rehearsed what he'd say to her, what he'd do. He visualized himself taking flight, soaring and then swooping down with the grace of the raptor he'd seen.

As she readied herself in the bathroom, he put a vase of daylilies in the middle of the mirrored bureau and slid into bed. He looked around the flowers at his reflection. His bare, hairless chest looked a bit pale, but he'd do. After a quick peep towards the door, he splashed on a bit more of the Old Spice he'd hidden in the bedside table. His teeth were brushed not ten minutes ago. When he lifted a hand to check his nails, she appeared behind his splayed fingers. He dropped his hand and grinned, "Come on then, get in."

Raising the blankets she noticed the lilies. "Oh, Alastair," she turned to him, "they're beautiful!"

"You like them?"

Expression wary, she asked, "They're from you?"

"Well, who else? Snuggle in, I'm freezing." He drew her close and pulled the covers over them. "I found a patch across the way growing wild."

She nodded, thoughtful. "I love them." Raised eyebrows wrinkled her forehead.

He smoothed the hair from her face. Tenderly, he kissed her brow. The furrows disappeared. When he had pressed closer, she'd sighed. He had been a hawk, strong and free. Alastair had closed his eyes, taken flight and claimed his wife.

❀ ❀ ❀

Lily hobbled through the bedroom door and Alastair set the quartz stone back onto the table. She made her way to the chair and collapsed. With a tired sigh, she balanced her cane on the arm of the chair.

Alastair cleared his throat.

"You all right?" she asked, frowning with concern over his strange pallor. "You look as though you've seen a ghost."

He shrugged. "Thanks for the mince and tatties," he said, grateful she'd never left.

"Mammy." Hearing Jennifer's voice, Lily struggled to open her eyes. "Why don't you let me help you to the bed?" Jennifer said. "You'll get a sore neck sleeping like this."

Lily sat up, scrubbed her face with her hands. "Ah...that's okay, hen. I was just resting." She peeked around Jennifer to Alastair. "How's your father?" Without waiting for an answer, she reached for her cane. "Still sleeping, I see. Well then, let's not disturb him with our chatter. I'd love a cup of tea." Leaning on the cane to stand, she said. "Come on, we'll go into the kitchen."

As Lily poured milk into her tea, she watched Jennifer move things around the fridge so that she could replace the milk carton.

Hands on hips, Jennifer reared back and peered in. She stacked the yogurt and shoved in the milk. The open carton toppled over. Spilled milk pooled on the shelf and dripped onto the floor.

How We Danced

Lily grimaced. She wanted to tell Jennifer she was putting the milk in the wrong spot; it belonged at the other side. Instead, she turned her back on the mess.

Jennifer ran to the sink and wrung out a dishcloth.

Lily chose not to watch as Jennifer cleaned up the milk. Instead she stared out the window over the sink and focused on the old rope swing that swayed in the breeze. But the scrape and clatter of bottles, jars and cartons being rearranged intruded. Just when Lily thought she couldn't stand the disturbance any longer, Jennifer closed the fridge door. Moments later, she joined Lily at the table. In her periphery, she saw Jennifer reach for the sugar and add two spoonfuls to her tea. She hesitated before adding a third. Lily knew her daughter was waiting for a comment, but Lily remained silent.

Reaching for the teapot, Lily recalled a day, years ago, when she had defrosted and cleaned the fridge. Jennifer was about four at the time. Back then it was big job. That's why she had sent her daughter outside to play. From the window over the sink, she had been able to keep an eye on Jennifer and still work. While emptying the contents of fridge onto the counter, she had found a ripe plum that got lost at the back of the fruit bin.

Lily called out the window, "Look," she said, "I found one of your favourites."

"A cookie?" Jennifer jumped off the swing.

Lily met Jennifer at the door and handed her the plum.

Jennifer scrunched her nose. "Can I have a cookie instead?"

"Maybe later." Lily smoothed her daughter's bangs. "Go and play," she said and went back to her cleaning.

She had the shelves out and was head and shoulders into the fridge when she heard a man's voice. Wondering who Jennifer could be talking to, she backed up and looked out the window.

The next instant she was out the door.

Jennifer's skinny legs were dangling from the swing's seat when Lily barrelled down the steps. Her breath quickened; her head spun. He was there with Jennifer, her little-girl face smiling and her blue eyes, his blue eyes, sparkling. He was there, looking at her, bending, reaching into their lives, and Lily was

77

shouting, crying, and stumbling. *In the house. Now!* Jennifer's confused fear crackled. *Not a stranger.* He was smiling, pleading, *Sweetheart.* The swing swayed, empty. He was still there. Her hands on his chest, hard, familiar, pushing, pushing no, just please, please, go, go.

Lily now looked at her adult daughter across the kitchen table, her posture as stiff and resolved as it had been when she was young. Lily yearned for her own youth, when David had pursued her, and her daughter adored her. These days she felt old and useless.

As though reading her thoughts, Jennifer scrutinized Lily's injured leg resting on a stool. "Is your ankle sore?"

Lily sighed. "It's not too bad."

"Are you worried about Daddy?"

"No more than usual."

Jennifer reached over for her hand. "Your ankle will heal."

Lily held on for a moment and then let go. As she did, Jennifer stiffened.

"You're right," Lily said, telling Jennifer what she assumed her daughter wanted to hear. Not the truth. That she felt as though, bit by bit, her life was being whittled away.

"You're managing better than I expected…" Jennifer's words trailed off.

The sincere concern in Jennifer's voice was gone. Lily's hand trembled as she poured another cup of tea.

"What were you doing in the hall earlier? It must have been urgent for you to venture that far without my help."

Lily felt as though her blood had been replaced by ice water. *Had Jennifer seen her return the box to the clock? No. If she had she would have asked about that. She must have seen me as I was heading back into my room.*

"I had to go to the toilet. I was going to tell you I made it there and back on my own, but I forgot."

It saddened Lily that they had learned to be so distrustful of one another. They'd been close when Jennifer was little, but as she had grown, so had the distance between them. It was hard to change ingrained habits. Even when you knew there had to be a better way.

"I see…" Jennifer drew out the words.

"Good grief. You make it sound as though I was up to no good." Lily feared the suspicion in her daughter's eyes. Still, she tried to sound lighthearted.

Jennifer heaved a sigh. After a moment she stood and started to clear the table. Lily drank her tea.

CHAPTER 10

Jennifer brought in a load of laundry as her mother plumped her father's pillows, tidied up the twisted blankets.

"Here," Lily said to Alastair, "bend your knees, turn on your side."

Jennifer smiled. Her mother was relentless when family was ill, but she did have a way of making you comfortable. At least once she was done. During the process you were at her mercy.

"I'm fine, Lily," Alastair complained.

Still grinning, Jennifer looked over at them. The covers on her father's bed were thrown to the end. He was on his back, knees bent. One pyjama leg had bunched up, revealing his damaged shin.

Jennifer's smiled faded. As always, she turned away. Beneath the scars, a secret plate of steel. She didn't want to bear witness to the damage. Once was enough.

"There. Isn't that better?" Lily asked.

Jennifer put the laundry basket down and left the room without waiting to hear her father's response. She walked to the front door and scowled out the window. Something was drawing her outside.

Crossing the porch, she bent over the railing. The walkway that ran between their house and the Albanese's was narrow and dark, even during the day.

Three men scurry out from between the houses, two with their faces turned away. The other is carrying something, a baseball bat? He glares at Jennifer, hawks, spits, keeps moving ... gone.

That night she hadn't been able to see what was happening, but she had heard the horrible accusations, her father's cry of pain. Afterwards, she had charged down the darkened pathway, found him in a sliver of light, writhing in agony, his leg mangled. She had run for her mother for help. When it was over, she had turned away, pushed that terrible scene into the recesses of her memory, never prodded, let it sleep. Lied and lied and lied until it became true.

Jennifer stepped back from the railing. She'd never spoken of the men, what they'd said, what they'd done. Never let her mind go there. Even at that young age she had recognized that once something was said, it lived and became fact. So she'd remained mute. And blind.

She grabbed the screen door, yanked it open, pushed the front door in, slamming it against the stop. Why must I remember these things now?

❀ ❀ ❀

The room was dark, except for the nightlight shining near Alastair's bed. Across the way, he discerned Lily's silhouette beneath the blankets; distinguished the slope of her slim shoulders rising and falling; the curve of her hip tapering to her thighs. He could tell her knees were bent, see the contour of her feet.

He missed Lily beside him. The smell of rose petal hand cream she applied before bed, the feel of her breath on his back, even the annoying way she moved one leg up and down the mattress, before sleep put a stop to it. Now he regretted the way he'd resented her and kept her at arm's length, as if his unhappiness had been her fault. Yet, once committed, she'd stayed the course. Lily possessed a resolve that eluded him.

Sometimes he believed he was cursed. No matter how hard he tried or how much he had wanted to stay faithful, he couldn't. He despised his weakness. Even when things were good between them, and God knew the woman did her best to satisfy,

Deborah Serravalle

something would happen to awaken his other needs. Forceful desires that repulsed and beckoned. Lily would have loathed him had she known.

As though disturbed by his turmoil, she stirred and murmured in her sleep. Alastair coughed, hoping she'd wake and ask if he needed anything. But instead, she settled, and her breathing began the monotonous hush of deep sleep. If only he could yank the covers off and stride across the room. Those days were gone.

Another woman might have asked more questions, but not Lily. Right from the outset she was guileless and kind, accepting his dismal excuses. He wished he could take back those times he'd disappointed her.

Fully awake now, he was restless. He sat up, reached for the house robe at the foot of his bed and struggled to put one arm in and then the other. Maybe he'd wander into the living room and read for a bit.

Before all this nonsense with the cancer, he'd started the Aubrey-Maturin's high seas adventure series by Patrick O'Brian. He'd enjoyed the first one, *Master and Commander,* and so he'd continued. He was just finishing the tenth installment, *The Far Side of the World,* when he'd gotten the bad news. From that point on, words on the page had scrambled, scattered and regrouped. *Cancer. Malignant tumour. Stage 4.* Alastair lost interest in the novel's characters. He had focussed on the battle facing him, not the romantic high seas, but something worse.

Suddenly he needed to know how the story ended.

Easing his legs over the edge of the mattress, he planted his feet on the floor, stood and scuffed into his slippers. Concentrating on the bedroom door ahead of him, he rubbed his hands together. *You can do this, MacAulay.* He stepped forward: one, two and three. He stumbled, grabbed hold of the back of his chair and righted himself. More steps. He stopped, caught his breath, straightened his back. Lily started to snore; a gentle, deep rumble that propelled him forward, through the door and into the hall.

After pausing several times along the hallway, he arrived at the closed door to the living room. Tentacles of fiery pain licked his torso, and slithered down his legs. Gripping the doorknob, he saw a reflection in one of the glass panes; not his face, but The Boy's. With a gasp he pushed open the door and slumped down on the closest chair. He took a moment to recover, wipe the moisture that had formed on his brow. Despite The Boy's appearance and the strength it had required to trek this far, he felt the best he had in days, perhaps weeks. He'd need to conserve his energy if he planned on making the return trip to bed unassisted. With this in mind, he looked around the room to gauge the distance between where he was, the bookshelves and the easy chair. That's when he spied the liquor cabinet.

Alastair licked his lips. A dram was just what the doctor ordered. Scotch and one of O'Brian's nautical novels; a match made in heaven. He turned in the chair and, with an extended foot, pushed the door until he heard a quiet click.

The most direct route to the bookshelves and cabinet was straight across the carpet. But in his condition he decided to go around the room. He could sit down on the love seat or on one of the chairs or footrests that lined the perimeter, if needed. Hoisting his body from the chair, he began his trek. At the love seat, his knees buckled, but he was able to right himself with the armrest and continued on. As he passed the piano, he plunked down on the stool, and using his feet, wheeled the rest of the way, arriving at the liquor cabinet winded, but elated. Remaining seated, he opened the doors and searched the contents. Gin, vodka, plum brandy. Where was his Scotch? Off to the side, he spotted a half-full bottle of Haig & Haig Pinch. Uncorking it, he took a whiff. *Hmph.*

The tumblers were in the glass case above. Clutching the cabinet for balance, he stood just long enough to retrieve one of the special squat goblets he reserved for whisky. As he lifted the bottle to pour, he spied another tucked way at the back. Re-corking the Haig & Haig, he pulled out The Macallan 18. A cigarette and a book of matches fell forward. Perfect, he thought, and pocketed them.

Alastair cupped the bottle in the palm of one hand and, with a tentative finger, traced the outline of the label. It had been a gift, sent special delivery when Jennifer was born. Alastair broke the seal, uncorked the bottle and poured four fingers into the glass.

After pulling his novel from the bookshelf, placing it on his lap with the goblet balanced atop, he wheeled over to his favourite easy chair. Drawing shaky fingers across his scalp, he looked back to where he'd come from. He was amazed that such a small task could leave him feeling drained. He waited to catch his breath before moving from the stool to the chair.

With a shaky hand he pulled the cigarette from his pocket, rolled it between his fingers. That would have to do. Smoking it would start him coughing, and he'd wake the house. Instead, he brought the glass of Scotch to his nose, closed his eyes and took a long, deep whiff. The peaty, long-ago fragrance brought to mind the first time he tasted The Macallan. It was before Jennifer was born. He had been working at Edward's Typewriter Repair. That day had started off like any other: fixing a machine in the upstairs workshop.

Alastair lifted the cover off the typewriter, removed the used ribbon spools and set them on the counter. He placed two new spools in the holders and threaded the clean ribbon through the wire in front of the roller. When he closed the cover, a loud snap reverberated round the empty shop.

All the guys were on calls, and he was grateful to have the place to himself. He liked the others well enough, but every once in a while it was nice to focus on the job at hand without interruption. He enjoyed concentrating on a repair, especially a complex one. Machines dropped in transit, or those that took a tumble from a desk, were the most challenging and required both skill and intuition. There were hundreds of tiny moving parts that could be damaged. Simple issues often revealed more complex problems. These difficult jobs were his favourite and one of the reasons he was sent on the tougher assignments. That, and the fact the customers loved him. Often he was requested.

Rising from the stool, he carried the repaired typewriter to the shelf near the stairwell for storage. It was scheduled to be picked up later today. Edwards, the shop owner, or Margaret, the secretary would deal with them. Rarely did a client darken the upstairs shop haunted by a miasma of ink with undertones of ammonia. They were sanctioned to the pristine store front below or relegated to orderly offices.

Facing the wall of windows that looked out over John Street, Alastair yawned and moved closer. Rivulets of raindrops streaked the glass like tears. He stretched his arms over his head, flexing his stiff back muscles. Maybe it was the rain or the oppressive humidity, but Alastair was fidgety.

Circling the heel of his hand against the window, he cleared a patch of condensation. Shoppers trod the sidewalk in the mid-afternoon gloom; mostly women in full skirts and high heels, their faces hidden by umbrellas.

He wondered how Lily was doing. She hadn't gotten up with him this morning as she usually did. Instead, she'd turned her back when the alarm went off and said she wasn't feeling well. He hoped that's all it was. If she was in some sort of huff, he was in no mood to deal with it.

Across the street in the doorway of a shop, a man with a fedora pulled low on his brow hovered for a moment to light a cigarette and then walked off. Alastair touched the packet tucked in his shirt pocket. Maybe he'd do the same. Probably all he needed was a break, and then he'd get back to work.

He climbed down the stairs and started through the store.

"Where are you going?" Mr. Edwards, his boss, came out of his office.

Alastair stood still but didn't turn around or answer. The secretary stopped typing.

"I need you to go on a call," Edwards said.

Alastair faced his boss.

Edwards looked him up and down. "Designs by Aaron. Aaron Trudel's a well-known decorator with a large client base. That could mean more business for us."

Edwards turned towards his office, but called out, "Put on a tie. Margaret, give him the details."

Although he didn't consider Edwards a fine judge of character, en route to the call Alastair couldn't help feeling influenced by his comments. The last thing he felt like dealing with was an uppity decorator. Besides, it was close to the end of the work day. He would have preferred to stay at the shop and repair that final job.

At least he had the company car. In what Alastair thought was a rare moment of generosity, Edwards had told him that since the shop would be closed by the time he finished his call, not to bother coming back, but to drive the car home and return with it in the morning. That was before he suggested Alastair had the choice to return and clock some overtime. The son of a bitch always had something up his sleeve. Alastair hadn't committed, but nevertheless had phoned Lily and told her not to hold dinner. Late calls weren't the norm, but every so often they happened. As usual, Lily was agreeable and offered to put a plate aside.

The address wasn't far from downtown, and he easily located the renovated Victorian home that housed Designs by Aaron. On a busy thoroughfare, the building was set right at the sidewalk. Just as he was about to look for a metre, he spotted a sign above an old brick archway that indicated parking was in the rear. Greenery threatened to engulf the lot, so the spots were tight. Alastair wondered why the shrubs and trees hadn't been trimmed. In contrast to the chic sidewalk front, the garden and parking lot had a tangled, fairy-tale feel. For a moment, Alastair wondered what this said about the proprietor. But then he shifted his concentration and backed into the spot without incident.

After retrieving his tool case from the trunk, he walked around to the front and climbed the stone steps. He stopped at the landing to shake off a premonition that he was at a crossroads.

Adjusting his heavy tool bag, he looked to his right, where a huge storefront window displayed the contents of an entire room. Gold, greens and several shades of orange were suffused with browns and taupey greys. Alastair sniffed, overdone.

As he opened the door and stepped into the shop, a bell tinkled, high and sweet. The place was full of lamps, love seats, chesterfields, fancy chairs that no one would ever sit on, and innumerable ornaments. He grimaced, "Dust collectors."

"Perhaps, but you'd be surprised what people will pay for them."

Alastair spun around and bumped into a large, bearded man with a wiry dog lodged in the crook of his arm.

The beast growled.

"Hush, Napoleon!" The man pulled his arm with the dog back and stuck out his other hand. Alastair took it, surprised by its warmth and strength.

"I'm Aaron. Don't mind Napoleon. Yorkies are possessive." He scratched the top of the dog's head. "You must be the typewriter repairman."

"Alastair MacAulay's the name."

Everything about the man was impeccable, from his tailored suit to his gold cufflinks to his leather shoes. Yet his relaxed welcome and firm handshake put Alastair at ease.

Aaron smiled. "Come, Alastair, I'll show you to the office."

Alastair shadowed him through a maze of furniture and fabric into a narrow hallway that led to the back of the shop. At the end, Aaron opened a door and, with a wave of a hand, invited Alastair to enter. Napoleon growled as he passed by.

Unlike the rest of the store, this room was soothing. No flashy colour. It was furnished with heavy, masculine pieces. A large desk sat by the window that looked out on the wildly beautiful back garden.

Aaron planted Napoleon on a square cushion atop the desk. The dog settled but kept his eyes on Alastair.

"Here we go." Aaron opened the side cabinet of the desk and sprung up the typewriter shelf. "I've a raft of invoices, orders to do and correspondence to complete. The keys are jamming and letters are skipping. Can you fix it? Or do I need to trash it and buy a new one?"

Alastair was already opening his tool case. "Come back in half an hour and I'll tell you." He glanced at the dog as he spread a soft cloth onto the desk to protect the surface.

"Would you like me to leave Napoleon for company?"

Alastair stopped what he was doing. Aaron smiled. Napoleon looked from one to the other and sat back.

If he was being tested, Alastair wasn't going to allow this spit-of-a-dog or toff-of-a-gentleman to best him. He held his hand out for the dog to sniff. Napoleon stretched his neck and licked his fingers.

"He can stay."

Deborah Serravalle

Alastair went back to retrieving tools from the case. He placed his tweezers, screwdrivers and a bottle of ammonia on the cloth.

Aaron scooped up Napoleon and laughed. A joyous sound it was, and Alastair suppressed the urge to join in. "I'll come back in thirty minutes, and you can give me your assessment."

Alastair waited until Aaron closed the door before getting to work.

He was packing up when Aaron returned.

"You're finished?" Aaron gave a dismissive wave. "Let me guess. She couldn't be saved and you put her out of her misery."

"No." Alastair snapped his case shut. "She's as good as new. Just needed a good clean, a few adjustments, and a fresh ribbon. When's the last time you had her serviced?"

"Hmm." Aaron plunked Napoleon on the leather sofa across from the desk. "I can't recall. Probably never."

"You may want to consider calling my office and setting up a maintenance schedule. Save yourself some trouble." Alastair lifted his case.

"A stitch in time saves nine?"

Alastair chuckled. "Something like that."

Often he had to state, repeat and defend his rationale for repairing or retiring a machine. The way Aaron accepted his assessment without question felt good. It was nice to be respected. Even Lily didn't show him this kind of deference.

"So you're done for the day then?" Aaron called over his shoulder as he walked towards a cabinet.

Alastair looked at his watch. He shrugged. "I am."

Aaron opened the cabinet doors. He stooped and reached into the back. "Fabulous. Have a seat. I have something I want you to try."

Alastair hesitated.

Aaron twisted his head round for a moment. "Oh, go on. Have a seat. I'll be right back." Aaron placed the decanter down and left.

Alastair set his tool case on the floor.

"Here we are." Aaron breezed back into the room carrying a full tray.

How We Danced

"What's all this?" Alastair asked.

"You are about to experience one of the finest single malt whiskies out of the highlands." Aaron sat down and poured three fingers in each glass. He handed one to Alastair. "And a little appetizer. Sláinte!"

Alastair raised his glass.

"Tell me what you think." Aaron lifted Napoleon onto his lap, stroking him as he waited.

Alastair closed his eyes, waved a cupped hand over the glass and inhaled. A beatific smile bloomed across his face, and he took a tentative sip.

Aaron leaned forward.

Alastair smacked his lips. This was without question the best Scotch he'd ever tasted. And he'd tasted a few. "You're a man of your word. What is it?"

"The eighteen-year-old Macallan."

Aaron took a drink.

That explained it. Alastair had tasted The Macallan before, but never this vintage. No wonder it was like drinking liquid gold.

Aaron handed Alastair a plate. "I hope you like chopped liver."

The man looked so expectant, Alastair wondered how he'd tell him if he didn't fancy the stuff. Lifting the cracker to his mouth, he returned Napoleon's jealous glare. "Mmm," he nodded, realizing he needn't have worried. "It's delicious."

Aaron leaned back with his Scotch. "As a rule, I drink a more modest brand."

Alastair was mesmerized by the lovely decanter. "Why serve this to me?" he blurted out.

"It was a gift," Aaron shrugged. "I thought it would be nice to share it with someone who'd appreciate it."

Something warm bloomed within Alastair's breast that had nothing to do with the Scotch. He helped himself to a cracker and then, like Aaron, relaxed into the sofa. The alcohol was meandering its way through his system, loosening him up. "Do you live here?" he asked.

"In the coach house." Aaron lifted a chin at the large picture window framing the garden.

Alastair had thought the ivy-encased building out back was for storage. "Alone?"

"Not really. Napoleon is excellent company. He's always happy to see me and he doesn't complain when I work long hours. However, if you mean do I have a wife, the answer is no. I did once but we parted ways—amicably, I might add. I'm godfather to her daughter."

"But I thought…" It was out before Alastair had a chance to stop it. He felt his face flush. There was something about this man that loosened his tongue.

"That I prefer men?" Aaron smiled without a trace of malice.

Alastair was horrified. He set his Scotch on the table, ready for a quick exit.

Seemingly nonplussed, Aaron continued, "I do. But it took the death of a dear friend to make me realise I wasn't going to live forever, and what time I did have, I wanted to live authentically. So I divorced Harriet, changed careers—I used to be stockbroker, can you imagine?—and the rest of the world be damned."

Impressed, yet a little horrified, Alastair stared at Aaron, unsure of what to say or do.

Aaron continued. "This is what I should have been doing from the outset," he waved a manicured hand around the room. "My poor mother, and then Harriet, suffered me endlessly decorating and then re-decorating their homes. Now I'm doing something I'm perfectly suited for and being paid handsomely for it." He topped off Alastair's Scotch and sat back with a grin. "The women love me, and the men aren't threatened. Besides," his voice went up a contrived octave, as he crossed his legs and flourished a limp wrist, "everyone knows we have impeccable taste."

He looked into Alastair's eyes. "Have I shocked you, Alastair? You look as though I have."

Alastair shrugged, steadied his hand, picked up his drink and took a big swallow. This character was toying with him and he didn't like it.

"I haven't put you off then?"

"What do you mean, put me off?"

"You haven't bolted. Am I to assume you're fine with sharing a drink, a meal perhaps?"

Once more he was being challenged. With sudden clarity, Alastair realised how difficult life must be for someone as openly deviant as Aaron. A sliver of envy slipped between his reflexive shock and ingrained disapproval. Aaron had guts.

"I run from no one," Alastair said with more bravado than he felt. With sincerity, he added, "I admire your confidence." Eyes cast down, he finished off his Scotch and put the empty glass on the table. "But I wouldn't say it's true—about all men of ..." Alastair faltered, "... your persuasion having good taste." He got up.

Aaron stood also. "Perhaps you're right."

Alastair reached for his tool case. He felt Aaron's eyes bore into him as he checked to make sure the straps were fastened. "Well, thank you for the drink." He extended his hand.

Aaron took it and held on. "Unless you have to be somewhere, why not stay for dinner? I have a couple of porterhouse steaks I can broil and some good imported ale in the fridge."

With effort, Alastair withdrew his hand. "I'm married." Meant as a statement, it sounded like a plea, and he blushed crimson. He'd made steps in the right direction. It had been ages since he'd wavered. Alastair glanced at the door. If he could just get out of here. To the car. Home. To Lily.

"It is dinner, not a proposition." Aaron had smiled and poured Alastair a fresh Scotch. "I'm not that easy. Now tell me, how do you like your steak?"

Alastair had looked at Aaron's open smile and accepted.

❀ ❀ ❀

Thunder cracked. Alastair flinched and the past disintegrated. A flash of lightning lit up the living room, rain lashed the windows. This wasn't good. Lily feared thunder and thrashing rain. It was time for him to get back to bed. He swirled and then gulped the remaining whisky.

Whether fortified by The Macallan or energized by the prospect of discovery, the slog back down the hallway was easier this time, even with his book in hand. He stopped outside their bedroom door to catch his breath. The patter of rain was muffled, and there hadn't been another clap of thunder. He hoped the storm had passed. Or that it would at least restrain its fury and not wake Lily until he was back in bed. Slowly turning the knob, he pushed the door open and stepped into the bedroom. Not a sound. He couldn't believe he'd gotten away with it. He looked at Lily. She slept on, oblivious.

❀ ❀ ❀

Lily was happy the family was over for a visit. Especially when she saw how it lifted Alastair's spirits. Cam and the girls had brought take-out, and they'd all sat around Alastair's bed chatting and eating chicken and fries. However, it wasn't long before Lily noticed Alastair's grey pallor, wan smile and drooping eyelids. At that point she suggested they go into the kitchen and let Granddad rest.

They sat around the table playing Monopoly. Lily's side still hurt from laughing during the latest round, when Emma insisted she take some money to pay for her second visit to Boardwalk, and then put a hotel on it.

Even so, Lily felt odd. The game, the laughing, none of it seemed right. "I better check on Granddad," she said.

"He's fine, Mammy." Jennifer glanced at the clock. "It's only been twenty minutes."

Lily half-stood, hesitating.

"Come on, sit down." Jennifer smiled. "I think Daddy was snoring before we'd all filed out. He didn't even realise we left."

Lily glanced around the table. Emma was counting her money, again. Lindsay and Cam were teasing one another about who'd get the chance to buy Park Avenue.

To leave now would disrupt the game. Lily sat down and tried to relax. She told herself Jennifer was right, that Alastair had always been a sound sleeper. In their younger years, his loud snores had often kept Lily awake. She had found the noise intolerable on the nights she had trouble sleeping.

After David turned up on their front lawn and approached Jennifer, sleep had been difficult, even when Alastair wasn't snoring. Lily had thought of David constantly. Fantasies of him had filled her days and kept her awake by night.

David's breath, warm on her neck … the feel of his lips brushing her cheek … his hand cupping her breast.

How We Danced

Her obsession with him began to intrude on simple pleasures. Taking Jennifer for an ice-cream cone or a walk with Alastair became a drudge. Often she imagined running into David. Sometimes she dressed up, certain she would see him. She rehearsed what she'd say, how she would act. Reading was impossible; she couldn't concentrate. Film stars at the cinema and actors on the TV became David. Many a night Alastair came home from a long day at work to a simple sandwich or bowl of canned soup. Dust collected along the baseboards and tables.

One evening, feeling particularly exhausted, Lily put Jennifer to bed early. It was summertime, still light out and Jennifer rebelled. Frustrated, Lily spanked her, told her to stay put and slammed the door.

Later, still angry and sleepless beside a snoring Alastair, she got up. Unsure of what to do, she wandered from the kitchen to the living room, back to the hallway. She grabbed a sweater from the front closet and pulled it on over her pyjamas, put on her shoes and went to sit on the porch. The breeze was cool and carried the scent of ripe grapes from the neighbour's pergola. Through the big maple, the moon hung full and bright. In the distance a train rumbled. She stepped off the porch, pulled her sweater tighter and walked towards the sound.

At the end of her street she turned west and picked up the pace. For the first time in ages, the tormenting questions and images eased. And so she walked faster. She focussed on the hard concrete beneath her feet, the glare of a streetlight, the slant of a roof in the distance.

When she thought she heard David whisper *Sweetheart*, she started to run. She ran past the golf course and then northwest, into Westdale. On one of the side streets a car approached and kept pace with her for a few feet. The driver pulled forward and then stopped. She ran into the backyard of the house closest to her, cut through the neighbour's yard and came out onto another street. Breathing heavily, heart racing, she stopped, placed a hand over the stitch in her side. Panting, she looked around and tried to get her bearings. She stood frozen for a moment, tried to grasp what she'd done. David lived a few streets from where she stood.

The walk to David and Catherine's home was farther than she had anticipated. Across the boulevard an engine roared; lights flashed on and the car drove off. A few seconds later, the scenario was repeated. This section of the avenue bordered the university grounds, so there were no homes. A perfect place for young lovers to park.

She'd been to David and Catherine's once before for a party. But then she'd been a guest and arrived by car. Tonight she was uninvited, on foot and tired. Regardless, she was certain she'd recognize the house. The imposing grey stone mansion was hard to forget.

Lily stopped. A cramp in her calf made it impossible to go forward. Her feet throbbed and her chest felt tight. *This is insane.* She was about to turn around and abandon her foolish quest when she spotted a familiar lamppost at the end of a drive thirty feet ahead. Within moments was standing in front of David and Catherine's home. Having stepped back from the gang after Jennifer was born, she hadn't heard much about David, but she knew they'd had a son, Michael.

The driveway leading to the house seemed longer than she remembered. The home seemed larger, a massive skull carved from black ice. The windows looked like gaping eyes; the cavernous front door, a mouth. Above the entrance, a nose cavity, the library. The night of the party she had been invited into that book-lined room, along with a few other guests, and was looking out onto the street when David, under the pretence of describing a detail about the lead glass casement, brushed her arm, his hand lingering longer than needed. Now the window was void of light or revellers.

A man with a dog appeared beside her. "Are you lost?"

Lily looked at the man and then back at the house. No longer a skull of ice. Merely chiselled stone. Upstairs, muted light in a small pane, perhaps a nightlight. Their son Michael's room. She thought of Jennifer asleep in bed while her mother stood outside a different child's home.

The dog yipped. The man spoke again, "Are you all right?" He stared at Lily's scuffed shoes and pyjamas.

She shrunk inside her sweater. The mix of fear and pity on his face reminded Lily of the way people looked at the woman, her face smeared with orange lipstick, who wandered downtown's Gore Park.

Lily took a step back from the man with the dog, and then another and another. Soon she was jogging down the street towards home.

Lily arrived home near sunrise, limping and chilled to the bone. Although the night was mild, her teeth had started chattering on the long walk back, and she was unable to stop them. She silently closed her front door, scuffed her blistered feet out of her shoes and went to Jennifer's room. Lily lowered herself onto the mattress and looked at her daughter's beautiful face. With a shaking hand she stroked Jennifer's hair. The child's eyes fluttered.

"What's wrong, Mammy?" Jennifer asked, her little-girl voice thickened by sleep.

"Everything's fine." Lily pressed her lips against Jennifer's brow and lingered a moment.

Leaving her daughter's door ajar, Lily tip-toed to her own room. Alastair was still asleep and snoring when she returned to bed. She moved close to him where it was warm and went to sleep.

CHAPTER 11

Jennifer had decided cleaning the windows on the outside would bring much-needed light into her parents' house. She finished polishing the final pane, climbed down the ladder and stood back a ways to admire her handiwork. The windows sparkled except for one tiny streak on the bottom pane, just out of arm's reach. Grabbing the cleaner and a paper towel, she climbed the first few ladder rungs. Her head was level with the ledge, so when something moved inside, it caught her eye. Curious, she stretched on tip-toes for a better look. Her mother was in the hall by the grandfather clock, the cabinet door was open. At first Jennifer thought her mother was adjusting the pulleys or weights. Then she saw her remove something from her pocket and place it inside. When she straightened, Jennifer ducked out of sight. After a moment, she raised her eyes above the ledge again. Her mother was gone, the clock face closed.

Jennifer returned the bucket and ladder to the shed. Then, as she gathered up her bundle of supplies, the glass cleaner tumbled from her arms. When she bent to pick it up an eerie feeling of déjà vu descended. She recalled sitting on the bottom cellar step a few weeks ago, a mishmash of dropped cleaning supplies on the floor; Mammy framed in the doorway above, a flashing glance one way and then the other, and the feeling afterwards that something was terribly wrong.

How We Danced

While her parents napped after lunch, Jennifer ventured into the hall to investigate. Her palms, and even the soles of her feet, were clammy. Telling herself she was overreacting, she pushed down her unease and opened the clock door. Except for the chains and balance weights, it was empty. She brushed the hair from her eyes and squinted into the dark corners. In one spot, a rim of unfinished wood protruded about an eighth of an inch. Intrigued, she squatted, ran a finger round it and lifted. With little effort the floor came up, revealing a compartment beneath. Fingers splayed, she reached into the hole and tapped about. Her fingertips brushed against something hard. She traced the square outline of the object and then, heart racing, removed it. She held a jeweller's gift box in her open palm. Her other hand, shaking, hovered over the lid. She glanced at her parents' closed bedroom door and then back at the box. Chewing the edge of her lip she considered whether or not to open it. Recently, after an incident where Emma had used Lindsay's body wash without permission, she'd lectured them about privacy and respect. Leaning forward, her hand still clutching the box, she lowered it into the hiding spot. But she couldn't let go. Pulling it out again for another look, it dropped and the lid fell off.

On a wad of cotton batting were a pair of earrings. Nothing extraordinary. At best, from the fifties or sixties. Underneath the earrings was a ticket stub. *The Wondergrove*. Thinking there must be more, she pried up the cotton liner. She found a book of matches and a note folded in half. The note read: *When you're in the mood, wear them and think of me*. No signature; initials: *DM*.

Jennifer flipped the cover of the yellowed matchbook. A phone number was scrawled in black ink. What would draw her mother to this cache now, when there were countless other things to consider? Jennifer memorized the phone number and closed the matchbook. After returning the stash to its hiding place, she went to her room and shut the door.

Phone in hand, she sat on her bed biting a fingernail, thinking about the note. The idea of her mother with an admirer seemed improbable. Romantic was not the first word that came to mind when Jennifer thought of her. Homebody was more appropriate.

Yet there had always been something she couldn't quite put her finger on regarding her mother. There was an underlying sadness that disappeared the moment Jennifer got close enough to ask, *Is anything wrong?* She peered at the old photo of her and Mammy on the dresser, taken at Niagara Falls. Mammy smiled weakly at the camera; Jennifer's small hand was reaching up, grasping her elbow. She glanced back to her phone and dialled the number.

"Ken's Fish & Chips," a man's voice boomed.

"Sorry," Jennifer hesitated, "I must have the wrong number."

"Elliott Steel, right?" The man sounded exasperated.

Jennifer didn't answer.

"I just opened this business, and I must have had ten of these calls. Why they don't retire numbers like this is beyond me. I'd request a new one, but all my advertising has been printed with this one. My website, too."

"Thanks anyway." Jennifer hung up and typed *Elliott Steel* into the browser.

Several pages of sites popped up: Information for salaried and pensioned employees; stock details; a shut down announcement. If *DM* worked in the factory, she had little hope of locating him. However, Jennifer clicked on *Shut Down Announcement.* If he was in management ... she scanned the article for a quote. Three paragraphs into the piece, she found one: "We are taking decisive action to improve the competitiveness of our stainless steel bar operations," said David Mallory, vice-president, Elliott Steel. "In addition..." Jennifer stopped reading.

Her fingers felt fat and clumsy as she tried to find more data on David Mallory. A raft of professional information appeared. She narrowed her search and his personal address and phone number came up on the screen. After adding this to her own contact list, she switched her search from *Everything* to *Images.* Hope turned to disappointment when six photos of six different men materialized, along with images of several homes and a gravestone.

Jennifer drummed her fingers on the mattress, checked the time. Mallory's address was about a ten-minute drive from here.

How We Danced

Her parents were resting. The nurse was available should anything happen. She scrawled a note—*Gone out, won't be long*—and put it on the kitchen table.

A sudden gust of wind created resistance when she tried to shut the front door. A sign? But she persisted, tugging harder, and it closed mutely.

Mallory's neighbourhood was by the university. It was bustling with traffic and students. Jennifer gave up on finding a parking spot and used the university lot. Mallory's street was only a short walk. She stopped; considered turning around. Even though she'd memorized the address, she pulled the paper she'd written it on from her pocket, stared at it for several seconds, put it back and walked on. *Eighty-eight, eighty-eight;* she repeated the mantra.

The properties were as manicured as she remembered and the homes as grand. Everything about the street represented old money. On the drive over she'd allowed the idea that her mother had taken a lover. Now she was struggling to imagine her with a wealthy, influential man. She wondered if money was the reason Mammy may have cheated. Perhaps this man had wooed her with promises of a better life, one her father had been unable to provide despite their coming to Canada. Walking a little faster, Jennifer decided it was all conjecture. Yet she couldn't shake the feeling that seeing this man's home might unravel a part of the mystery.

She checked the house numbers and figured eighty-eight should be next, just past this row of tall hedges. She quickened her pace. As the massive home came into view, she walked faster still. The day was warm, and her feet were sweaty in her flimsy sandals that slapped and slid on the hot asphalt. She wished she had worn more sensible shoes. No sooner had the thought crossed her mind, than she tripped and stumbled. Unable to save herself, she landed painfully on her hands and knees. Stunned, she sat back on the asphalt and looked down at her skinned, bleeding palms.

"Are you okay?" a voice called out in alarm.

An older man was kneeling in a garden close to house number eighty-eight.

Jennifer examined his face and wondered if this was him.

He stood, brushed the front of his pants and repeated his question.

"I'm fine," she called back, but faltered when she tried to stand.

"Wait," the man said as he came towards her, "I'll help you."

In a moment he was there, crouched beside her, hand on her elbow. "Try now. Take your time."

"Thanks." She was on her feet. His hand still cupped her elbow. "I don't know what happened."

"Come and sit for a moment."

She allowed him to lead her up the long drive to one of the chairs by the front door. He told her to take her time; catch her breath.

"I'll get a washcloth," he said and went into the house.

Sitting back, she looked around. The garden stretched from the entrance, part way down the lawn, curving around the corner of the house. There were several varieties of hosta, dogwood, azalea, and by a clump of cedar, numerous rhododendron. One area was devoted to roses: red, pale lilac, soft pink, cheeky fuchsia. Thick vines of purple clematis ran riot up and over an arbor. There were no lilies. She tried to imagine her mother working in this garden, but couldn't. Acidic soil, too much shade; lilies would never thrive.

He was back. "I've brought Band-Aids as well." He set them on the arm of her chair.

The cloth was cool and soothing. She dabbed the dirt from the heel of her hand. "I feel silly." She folded the cloth to conceal her blood and hide the dirt, and then held it out to him.

Without moving his blue eyes from hers, he took it. She realised she'd seen him before. If he was Mallory, how had their paths crossed? Her parents rarely entertained. She would have remembered a party and the people who came. She pushed away the idea of her mother welcoming a lover at their home.

"You look familiar," she said.

He put the washcloth aside. "I'm always here." He lifted his chin in the direction of his garden.

"It's beautiful," she said.

He sighed and looked around. "It's more than I ever wanted. My wife's house, you see. I inherited it."

"Still—" Confused by his comment, she examined the stonework, "it's a spectacular home. You must love it."

He shrugged. "A home is what you make it."

For a moment neither of them spoke. Finally, he patted his chest. "I can't do as much as I used to. A couple of heart attacks. But thank you." He smiled.

Feeling awkward, she said, "I should be the one thanking you. I'm Jennifer. I'd shake your hand but ..." Her laugh was tremulous.

He sat on the chair opposite. "David Mallory."

It was him. He was different from her father, taller, slimmer, more relaxed and self-assured. She imagined the tiny box tucked away in the clock of her parents' home; words that this man had penned years ago to her mother, hidden from sight, perhaps forgotten by him.

"My mother has a garden." She wanted to mention her mother to place her in his mind.

"Does she?"

"It's brighter and not quite as elaborate."

"I know," he exhaled slowly. "Too much shade, but I can't bear to part with the trees; so much history."

"She grows lilies, her namesake."

He nodded. "I see." He drew the words out as though to illustrate he understood more than she'd said. She waited, heart pounding, hoping, yet afraid he'd ask or offer something more. When it was clear that he wouldn't, she said, "Of course my mother's garden is much smaller."

"Would you like to tell me about it?" He shifted in his chair, acknowledging the conversation would continue for a while.

She wondered if he meant the garden or something more. All at once she lost her nerve. What if he told her something that turned her world upside down? "Do you live here alone?" seemed a safer question.

"I do now. My wife passed a few years ago."

"I'm sorry."

He accepted her polite expression of sympathy with a nod.

"Do you have any children?"

"I had a son, Michael. He died just shy of his fifth birthday of a congenital heart defect. If he had lived, he would be about your age."

"It's a terrible thing to lose a child. I can't imagine." She looked away, not knowing what more to say. He'd suffered terrible losses; his health was fragile. She had no right to intrude, to impose her curiosity on him. It was wrong to have come. Any questions she had should be directed to her mother.

"I have a daughter." He said this almost as an afterthought. "But sadly, we ..." he seemed to search for the right word, "we're estranged."

"That's a shame."

His speaking out had somehow shifted the balance of conversation. Now she sensed he wanted to say more, to unburden himself. The loss of control made her uncomfortable and she wanted to leave, fearing he'd tell her more than she could handle.

"It is," he said. "But the fault is all mine."

"I better go. Thanks again."

He reached across the space between them. Breath caught in her throat. He picked up the Band-Aids, handed them to her.

At the end of the drive she stopped and turned around. He still stood at the entrance, clutching the folded washcloth. She lifted her hand and then walked on.

Perhaps she had known throughout their conversation where she had seen him before. But it wasn't until she was buckled in her car that she allowed the memory to crystallize. It was a snapshot on the front lawn of her parents' home, the empty swing swaying, her mother's back rigid, as she pointed and yelled, "*Go and never come back.*"

❀ ❀ ❀

The nurse pointed to the mottled scar on Alastair's shin. "Did you get this in a fight?"

He looked away, scratched the back of his head and waited until she had finished helping him pull on his track pants before he answered, "Something like that."

"I'd love to see the other guy," she said, as she walked away.

"No you wouldn't."

How We Danced

Alastair wouldn't have wished that mean little bastard on his worst enemy.

It had been a winter's evening, too cold even for snow. He'd worked late and taken the bus home. Tired and cold, the trek from the stop to home had seemed longer than usual.

As he neared the house, three men came out from between his place and the Albanese's. The one in the middle, carrying some sort of steel pipe, was shorter than the two who flanked him. Alastair knew his next door neighbour, Gaetano, had been busy installing a second kitchen in his basement and figured the men had been helping put in the new plumbing.

Alastair faced the three men as he was about to turn up his front path.

"Alastair?" the man in the middle said. His breath rose between them in the cold air.

Alastair stomped his feet and rubbed his gloved hands together. "That's me."

He assumed they wanted to borrow a tool or enlist his help in some way. He thought the little guy looked familiar. Perhaps he was a relative of Gaetano's. Family was always coming and going from the Albanese's. Or did he know him through work?

Feeling certain he'd eventually place this fellow, Alastair responded in a familiar tone. "You're in helping Gaetano with the kitchen?"

When the three men glanced at each other and snickered, the fine hairs on the back of Alastair's neck bristled. He doubted these men were friends of Gaetano's. Alastair glanced at his house. Lights were on in the living room. Lily was probably watching TV. Jennifer's bedroom windows were also lit up. He pictured his daughter at her desk doing homework. The front door was about thirty feet from where he stood. If he dashed, he might make it.

The little man with the pipe slapped it threateningly against his open palm. "Don't even think about it."

The two on either side lunged forward and grabbed Alistair by the arms.

"Take him in there." The middle man lifted his chin towards the dark pathway between the two homes.

"W-what?" Alastair stuttered.

"You heard me, you fucking fairy!"

Alastair cringed, turning his face as though he'd been slapped.

"Cooperate or I'll tell your wife." His mouth contorted in a cruel smile. "Maybe I'll pay her a visit anyway."

Fear cramped Alastair's bowels. "I don't understand," he said, thinking that perhaps he did.

"Shut up," the guy on Alastair's left said. "Let's go."

Frightened, Alastair was frog-marched between the homes.

"Look guys," he tried his best to sound conciliatory. "You've made a mistake."

And he believed they had. Since his break with Aaron, and Jennifer's birth thirteen years earlier, his dalliances had been sporadic, discreet and only with consenting strangers at places he knew to be safe. He would never risk his family and reputation with a relationship. Neither would the others. They had as much to lose as he did.

"Oh, there's no mistake, Alastair." The middle man mocked his name in a falsetto. "You're the queer who hit on my kid brother. I had him point you out to me."

Alastair realised who this man resembled: Peter, from the King Eddie.

"You'll be sorry."

Before Alastair had an opportunity to respond, the two men had slammed him against the brick wall, pinned him to the spot.

Peter's brother was now threatening him with a steel pipe. Alastair strained against the hold the other two had on him, but it was useless.

He needed to set this guy straight, but he decided to keep the facts to a minimum. "Look buddy, whatever your brother told you, it's not true," he said in a deep, clear voice.

The little man snorted like an enraged bull. Puffs of cold air hung between them.

"Don't call my brother a liar, you filthy pervert!" He swung the pipe low and hard.

Alastair cried out in agony, slumping between his captors who continued to hold him up.

"Daddy?" Jennifer called into the walkway.

The thugs let go of Alastair's arms, and he collapsed to the ground. Even through his pain he wondered how Jennifer had known to come outside and where she was now.

"Let's get out of here," the middle man said, dropping the pipe. Alastair rolled out of the way as it hit the concrete with a clang that echoed between the brick walls. The men ran off.

Jennifer was beside him. "Daddy! Oh, Daddy, are you okay?"

Alastair tried to form words around the pain. "Go inside." He grunted and attempted to get up. Dizzy, he stumbled and would have fallen had Jennifer not steadied him. They made it as far as the front steps where he collapsed in a cold sweat.

"I'll get Mammy," she said and ran off before he could protest.

Alastair heard whimpering and followed the sound. Across the road, The Boy stood staring, his eyes wide with fright. Alastair wanted to let the child know he'd be okay, so he raised his hand. When he did, The Boy vanished.

Lily came rushing out the front door. With her help he made it inside. She brought a chair from the living room into the hallway.

When Alastair sat, a fibre of hot pain shot up his leg, making him feel sick to his stomach. He moaned and rocked back and forth, frantically thinking of how he'd explain.

"Let me have a look." Lily squatted in front of him, rolled up his pant leg and gasped.

Jennifer cried, "Oh no!"

Alastair looked down at his shin. Jagged bone protruded from split skin, blood streamed down his leg, soaking his socks.

Horrified, he looked at Lily. What a mess he'd made of things.

"What happened?" she asked.

Stunned, Alastair stared at her. He opened his mouth to speak but couldn't think of an appropriate response.

Jennifer came behind him, laid a protective hand on his shoulder. "I saw Daddy coming up the front steps. Then all of a sudden, he went down and I could tell he was hurt badly. That's when I ran out."

"You mean to tell me this happened from a fall?" Lily looked from Alastair to Jennifer.

"That's right," Jennifer said. "He must have hit the edge of the step."

Lily's eyes widened, and Alastair thought she was going to dispute their daughter's explanation.

After a moment, she stood. "Stay with your father, while I call for an ambulance."

When Alastair heard Lily talking to the dispatcher, he looked at his daughter who was still standing behind him, hands cupping his shoulders. Her mouth was set in a firm line. When their eyes met, she put both arms around him, and leaning down, pressed her cheek against his. That's when he knew he should be a man, tell Lily the truth. It was cowardly to remain silent and allow Jennifer to lie to protect him. But when Lily returned and announced the ambulance was on its way, he continued to cling to Jennifer and said nothing.

❋ ❋ ❋

Lily placed her palm on Alastair's thin face and hoped her touch offered some comfort. He'd suffered throughout the spring and summer, a little more of him fading with each season's passing. Now he did little more than sleep. She looked out of the window at the bare tree and the dry leaves littering their yard. When she turned back to Alastair, his eyes fluttered. Not wanting to disturb him, she removed her hand and stepped back.

She glanced at the nurse who sat across the room knitting. The click of her needles grated on her nerves, but she said nothing. It was best to keep the peace. What if the nurse vented her spleen on Alastair when she was out of the room? That's why she hadn't wanted the help of outsiders. But now she had no choice. Alastair's temperature had spiked, and he couldn't get out of bed. After that they'd called the doctor. An infection, he'd said, and then altered Alastair's medication and arranged for full-time home care.

The stainless steel pole was now positioned at his bedside. A half-empty bag hung limp from a hook. Lily watched as the liquid relief dripped, slithering down and around the clear tubing into his body.

She blinked and sighed. Neither she nor Jennifer was capable of dealing with all the bags, hooks, intravenous tubing and needles that had invaded their home.

How We Danced

Lily looked again at the nurse. With her stout legs crossed at the ankles, her tiny feet barely touched the floor. She was too short. How could someone the size of her handle Alastair if he had to get up? Or worse, if he fell? The way she worried her bottom lip as she knitted wasn't a good sign, either. Obviously the woman had difficulty with her nerves. She'd probably fall to pieces at the first sign of trouble.

Even if they did need the nurse's help, she wouldn't allow these strangers much leeway. At least this daytime one wasn't too bad. The night shift replacement was worse. Lily crossed her arms. She'd tolerate no interference. This was her home.

Jennifer came in and stood alongside her. "I've made lunch."

The cricketing needles stopped. The nurse said to Lily, "I'll call you if he wakes."

Lily walked into the kitchen and saw the exquisitely set table. Unshed tears blurred the flower pattern on her good china and made her silverware glisten.

"Do you like it?" Jennifer asked.

Lily cleared her throat. She didn't feel the situation warranted Jennifer pampering her. She felt bad enough that she'd taken her daughter away from Cam and the girls.

"You shouldn't have bothered."

"I thought we could both use a bit of cheering up."

Lily regretted the disappointment on Jennifer's face as she pulled out a chair and without energy said, "Have a seat."

Lily looked at the stove, but there was only one pot set out.

Jennifer followed her gaze. "It's just tomato soup and grilled cheese."

Embarrassed by the tears welling in her eyes, Lily reached for a napkin to dab them gently. She was touched that Jennifer remembered. This was their special meal when Jennifer was a child; on the evenings Alastair had worked late, or chosen not to come home. Back then, the simple meal had been a comfort to both of them.

Jennifer ladled soup into the bowls. She placed one in front of Lily, another across the table.

When the ripe scent of tomatoes drifted up, Lily's mouth watered. As soon as her daughter sat, she dug in. But after a few mouthfuls, her stomach turned. She put her spoon down and peeled away the crust of her sandwich, nibbled on that, hoping the sick feeling would pass.

The first time she had discovered dry toast helped nausea was when she was pregnant with Jennifer. She was too ill to keep anything down. Her friend, Carol, had made her some toast and then insisted she go to the doctor's and confirm what they both suspected.

After leaving Dr. Henry's office, she walked downhill towards Main Street to catch the bus. Looking up at the ominous thunderheads, she shuddered. What an autumn it had been—rain, rain and more rain. Now it appeared that the remnant of a storm was going to touch down this evening. But she didn't care. She was having a baby and she was elated.

Careful not to slip on the wet leaves that covered the sidewalk, she yanked up her collar and bent forward against the wind. Clutching the knot of her kerchief, she wondered what to do next. With the weather the way it was, the sensible thing would be to get back to the apartment. Yet the urge to share her thrilling news tugged at her like the scent of home cooking.

She was sure he'd be happy. After all, she and David would be together already if Catherine's father hadn't passed away. Catherine had been close to him, and David claimed she was devastated by his death. For this reason he had begged her to allow time for Catherine to heal from one loss before he announced another. Lily admired David's compassion for his wife. And why not be generous? Lily knew he truly loved her. They would have the rest of their lives together. So of course she'd agreed to wait. But the baby changed everything.

She checked her wristwatch hoping that she could get to a telephone booth before David left his office.

Still undecided about what to do, she crossed Main Street and took her place at the bus stop in front of Designs by Aaron. This shop, with its jutting window display, had always intrigued her, but intimidated by the posh look of the place she'd never ventured in to browse.

A funnel of leaves swirled, and the first few drops of rain splattered. She turned her back to the road and opened her umbrella. Within moments, thousands of droplets sliced the air like sharp, angry needles.

She saw something move in the store's window. A man, who had been crouched on the floor, stood up. Lily was startled at his height and girth. Something in her face must have given her thoughts away because he smiled and winked.

Laughing, she twirled her umbrella.

He held his arms up as if to say, why are you standing there?

Lily shrugged and then raising her brows, mimed having a telephone conversation and pointed at the entrance to his shop.

He motioned to come inside.

Lily dashed up the steps, closed her umbrella and pushed in the door to the shop. There was an umbrella stand right there, and she plunked hers in as the big man came round the corner, followed by a little dog.

"Come in, darling. Don't be shy." Aaron stooped to pick up the dog.

"This is very kind of you." She shook the rainwater from her hands. "It's pelting down."

There was a flash, followed by a loud crack of thunder. Lily flinched. The dog started to pant.

"It's supposed to go on all night." He looked passed her and out the window. "For Napoleon's sake, I hope not." He scratched the dog's head. "You don't like storms, do you, little man?"

Palm up, Lily extended her hand. The dog stopped his nervous panting, sniffed her fingers and then looked at his master.

"He likes you."

"How can you tell?"

"He didn't bite."

Lily laughed, "Oh, away with you!"

"The rain will ease in a bit. In the meantime, you can make that call." He held out his hand. "Here, give me your wrap."

With chilled hands, she slipped off her sopping trench coat and passed it to him.

He slung it on a hook by the door. "Come, follow me. The phone's in my office."

Lily took big strides to keep up.

"Take as long as you need. I'll be up front." He closed the door behind him.

The big oak desk was framed by a huge window that overlooked a garden. Even with the autumn leaves strewn about and the rain hammering down, it was beautiful. It was the perfect spot to call David with her news. Her hand trembled as she dialled, but her heart raced towards the sound of his voice.

"Mallory here."

"David. It's me." Lily said.

"Hold on."

There was silence, the sound of a door closing and then, "I'm so glad you called, sweetheart. I've been desperate to talk to you."

"You have?"

"Yes. Something's happened. Something unexpected."

Lily pulled out the desk chair and sat down. "What?"

"Catherine's pregnant."

Lily closed her eyes and, slumping over, put a hand to her forehead. "I thought you weren't sleeping together."

"This is difficult for me."

Lily swallowed hard. "I can imagine."

"I'm devastated." When Lily didn't respond, David continued, his voice sharp. "I can't very well leave her right now."

Lily placed a protective hand against her abdomen. She envisioned the tiny form within her.

"Lily, are you there? Say something?"

"Goodbye, David."

"Don't hang up. Please—"

❀ ❀ ❀

Jennifer's voice was raised, "Mammy, did you hear me?"

Lily blinked. "Sorry, no. My mind wandered."

"You're not eating."

Lily glanced down at the abandoned soup, the crust in her hand.

"You shouldn't be skipping meals. I've told you—"

As Jennifer lectured her about the necessity of keeping up her strength, Lily thought of how she could have told David, could have begged him not to abandon her. But she hadn't. She assumed he'd eventually figured it out. Or at least he'd had an inkling. That's why he'd shown up at the house a few years later and approached Jennie. Lily had maintained her silence and kept the peace.

Jennifer had stopped talking. No doubt her daughter interpreted her silence as agreement. For a few moments the only sound was the chime of silverware on fine bone china.

Lily swallowed. "All your father does now is sleep. I just don't understand it." She picked at the crust of her grilled cheese sandwich. "He wasn't that bad before."

"But you knew it would get worse."

Lily pushed the sandwich away. She nodded and stared at a spot above Jennifer's head.

CHAPTER 12

Jennifer tossed the loaf into the grocery cart and crossed *bread* off the list. Three cans of soup and saltine crackers were the only two items left, and they were in the next lane. She pushed the cart around the end-aisle display and stopped in front of the shelves that held cans and Tetra Paks of soup. She read her mother's neat script, a little surprised she hadn't specified what kind to buy. Jennifer scanned the can labels, considering which her mother might prefer, and decided on their old standbys: celery, mushroom and tomato. As Jennifer picked up the can of tomato soup, she recalled the evening, not that long ago, when she had prepared this for her mother and served it in their good tableware. She'd hoped that her mother would be pleased, but instead she'd chastised her about the china and then sipped her soup in silence, miles away.

At the recollection, Jennifer's stomach soured. She thought of Emma, who was prone to tummy aches at life's ups and downs. Suddenly she wanted to hold her, and Lindsay; to tell them how important they were to her, how much she loved them. Cameron as well; she needed to hear his voice. Jennifer plucked the celery and mushroom soups from the shelf and put them into the cart. Across the aisle she spotted the saltines, tossed them in also and headed for the check out. As soon as she was done, she'd phone her family from the car.

Minutes later, Cameron answered. "Hey, I was just going to phone you."

At the sound of his voice, Jennifer's eyes filled. "Great minds think alike," she said, hoping the playful comment offset the catch in her voice.

"Yeah," Cam continued. "You'll never guess—Lindsay started her period."

"Oh my," Jennifer's heart sank. This was a major milestone in her daughter's life. She'd looked forward to sharing this special time with her, and now she'd missed it.

"It's okay," Cam said. "Everything's under control. Thank goodness for Isla. Honestly, Jen, she was amazing with Lindz—"

"Isla?" Jennifer said. A flash of anger warmed her cheeks. "Why wouldn't you call me?"

"Calm down," Cam said.

"Don't tell me to calm down," Jennifer tried to keep her voice even. "*My* daughter gets her period, a pivotal event in a girl's life, and you call another woman to help? Yeah, I'm upset. I have every right to be."

"First of all, she's *our* daughter. Secondly, Lindsay was the one that went next door to Isla, who is *your* friend I might add, and told her, not me."

"Oh." Jennifer's throat tightened; tears stung her eyes.

"Yeah, *oh*," Cam said. "I know you're under a lot of stress with your parents. I get it. But what *you* fail to realise is that I'm stressed as well. I'm more than some bit player, Jen. My life is affected, too. I'm doing as much work from home as I can, but my Inbox is a disaster. I'm so far behind in correspondence it's frightening. I haven't been to the office nearly as much as I need to. Others have had to step in and connect with key clients, a few of whom weren't impressed. When they were expecting to meet with the Senior Manager, they feel shortchanged. This is all catching up with me *and* my team. I've missed meetings, pivotal ones that have affected their morale and our bottom line. To top it off, yesterday I found out that we failed to meet our quota. Now the VP is on my case." Cam drew a breath and lowered his voice which had gradually increased in volume. "Listen, I'm doing my best to hold down the fort here, but I'll be damned if I'm going to to listen to you bitch because we dealt with something and you missed it."

"We. You mean you and Isla." Jennifer said.

"What?" Cam said. "You can't be serious. It wasn't—"

Jennifer cut him off. "You don't understand, this was important. Why didn't Lindsay call me? I'm her mother. Why didn't you call me?"

"Damn it, Jen. I was going to call. I told you that when I answered the phone." There was silence and then Cam let out a long breath. "It's not like we planned any of this. The kid was taken aback. She went next door, spoke to Isla, and then they both came back here and told me. I didn't know what the hell to do. Isla gave her a, you know, a pad or whatever."

"Let me speak to Lindsay," Jennifer said.

"She's not here. Isla took her to the store to buy what she needs."

"It should be me taking her." Jennifer heard the petulance in her voice, wanted to somehow take it back but couldn't.

"What is wrong with you?" Cam raised his voice again. "This isn't about you, it's about Lindsay. You should be grateful Isla stepped up to help us. Instead you're acting like a—" Cam spluttered, stumbled and finally let out a long breath. "Look, I refuse to fight about this. You're not being fair. Call me later, when you've calmed down."

He was gone. She stared at the silent phone in disbelief. Her heart raced; she was short of breath. What right did he have to hang up? For a moment she considered calling back but then dismissed the idea; what would she say? She tossed the phone in her handbag and sat back. Her queasy stomach now felt as though it had been hollowed out with a dull spoon. The tears she'd been holding back while talking to Cam rolled down her cheeks. She took a tissue out of her purse, blew her nose, wiped her face and then glanced around to see if anyone was watching.

In the parking spot next to her, the driver's door slammed. A woman emerged who was fixated on her car keys and shopping bags. Nearby a cart rumbled across the asphalt, a child cried. As she dabbed her nose, a sedan headed for the exit slowed down, almost coming to a stop directly in front of her vehicle. The man driving glanced her way. Her instinct was to bolt. Since that wasn't possible, she turned her face away and, hunching her shoulders, pretended to search for something in her purse. Even as she rummaged through her handbag, she questioned her fearful reaction. Her response had been visceral, not rational. When she looked again, the car was at the exit, its signal flashing. Jennifer narrowed her eyes at the car's lights. The scene was disturbingly familiar. Suddenly she knew why.

When she was a child, a similar car had slowed down and a man, wearing a fedora low on his brow, had driven by as she'd played on an ice patch. Now the stranger behind the wheel from back then had a face. *David Mallory.*

Jennifer shivered as the sedan turned onto the street and disappeared. It was time for her to go also. She pulled her keys from her purse and stuck them into the ignition, turned it. As the engine roared to life, her rage subsided. Driving out of the lot, she decided to call Cameron when she got back to her parents' place, tell him she was sorry, hoping that, in time, she really would be.

❀ ❀ ❀

Cautious fingers stroked Alastair's brow. The scent of rose hand cream hovered over him.

"Alastair," Lily whispered.

He tried to open his eyes but his lids were weighted shut, immovable. There was another flutter of her hand, a sigh and then the rustle of fabric, scrape of chair. She was gone. Her touch had been pleasant and now, in the absence of it, he was lonely. But not bereft. Only one person could produce that depth of emotion in him.

Aaron's touch had never been tentative. Alastair recalled the first time they'd made love. Perry Como's "Wanted" softly played in the background. Afterwards, Aaron's firm hand had wiped his dampened forehead, the self-assured kiss had followed.

"Wonderful," Aaron had said, rolling onto his back and clasping his hands behind his head.

When Alastair didn't respond, Aaron turned to face him. "And for you?"

Alastair eased onto his side and drew closer to Aaron. It was difficult for him to speak of such things, to share. "Aye. It was that and then some." He placed a hand against Aaron's cheek, drew his thumb against the rasp of late afternoon beard; he briefly closed his eyes with pleasure. *This is where I belong.*

A siren whined, a door slammed, someone called out.

Alastair bolted upright. "Who's that?"

Aaron put a hand on his shoulder and tried to draw him back down. "It's okay."

Alastair's heart hammered and he resisted Aaron's tug.

"Trust me, I'm discreet," Aaron's tone was as firm and self-assured as his touch. "The carriage house is private *and* safe—you saw my overgrown garden. The door's double-bolted. We'd have time to move to the table. You can't arrest two friends for sharing a drink, now can you?"

Alastair settled back onto his pillow and exhaled.

"Your first time?" Aaron searched Alastair's face.

Aaron's expression was quizzical, and Alastair realised he was serious. He chuckled. "I'm no virgin. There have been men—here and there—" He struggled to find the right words, "Nothing serious," his face flushed at the admission. "And I've been with Lily, not often, mind you," he hesitated. "It's difficult."

"I get it," Aaron said.

Alastair felt his eyes begin to fill and he turned away. He tried to laugh, but the sound he made was humourless. He swallowed. "I love her. I never meant to deceive the woman."

"Is it deceit if you're not aware?" Aaron asked. "For years I convinced myself I could be happy with Harriet. And we were, in a way. Although I nearly drove the poor girl mad with my compulsive decorating and re-decorating of our home." Aaron laughed and then grew silent. When he continued his tone was more serious. "In hindsight, all that wallpapering probably had more to do with my repressed sexual energy than artistic expression. But Harriet was a good sport about it; just like she was a good sport about our lacklustre sex life."

Alastair sensed Aaron was struggling with strong emotion and that he hadn't finished his story. While Alastair waited, he thought of Lily, wondered how she felt about their scant love life. *Was she happy? Or, like Harriet, was she just being a good sport? Why had he never considered her feelings before?*

Aaron continued. "Everything changed when Ben was killed."

"Ben?" Alastair searched Aaron's eyes. "Is that the friend you mentioned? The one whose death changed your life?"

Aaron nodded. "When he died I started living."

"Were you two together?" Alastair asked.

"No. Best friends." Aaron grinned. "Since we were kids."

Alastair noted the faraway look in Aaron's eyes, as though he was remembering something pleasant.

"I loved everything about him," Aaron said. "I wondered if that's why."

Alastair laid a hand on Aaron's arm.

"My life fell apart afterwards. I suppose I lived through him," Aaron said.

"What do you mean?" Alastair said.

"If my best friend was accomplished, and heterosexual, I was, too. Then, just like that," Aaron snapped his fingers. "Ben was gone. A motorcycle accident; he loved to ride." Aaron frowned at Alastair. "When I lost him, I lost myself. Make sense?"

Alastair nodded. He thought of The Boy, the way he randomly appeared.

"What?" Aaron drew himself up against the bed's headboard. "You look spooked."

Alastair sat up. He placed his hands over his face and then rubbed his eyes. He was tempted to tell Aaron about The Boy, get his opinion on him. He yawned, stalling. Was this a risk he was willing to take? He'd reluctantly acknowledged The Boy, never mind share his existence. He removed his hands, opened his eyes.

Aaron stroked his hair. "Tell me."

Heart pounding, Alastair told Aaron about The Boy's appearances, how he came without warning, ran off when he pursued and disappeared when Alastair tried to pin him down. When Alastair was finished, his mouth was parched and his face felt flushed. Aaron had listened attentively without interruption. Alastair had appreciated his silence then, but now it was making him uncomfortable.

Aaron scratched the stubble on his face. His gaze was focussed not on Alastair, but past him.

He couldn't stand the silence. His gut ached. *Why had he risked Aaron's respect? It was stupid, he was stupid. He'd only just found him, now he was lost.* "You think I'm daft, don't you?"

Aaron blinked and quickly reached for Alastair's hand. "Of course not. I was just thinking, trying to puzzle it out, The Boy, what he means."

Alastair's brow wrinkled.

"You know, represents," Aaron reached for a water pitcher on the bedside table, poured a glass for Alastair and then one for himself.

Alastair was grateful Aaron's comment and tone weren't judgmental. Alastair had accepted the proffered glass, but was too anxious and curious about Aaron's thoughts to even consider taking a sip.

Aaron pulled his knees into his chest and drank deeply. He put the water glass down with a solid *thunk.*

"The way I see it, there are only two choices: *One*—The Boy is a ghost, spirit, what have you. Or, *two*—he's a figment of your imagination—"

"Great. Either option doesn't bode well for me."

"Hold on, I'm not finished." Aaron chuckled. "I think The Boy is important to your well-being."

Alastair's Glasgow brogue, which he usually kept in check, kicked in. "So seein' a wee boy, that doesne exist, dashin' to and fro amongst real folk—at least *I think* they're real—is somehow for the benefit of my health?"

Aaron laughed then, long and hard.

Alastair remembered the first time he'd heard that sound, only a few weeks back, how he'd wanted to join in but suppressed the urge. This time he didn't.

Alastair wiped tears from his eyes. "I can't believe I'm laughing about this. I've felt so ashamed, and alone for so long."

Aaron drew him close. "No shame here, Alastair. Nor judgement. Just us."

They sat quietly for a bit and then Alastair said, "There's a reason The Boy came to mind when you talked of Ben."

"You're saying The Boy is your Ben?" Aaron asked.

"Maybe," Alastair said.

"Let's break it down." Aaron suggested. "From what you've said, it's clear that The Boy visits when you're worried or sad or even depressed, right?"

Alastair considered this for a moment. "I suppose."

Aaron continued, "But when you get near, he runs off."

Alastair nodded.

"When you're almost there—*Poof!*—he's gone, vanishes into thin air."

Alastair scrubbed his scalp. "It's so confusing. What does he want?"

"Did he follow you from Scotland?" Aaron asked.

Alastair's eyes widened. No one had ever understood him, read him, the way Aaron seemed to. He nodded.

"Is that why you emigrated?" Aaron asked. "Were you running from The Boy?"

Alastair snorted. "No. In truth I came for the work. There were more opportunities here." He was silent for a moment then added, "But I had hoped I'd left The Boy behind."

"Tell me this, how do you feel right now, here with me?"

Alastair exhaled slowly. "I haven't the words. Happy, isn't enough. Contented, as well." He reached for Aaron's hand and squeezed it. "Satisfied."

Aaron threaded his fingers through Alastair's. "Maybe The Boy appears to encourage you to be yourself, the person you were meant to be. And when you do, his work will be done."

Alastair gazed into Aaron's sparkling eyes, searched his beautiful face. Alastair saw love and acceptance. "Like who I am now, here with you?"

Aaron pulled him close and tenderly kissed him. As his lips parted and he responded to Aaron's gentle urging, thoughts of The Boy drifted away.

❊ ❊ ❊

Lily closed the bedroom door and stepped into the hallway. Alastair was resting comfortably. The nurse was there in case he woke and needed something. Jennifer had gone to run errands. Lily's time to herself had become rare and felt awkward. She stood for a moment and weighed her options—she could tidy up a bit, rest and watch some TV, or go for a walk. Undecided, she went to the door and opened it. Cool air rushed in, along with the scent of freshly cut grass. A lawnmower droned. She glanced across the street at Diane's house.

A new couple, the latest in a long line of families to own the Stoneham's old place, had moved in. Odd how some houses were like that, new owners or tenants coming and going. No permanence. Lily was comforted that she and Alastair had provided a stable home for Jennifer and themselves. She hoped that Diane had succeeded in finding peace for her and Johnny. Big John's death hadn't been easy for her or for their son. She and Alastair had done their best to be supportive.

For the first few years after they moved away, Diane had kept in touch, a note included with her annual Christmas card. After a while, the notes stopped, and eventually the cards petered out. Lily still thought of the house as Diane's. Odd, since Johnny now would be older than Jennifer. It is hard to imagine. Lily still pictured him as a little boy trailing after Big John.

The lawnmower grew louder, and a man in a sleeveless t-shirt and shorts came around the corner of the house and started mowing the front lawn. Near the sidewalk's edge he stopped and, with the back of his forearm, wiped his brow. The fellow was young and fit. His upper arms were thick. Lily glanced down at strong thighs and muscular calves. Although he was shorter, this fellow reminded her of Big John.

She must mention him to Alastair, ask if he sees the resemblance. The thought was there before she had time to censor it. Conversation with Alastair was almost impossible now, his opinions beyond her reach.

Filled with a sudden, strong ache, she pressed a hand to her breast as if to staunch the flow of sorrow. Her mind rushed through the years, landing on a memory of Alastair. He stood in this doorway, body tense, the fingertips of one hand pressed on the glass. She came up behind him, curious to see what he was watching. Across the street, Big John, shirtless and sweating, was pushing a lawnmower through the grass.

"That John's a bit of an exhibitionist, isn't he?" she said, laughing.

Alastair jumped; he turned to her, his face white to the lips. "Don't sneak up on me like that!"

"Sorry." Lily took a step back. "I assumed you knew I was—"

He made a guttural sound that indicated he didn't accept her explanation or apology. And then he stormed off through the hall and stomped down the basement stairs. She felt the slam of his workshop door reverberate through the house.

His angry response didn't make sense then or now. The new neighbour's lawnmower suddenly stopped. The silence was uncomfortable, and Lily withdrew into the hallway and shut the door. She went into the living room and turned on the TV. *Oprah* had just started. Lily eased into her chair and put her feet up. Her hand was poised over the remote, waiting to see if the guest was worth watching. Nate the decorator, one of Oprah's regulars, was getting married. A photo of him and another handsome fellow flashed on the screen.

How times have changed.

As Nate talked to Oprah, the memory of Alastair poised at the door all those years ago returned. They had never discussed it. He'd come upstairs from the basement a few hours later, and life had continued as though the odd interchange never occurred. Had he simply been angry because she startled him?

The new neighbour's biceps flashed across Lily's mind; Big John's bare chest, gleaming with perspiration.

Nate laughed at something Oprah said. Lily turned her attention back to the program. Nothing in Nate's demeanour indicated he preferred men. A vision of Alastair in Big John's embrace flashed into her mind's eye. Lily shuddered. Absurd. She and Alastair hadn't slept together often, but it wasn't as though their marriage had *never* been consummated. They'd managed.

But that's all they'd done. They'd never shared the deepest, truest part of themselves with each other.

She's in bed with David, lying in the crook of his arm, laughing. He's telling her about his first love and an awkward kiss.

She'd never shared a moment like that with Alastair. Once more Lily glanced at Nate. A voice within her bubbled up and whispered, *'It would explain things.'*

Deborah Serravalle

Lily turned off the TV and got up. Her stove was filthy, the oven was worse. She hadn't cleaned either of them in ages. She headed for the kitchen, hell bent on erasing every bit of grime.

CHAPTER 13

The moment Jennifer stepped into her foyer she knew something was off. Perhaps that's why she closed the door and chose not to call out, *Surprise, I'm home,* as she'd planned.

A savoury scent, gamey and rich, hung in the air. The lights were on in the kitchen, Cam was talking. She couldn't hear what he was saying, but his tone indicated it wasn't with one of the girls. Her heart lurched, sped up, and the rhythmic pace thrummed in her ears. She stood frozen in the hallway; pressed her hand against the wall; rubbed her thumb on the rough, dry surface. The table was set for four, with wine glasses at two places. There was even a small bouquet of flowers in the centre. Perhaps Cam had called her parents' place and knew she was on her way home for a visit. Deciding it was the only explanation that made sense, she walked into the kitchen.

Isla Lafferty turned from the pot she was stirring. A mass of long, ginger curls swung onto her beautiful face, and she brushed them aside. "Jennie!" she called, looking both surprised and happy.

Why is she here? was Jennifer's immediate thought, followed by a memory of how Isla had stepped up and in; how'd she'd taken Jennifer's place when they'd needed her. She didn't want Isla anywhere near Cam or her girls, even if she was helping. Feeling guilty, she forced a smile. *Be gracious*, she told herself.

A stage actress, Isla's leisurely routine was punctuated with times of great activity. If playing London or New York, she'd be gone for months; if Toronto, she'd come and go at odd hours. Unencumbered by husband or children, she lived a life Jennifer considered carefree and glamorous. When Jennifer had said this to her once, Isla had laughed, admitting she secretly envied Jennifer's teaching career and family. It was then they decided that, between the two of them, they had the perfect life. After Isla's admission, Jennifer had felt a little sorry for her and invited her for dinner or other family activities when she was on hiatus. She liked the way Isla interacted with the girls. And Jennifer knew Cameron didn't mind.

Cam walked in from the dining room, a bottle of wine in one hand, corkscrew in the other.

Jennifer stretched her lips into a smile. "It looks like I arrived just in time." She hoped she sounded lighthearted, teasing; that the resentment she felt for Cam wasn't obvious. That way she wouldn't have to deny it later, to Cam or herself.

Cam put the wine and corkscrew down, walked over and pulled her into his arms. "This is a nice surprise." His breath was warm on her neck. She'd missed Cameron and had longed for this moment, yet she couldn't relax. When the girls came in from the family room, she was glad of the excuse to pull back. Her thoughts turned to Mammy, of the times she'd seen her hold back from Daddy's embrace. It's not the same, she thought, Mammy and I are different. Or were they? Families had a way repeating their dysfunction. What if it was in her DNA? Or that she tried so hard not repeat her mother's mistakes that she did anyway; a self-fulfilling prophecy?

Emma came running. "Mommy!" she called out.

Lindsay waited, watching. After cuddling Emma, Jennifer called Lindsay over. She was stiff for a moment but gradually softened. Jennifer closed her eyes, enjoyed the sensation of Lindsay's hair against her cheek, the fragility of her slim shoulders.

Isla was there, beside them. "Have a seat, girls," she said. "Oh Cam, can you set another place for our guest of honour?"

How We Danced

Without their usual grumbling, both girls took their chairs at the table. Cameron went to the cupboard for another plate. Jennifer wasn't sure what to do. Sit, stand, help? Nothing seemed right. In the end she stayed rooted in the middle of the room, watching Isla. She was stunning as always—something that had never bothered Jennifer before, but now made her feel uncomfortable about her own appearance. She smoothed a hand over her hair, regretted not applying an extra layer of mascara.

"I've made the only meal I know how, lamb stew with a wallop of Guinness." Isla hugged her and laughed. "Nothing like the gourmet meals you prepare, but it'll fill our bellies."

She smelled like the outdoors, green and fresh. Ironic, Jennifer thought, considering most of Isla's time was spent in dark theatres. "I thought you were in London until October?"

Isla stepped back and waved her hand in dismissal. "Miserable reviews. We closed early."

Jennifer knew how much Isla had wanted that part, how disappointed she must be. "I'm sorry," she said, meaning it.

"Don't be. Now that I'm home I can help Cam with the girls."

Jennifer's heart sped up. "That's kind, but you have enough to do." The truth was, without commitments, Isla was the perfect person to help.

"Nonsense, we're friends. Of course I'll help." Isla took both her hands in hers. "Tell me, how's your father?"

When Isla continued to look at her expectantly, she tried to speak, but painful thoughts of her father lodged in her throat, making it impossible to talk.

"Never mind. Come and have a nice glass of wine and relax. You've earned it." Isla led her by the hand to the table. "Cameron?"

Cameron stopped arranging the extra place setting and poured Jennifer's wine. Not knowing what else to do, she sat back and took a sip. It was especially good. He tended to be particular about using his finer stock. She wondered how spontaneous their meal was or if this was something he and Isla had planned. *You're being ridiculous*, she told herself, brought the glass to her nose and inhaled before taking another small sip.

125

Deborah Serravalle

Isla set the pot on the table and ladled out the stew. "Lindsay, do you mind grabbing the bread and butter on the counter?"

Lindsay jumped up to do as Isla asked. Jennifer took another swallow of wine, determined to enjoy her visit home.

"There we go." Isla sat back and looked around the table. "Tell me what you think."

Head down, Jennifer blew on a spoonful of the fragrant stew.

Cameron was the first to speak, "It's fabulous!"

Emma chimed in with, "Yummy." And Lindsay, sounding surprised said, "This is *really* good. Pass the bread."

"Aren't you hungry, Jennie?" Isla laid a hand on her arm. "Or don't you fancy it?"

"I was just waiting for it to cool," Jennifer said bringing the spoonful to her lips. It seemed absurd that beautiful, globe-trotting Isla was seeking her approval for something as mundane as a home-cooked meal. Chewing enthusiastically, she nodded her appreciation. Apparently satisfied, Isla turned her attention to her own bowl.

As the girls answered questions about their day from Isla and Cameron, Jennifer tried to listen, tried to eat. But she could do neither. The stew was good, the meat tender. Yet she found she couldn't swallow. It was as though her throat was blocked.

Isla was laughing at something one of the girls or Cameron had said. Is this how it had begun for Mammy and David Mallory, an innocent joke across the dining table? Judging from the paraphernalia her mother had kept, she and Mallory had travelled in the same circle. Although how someone like Mallory and her parents were socially aligned, Jennifer couldn't figure. Maybe his wife had been Mammy's friend. Jennifer looked over at Isla still laughing and talking to Cam. Jennifer gave up trying to swallow. Feigning a cough, she spat the masticated lamb into her napkin.

Isla pushed her bowl aside, brought her wine glass closer. "Jennie," she began, "let me tell you about my time in London." She went on to say that she'd befriended one of the lesser royals—a cousin three times removed or something—she was unclear on this detail. After seeing her performance, he'd asked for an introduction. And then for the next few weeks he'd shown her all around London and, she nudged Jennifer conspiratorially, "taken her out to his country estate."

As Isla took a break from her story for a sip of wine, Jennifer noticed her friend's cheeks were mottled a silky shade of pink. The blush extended down her neck, branching out across the delicate skin underneath her collar bones. She looked across the table at Cameron to gauge his reaction. He was busy wiping Emma's face and hands, then excusing her to go play.

Isla continued, "Too bad the show was cancelled," she sighed. "For once I was getting out and seeing more than the inside of my hotel room and the backstage of the theatre."

"It must be so exciting being an actress!" Lindsay said.

"Sometimes," Isla confided. "But it's tough on relationships."

"Is that why you're not married anymore?" Lindsay asked.

"Lindsay!" Cameron and Jennifer spoke at once.

Isla laughed, "Partly." She turned to Jennifer and said, "I'm thinking of packing it in and teaching theatre classes at the university. What do you think?"

"If it's what you want." Until recently Jennifer would have been thrilled to have her friend stay home. Now she wasn't sure.

"You know I've travelled for years. I'm looking forward to putting down roots." Isla squeezed Jennifer's hand. "And spending more time with friends. Just think," she gushed, "you and I will both be teachers!"

The muscle between Jennifer's shoulder blades tightened into a painful spasm. "That's wonderful," she said.

❀ ❀ ❀

Alastair watched Althea, the new daytime nurse, wring out the washcloth. Her hands were the colour of melted chocolate and just as smooth. As she leaned over him, he noticed she smelled like a confection, too, a blend of coconut and something else tropical he couldn't quite place.

Today was a good day. He wasn't energetic per se but alert and awake, at least. A bit of the fog that he now lived in had lifted. That in itself was miraculous.

"You're doing fine. Now turn onto your side. That's right." She wiped his back. "You'll rest better once we get you washed up."

If the massive doses of morphine didn't ease his discomfort, he doubted a sponge bath would do the job. Warm water trickling down his back contrasted with the chill on his exposed chest. His teeth chattered but he did his best to cooperate, not wanting to draw further attention by complaining.

He ached all over. His skin felt tender. Even a swipe from the terrycloth was painful. He envisioned raised blue welts lashed across his back, though in truth he knew she was being gentle. To console himself, with each stroke he imagined being closer to the warm comfort of his pillows.

Althea rubbed his back with a towel. "There, you're dried off. We'll get your pyjama shirt on and you can rest. Would you like me to turn on the TV?"

He eased onto his pillows and sighed. The draw to watch mind-numbing television was great. Lately that's all he'd done. But if he wanted to stay alert, he'd have to do more. As she buttoned his pyjama shirt he closed his eyes. "No, I think I'll read for a bit."

As Althea handed him his novel, he groaned. "I need to use the toilet."

"I'll get the urinal."

He was tempted. But it was a slippery slope. "No," he said, pulling himself up. He tottered at the edge of the bed.

She moved to his side. He started to say he was fine but reconsidered when his feet hit the floor and his knees threatened to buckle. She slipped an arm around his back and steadied him.

All was well for several feet. And then halfway to the door the room contorted. When he stopped to collect himself, beads of sweat popped out on his brow. He wondered if the urinal might have been the wiser choice and looked at his nurse.

"Would you like to get back in bed?"

He hesitated, but decided to push through. "No."

Althea continued to support him as he shuffled forward and then stopped again.

"When you're ready," she said.

As he waited for his equilibrium to return, he looked out the window. Across the street, the neighbour's flowerbed of mixed annuals was in full bloom. It was beautiful, a dazzling riot of colour, texture and shape. Now he understood why Lily spent so much time in her garden. He wished he'd realised sooner.

He yearned to feel the breeze on his skin, take a deep, cleansing breath of sweet, fresh air and exhale this horrible disease. This past winter had been a dark journey of tests, doctors and hospital visits. Now it was summer. And for him, there would never be another. The flowerbed blurred; the colours blended. What else had he missed?

Alastair turned away, tried to wipe his eyes without the nurse noticing.

"All set?" she asked.

There was little he could do now to change the past. He shrugged and moved forward.

Outside the bathroom door he stopped and leaned against the wall. His legs would take him no farther.

"We're almost there." Althea held onto his elbow.

With a silent plea he looked to her. There was nothing she could do. No one could save him. He was alone and helpless. Frightened, his heart quickened, his breath reduced to sharp exhalations. He tried to steady his breathing, but the air felt as though it was filled with jagged particles of dust that caught in his throat. He started to cough.

In an instant she whipped an arm around his back and stuck her shoulder in his armpit. "Lean on me, it'll pass."

He followed her instructions, but she was wrong, the coughing didn't subside soon enough. He felt a release as the warm gush of urine skittered down his leg, soaking his pyjamas and socks. Horrified, he looked at the puddle surrounding his slippers and Althea's practical shoes.

"Is everything okay?" Lily came into the hall from the kitchen.

Lifting his head, he looked at his wife in her kerchief and garden gloves.

Jennifer came up behind her mother. She glanced from him to Althea and then down at the puddle.

When he saw the comprehension dawn on his daughter's face, he turned away.

Althea adjusted his weight.

"I heard him coughing from the yard," said Lily. And wait, isn't—?"

"Come on, Mammy. The nurse has everything under control."

Alastair's head felt light, his limbs heavy. His peripheral vision was getting smaller and smaller. And then it occurred to him: *I'm dying.*

Seconds passed. Or was it minutes? He wasn't certain. Something wasn't right, but he wasn't sure what. He looked down at his feet and tried to remember what was wrong, knowing that something was.

Rainwater pooled around them. Confused, he decided there must have been a storm. Hadn't he heard that on the news? It was the worst one in years, rain and flooding everywhere. He remembered he wanted to check on Aaron. Make sure he was okay. He missed him. The storm was a good excuse.

Wait. Now he was in Aaron's shop. Odd that he couldn't remember arriving.

"Napoleon, look who's here!" Aaron tossed a leopard print cushion onto the sofa in the display window, stepped through the opening and back into the shop. "We haven't heard from you in ages. We assumed you were through with us."

The terrier started barking. Welcome or warning? Alastair was unsure. But when he ventured closer, hand extended, the dog growled. He took a step back.

Aaron laughed. "He doesn't trust you anymore. You led him on and let him down."

Alastair wanted to rush over to Aaron but he remained rooted in the puddle. "He's right to feel betrayed, but I had no choice."

"Why are you here?" Aaron asked.

"I wanted to make sure you were okay. The storm, there's flooding all over the city, especially in this area." As the words tumbled out, Alastair knew they were absurd. Aaron had been so good to him. He shouldn't have run. He should have come sooner.

"How gallant. Well as you can see, I'm fine."

Aaron's tone was sharp. Alastair knew he was angry and hurt. He had every right to be. Alastair wanted to take him in his arms. Beg to be forgiven. For things to go back to the way they had been.

"I wasn't certain you'd open the shop today." Alastair stalled for time.

"I probably wouldn't have, but my buying agent arrived last night with a shipment we need to unload." Aaron lowered himself onto a settee, tucked the dog in a corner. "So how are things with you and the lovely Lily?"

Alastair shifted his weight from one foot to the other. It was a mistake to show up this way when he had nothing to offer.

Aaron flipped his cigarette case open. "Why are you here?"

"The storm, I told you. I was concerned."

"Smoke?"

Alastair reached and took a cigarette from Aaron's monogrammed case.

"So you're concerned about my well-being." Aaron motioned for a light.

Alastair pulled a matchbook from his pocket. His hand trembled as he lit Aaron's cigarette and then his own.

"She's pregnant."

Aaron blew out his first drag. He settled back, his expression hard and closed. "Congratulations."

Alastair puffed on the cigarette. "I wanted to explain—"

There was a rap at the side entrance. A young man gripped the door frame with both hands. "Sorry to interrupt. Whenever you're ready, Aaron. Everything is unloaded."

Alastair drew a quick breath. This was the new buying agent. He noted his broad shoulders, the shirt sleeves rolled up to the elbows over thick forearms. Why would he hang around and help set up? A sudden and swift dose of jealousy left Alastair feeling hollow and rejected.

"I'll be there in a few minutes, George." Aaron said.

The new buying agent, started to retreat to the back room.

"Oh wait," Aaron said.

George stopped in his tracks and raised a brow at Aaron.

Aaron smiled. "Would you be a love and bring out that cardboard box I have in the office, the one behind the desk?"

"Sure." The young man rushed off.

"I have something for you." Aaron said.

"For me?" Alastair's mouth was so parched he had trouble forming the words.

Aaron rose from the settee as George reappeared.

"My typewriter was causing me grief again. I didn't want to bother you, so I went out and bought new one. I recalled you had a way with the Smith Corona. She's of no use to me anymore." Aaron turned to George. "Do you mind carrying that out to Alastair's car?"

Alastair's face reddened. He'd taken the bus, arrived on foot. He found his voice. "I can manage." He took the box from George, the weight of it pushing him down.

"As you wish." Aaron stubbed out his cigarette, picked up Napoleon and walked out the side door with George at his heel.

"Not to worry," a woman spoke.

Alastair turned to the voice. It was Althea, his nurse.

He looked around. Aaron's shop was gone and he was standing in his own hallway.

"Let's get you back to bed," she said.

Not knowing what else to do, he nodded. As he shuffled down the hall with Althea leading, he tried to sort out what had just happened. The fog wouldn't lift. He began to tremble. By the time they reached the bedroom he was shaking uncontrollably.

He remained silent as she offered reassurance that he was fine, that there was no shame in wetting yourself when seized by a coughing fit. She said these things as she stripped, washed and changed him. He agreed; compared to losing his mind, pissing himself seemed trivial.

She plumped up his pillows and helped him swing his legs up, over and onto the mattress. Then she picked up his book from the nightstand and handed it to him. He stared past her.

"You don't want to read?"

He shook his head.

She placed the novel beside him. "In case you change your mind."

He turned his face to the wall. It was too late for any of that.

"Come on, Mammy," Jennifer said. "You could use a break. Besides, you said you needed to get to the library. Afterwards, we could go for lunch."

"Mmhm," Lily nodded and looked at Alastair. He was asleep or unconscious. These days it was getting harder to tell. The nurse was fiddling with a tube on his intravenous pole.

How We Danced

Lily changed her clothes. She put on a little lipstick and blush. When she checked her reflection, she was pleased. Fluffing her hair, she realised she was singing. She stopped and glanced around the empty bathroom. She hoped Jennifer or the nurse hadn't heard. Again she looked in the mirror. The blush on her cheekbones that was perfect moments before, now seemed too bright. She grabbed a cotton pad, rubbed off some colour.

They were lucky to get the last spot in the small library parking lot. All of Westdale seemed busier than usual for a mid-week afternoon. Lily wondered if it was the pleasant weather. The library was crowded. A program for new mothers was ending. Strollers and babies were scattered everywhere. She stepped back to allow a young woman with a howling bundle to pass. There were people at computers, people asking questions at the front counter, people milling the stacks. As an attractive middle-aged man drew near, she tucked her cane into the folds of her skirt. She despised the weight of it against her leg, a nagging reminder of her diminished capacity.

Normally, a trip to the library was a relaxing outing. Today she found the commotion distracting. Wandering the fiction section, she couldn't find anything that appealed or muster the energy to do a proper search.

Jennifer came alongside holding several books. "You haven't chosen anything yet?"

Unsure of how to respond, Lily lifted a shoulder. She hoped she appeared nonchalant. But then she saw the concern cross Jennifer's face and felt foolish.

"Well, I found more than I need. We can share. I got some good ones, look." Jennifer held out the pile like an offering.

After dividing up their reads, they checked out and drove the small distance to the restaurant. Feeling tired, Lily leaned on her cane inside the bistro's door while Jennifer parked the car. She scanned the crowded room. Everyone appeared to be Jennifer's age or younger. They were all talking loudly, to each other or on one of those smart phones. Two servers wove between tables. She tried to make eye contact, but neither of them glanced her way. Blushing, she looked down.

The door opened and Jennifer was beside her. "Is there a table free or do we have to wait?"

"I don't know," Lily said as she shrugged.

Jennifer lifted her brows. "You mean no one spoke to you?" Lily shook her head.

Jennifer raised her arm and caught a server's eye. "Excuse me," she said in a sharp voice. "Do you have a table for two?"

Lily rubbed the handle of her cane. She whispered so only Jennifer could hear. "It's okay."

"No, it's not okay, Mammy. Don't worry, though. I won't make a scene. But I don't appreciate you being ignored like that. It's not fair. In fact, it's rather unkind."

"Really, it was nothing," Lily said. Yet as Jennifer peered around the room looking for a free table, Lily couldn't deny the overwhelming urge she had to touch her daughter and say *thank you*. As she steadied her cane and reached out, a young server with black curly hair came up to them. Lily pulled back.

The server rubbed his palms down the length of his apron. "Sorry," he smiled. "It's crazy in here today." He grabbed some menus and started winding his way around the tables.

Jennifer folded out her arm indicating Lily should go first. She trod cautiously, not wanting to catch her cane on the wrought iron table legs and chairs spidered at random angles. The young man was waiting for them at a small table at the back of the bistro, right beside the open kitchen and near the stairs with a sign that pointed down, *Bathrooms*. He put the menus on the table, said, "Enjoy," and then scurried off.

Lily tried to pull out her chair. It was awkward and heavy. The foot caught on a lip of the old hardwood.

"Here, Mammy, let me get that." Jennifer lifted the chair out and helped Lily get settled.

Lily scanned the menu. Some of the items made sense, but others were foreign. "What are tapas?"

"Finger food, like canapés." Jennifer said.

"Hmph." Lily went back to reading the menu.

"They have a soup and sandwich special." Jennifer pointed up at a chalk board. "Why don't we get that? You like asparagus soup, right?"

How We Danced

Lily shut the menu. "I do." All of a sudden she was hungry.

She recognized Jennifer was trying hard to make their outing pleasant. Before this business with Alastair, Lily would have enjoyed a trip to the library to choose books and a lunch somewhere new and different with her daughter. But for some reason, today she felt strange and out of place.

The server returned, flipped open a pad. "You ladies ready to order?"

As they waited for their food to arrive, Jennifer took a call from the girls' school on her mobile. While Jennifer talked, Lily noticed two young women across the aisle and soon realised one was nursing her baby. When she was younger, women never did that. It took her ages to even leave the house after Jennifer's birth. When Jennifer could last a few hours without feeding, Alastair had offered to mind her. Lily had jumped at the chance to go downtown, only to find she felt overwhelmed by the crowds and commotion. Much like today, she thought.

Jennifer put down her phone as the waiter placed soup bowls in front of them. Lily noticed she looked pale, the lines of her mouth were tight.

"It smells wonderful," Jennifer said and dug in.

Lily enjoyed the asparagus soup, but the sandwich was the real treat. Filled with brie cheese, apples, sprouts and walnuts, it was like nothing she had ever tasted.

"I have an idea," Jennifer said. "Rather than order dessert, why don't we get some frozen yogurt across the street and go for a little drive. The university is just around the corner, and I haven't been through the campus in ages. I'd like to see how it's changed."

"Do we have time?" Lily looked at her watch.

"The nurse is with Daddy. I left my number. If there's a problem she'll call."

"I don't know ..."

"Come on," Jennifer teased. "You know you want to."

Although the morning had been cool, the afternoon had warmed. Jennifer opened the car's sunroof and all the windows. She cruised up one street and down another, commenting on particularly nice homes or gardens.

Lily had put her sweater on and enjoyed the breeze while she ate her yogurt and listened to her daughter reminisce about her youth.

They emerged from one of the meandering side streets and turned onto the main thoroughfare. The university came into view. It was then Lily remembered David's home was nearby. She wondered if he and Catherine still lived there.

They pulled up to the three-way stop at the entrance to the university. On the right was David's street.

Lily's heart sped up. "Turn here," she said on impulse and pointed right.

Jennifer's eyes were wide with surprise. "Why?"

Lily decided to tell the bare truth. "Years ago, your father and I went to a party there."

Someone behind them honked. Jennifer turned.

"It must have been a nice party ..." Jennifer trailed off.

Lily tried to appear nonchalant. "It was," she said while forcing a smile.

"I remember this street from my university days," Jennifer said. "There are some beautiful old homes down here."

Lily didn't respond. Nor did she look in Jennifer's direction. The yogurt she'd eaten curdled in her stomach. She set the dish on her lap and gripped the door handle.

There was a moment of silence and then Jennifer said, "Well, let me know if you recognize the house."

They passed several properties before Jennifer slowed down in front of a sprawling ranch-style home. "Look at that one. The garden is nice and you can't fault the architecture, but I prefer the older, stately designs. Don't you?"

Lily nodded as she drove on. The homes looked smaller, less opulent, than she remembered. She tried to recall where David and Catherine's place was in the looping avenue. She thought it was farther down, where the boulevard strip narrowed.

"See that open space?" Jennifer pointed at the grassy area that divided the street. "When I was in school, a group of us used to play touch football there. And at night," Jennifer turned to face Lily, smiling, "the kids used to go parking at the other side. Cops would cruise the circle and chase them off."

How We Danced

Lily recalled the glaring headlights the night she'd walked this boulevard in her pyjamas and sweater. She thought of the man with the dog. Looking back, she felt lucky it was him she'd encountered. A police officer would have been worse.

Jennifer prattled on about a red-brick Georgian two-storey she felt sure Emma would love and a stately Tudor set back amongst the trees that she figured would be more to Lindsay's liking. When they rounded a slight bend, the imposing grey stone of Catherine and David's home came into view. There was a realtor's sign on the lawn.

"This is it." Lily's mouth was dry and her heart pounded. "It's for sale."

She wondered if it was David and Catherine leaving. Or perhaps they'd gone years ago and now another family was moving out. It might even be their son. Lily stared out the windshield; studied a clump of birch on another property.

"I see that," Jennifer said and then drove on in silence, her mouth a thin line.

On the opposite side of the boulevard strip they passed the stone mansion for the second time. They both turned and looked at the home and the realtor's sign. Lily waited, thinking Jennifer might comment. But she stayed silent. There was only the hum of the car engine as she pressed the accelerator.

CHAPTER 14

Jennifer was curious, even worried, about David Mallory's home being for sale. When they'd met, he'd made it clear he admired the place; if not the grand house, certainly the manicured gardens. It was visible in the way he'd reached out to run a hand over the petals of blossoming shrubs, the contented smile that crossed his face at the time. *So much history,* he'd said.

Unless something catastrophic happened, why would he leave? Despite her concern, it took several days before she could think about returning. Even then she felt guilty. Her father had suffered a serious setback, an infection that required a vigorous round of antibiotics. She hadn't wanted to leave her mother, especially to snoop around Mallory's house. It felt disloyal. But then her father had turned a corner, rallied, and his prescriptions needed filling. They were running low on a few basics. After stopping at the pharmacy and grocery store, Jennifer made a detour by Mallory's street, promising herself she would hurry.

She drove to the end of the looping boulevard and parked on a small, concealed cul-de-sac. From there she walked back, toward his home. A car stood in the driveway, and as she drew closer a van pulled in beside it. A woman got out and began unloading cleaning equipment.

How We Danced

Hovering at the end of the drive, Jennifer tried to muster the courage to walk the short distance and ask the woman a few questions. As the cleaner started towards the house, Jennifer rushed forward and said, "Good morning."

The woman looked at her and smiled.

Encouraged, Jennifer drew closer. "I was talking to Mr. Mallory not long ago. He never mentioned moving."

The cleaner's smile faded. She looked back at the house for a moment. "You knew him?" she asked, hefting a vacuum hose over her shoulder.

Jennifer's stomach flipped at the woman's use of the past tense. Mallory's comment about his damaged heart came back. Perhaps he'd suffered another attack and could no longer manage alone. Or perhaps; she blocked further conjecture. "I met him recently when—"

Jennifer and the cleaner turned as two women came out the front door and started down the walkway towards them.

"There's Ms. Foster with the realtor, she'll help you." The cleaner walked away.

The two women stopped their conversation when they reached Jennifer. They looked at her, their faces open but curious. Wishing she'd worn something more impressive than capris and a t-shirt, she forced a smile. Perhaps one of these women was the estranged daughter Mallory had mentioned. She searched each woman's face for some resemblance to him, but found none.

The taller woman nodded at Jennifer and then addressed her friend. "I'll call you after the showing on Thursday." She got into her car and backed out.

The remaining woman faced her. "How may I help?"

Nervous and tongue-tied, she wasn't sure what to say. She surmised this was Ms. Foster. In a tailored coral dress and matching jacket, she was about her age, maybe a bit older.

Not knowing what else to do, Jennifer stuck her hand out. "Jennifer Roberts."

"Elizabeth Foster," the woman trailed off while still holding her hand. "Forgive me, but do we have a meeting?"

"No, I'm sorry." Jennifer withdrew her hand. "Let me explain. I met Mr. Mallory under rather unusual circumstances a few weeks ago. I fell there," she said with a self-deprecating chuckle and pointed to the end of the drive. "And he helped me. I wanted to thank him, but it appears he's up and moved."

She could tell Elizabeth was trying to decide how to respond.

Allowing it may be guilt surrounding their estrangement, she softened her voice. "Are you his daughter?"

Jennifer wasn't sure if it was shock, fear or a combination of both that flitted across Elizabeth's face before she assumed a demeanour of neutrality.

"If you met him by chance, how would you know if he had a daughter?"

Elizabeth's cynicism was valid. Jennifer realised she had no right to her questions. What was she thinking, barging in assuming she'd find answers? She was nothing to Mallory and even less to his daughter. Deciding she wouldn't learn anything from Elizabeth, whatever her relation to Mallory, she said, "I'm sorry to have disturbed you," and turned to go.

"No. Wait." Elizabeth placed a hand on her arm.

Surprised, Jennifer turned around.

"I'm David's niece." She smiled solicitously. "Forgive my being defensive, but one can't be too careful. My uncle was a wealthy man, and, well, you can imagine—"

Jennifer felt her face blanch. "He … died?"

"Yes, I'm sorry to say." Elizabeth's shrug defied her words.

"When?" Jennifer gasped.

"A few weeks ago now." Elizabeth glanced back at the house. "A neighbour found him sitting in that chair. Massive heart attack."

It was the chair in the entrance alcove where she and Mallory had chatted.

"You say you fell and hurt yourself?" Elizabeth frowned, pondering something.

"Yes, why?"

"When they found him, he was holding a blood-stained facecloth. We had wondered—"

Jennifer clapped a hand to her mouth. She remembered folding the cloth to conceal her blood, handing it back to him.

"You look upset. Are you okay?" Elizabeth's voice seemed far away. The home, the lawn, the driveway started to blur and converge. Without waiting to hear if she was all right, Elizabeth shifted to another question. "He mentioned a daughter?"

Jennifer heard herself say, "I'm sorry about your uncle." She willed her feet to move, one after the other.

Elizabeth followed behind. "Is there a number where I can reach you?"

Jennifer shook her head and kept moving. Her heart pounded against her ribs like a caged bird. She needed to catch her breath and get away from this woman. Someplace safe. Somewhere to think. To make sense of this news.

By the time she reached the car she was no longer gasping for air, but her heart continued its irregular rhythm. After taking a few deep, slow breaths, she started the engine and drove off. As she passed Mallory's house she noticed the garden, bursting with new rose blooms.

That's when the tears began. She turned into the nearest parking lot, pulled out a pack of tissues and blew her nose.

It must have happened that afternoon, soon after she'd left him. She imagined Mallory as she'd last seen him, sitting by his front entrance, the garden he tended spread before him, holding the folded facecloth. She blinked, swallowed hard.

Maybe he knew more than he let on.

She replayed their conversation, broke it down sentence by sentence, word by word. Now his comments seemed cryptic and full of meaning she'd missed. Squeezing her eyes shut, she tilted her head back.

What have I done?

She buried her face in her hands. His gentle smile and curious expression swam before her closed eyes.

Sitting up, she blew her nose one last time. Her parents were at home, waiting for her. Mammy would worry if she was gone too long. She put the tissues away, started the car and tried to push David Mallory from her mind.

Back at her parents', as she unloaded the grocery sacks from the trunk, thoughts of Mallory returned. The bags seemed heavy, weighted with unasked, unanswered questions.

Who was this man who had died holding a cloth stained with her blood?

❋ ❋ ❋

Alastair was comfortable. For now that was enough. When pain free, he had learned to focus on the present: cool, clean sheets draped across his chest, a beam of morning light, the rhythm of his heart. After his sponge bath, Lily had separated the newspaper into sections, set it within easy reach and then opened the blinds and the window. He savoured the light breeze, the earthy scent of grass mingled with damp soil, and waited.

A moment more and then, *woo-OO-oo-oo-oo*. He smiled and waited for the mourning dove's mate to arrive, confident it would. Listening to the bird cooing on the ledge, he closed his eyes. When they had first started coming to the window, in the days before his illness, he researched the species, learned they mated for life, both parents caring for the young. There was something extraordinary about their commitment to each other. Just like us, he'd thought. Since he'd been confined to bed, their predictable presence marked something more: the beginning of another day, a reason to be grateful.

He recalled a time when pigeons were so numerous in the city their presence became a problem. They'd been rounded up, caged and moved elsewhere. The starlings had been dealt with more harshly.

Back then, the birds had congregated by the hundreds downtown in Gore Park. The experience had been miserable for anyone daring to venture into the treed enclave. Perched within the branches, the birds had created a feathery canopy, so high and heavy the trees looked liked inside-out umbrellas. Their excrement covered everything in slick, green-grey slime. Sitting on a park bench was impossible; the pathways around the fountain, filthy. City Hall banned feeding them, but it did little good. A radical solution was announced: the starlings were to be culled, shot as they roosted in the trees.

Alastair, although well aware of the culling date, had forgotten about it. Or at least it had been overshadowed, as it was also Robert Burns Day. Late that afternoon, he had left the typewriter shop on foot, tool case in hand.

His call was just past the farmers market. To avoid the foot traffic of King Street, he headed north and cut along King William at a brisk pace. As he walked, he estimated how long his appointment would take. He wondered if he'd have to go back to the shop or if he'd finish up his day there. Considering the time, the latter seemed likely. In which case, he'd lift his glass in honour of Robbie at the King Eddie.

He was approaching a crosswalk when he was startled by the crack of gunfire. The tool case slipped from his hand, hitting the sidewalk with a thump. More shots followed in rapid succession. Looking south on Hughson Street, Alastair glimpsed the gunmen, lined up like a military firing squad, in Gore Park. Tossing his cigarette away, he grabbed his tool case and ran towards the carnage.

The news agent's shack on the corner of King was closed. No cars, other than police cruisers, were on the road. He glanced east and then west, saw the barricades several blocks off in each direction. The rapid, staccato fire was deafening, the scent of hot copper, hellish. He pulled a handkerchief from his pocket, held it to his nose as he crossed King Street. Policemen stood guard at strategic points, holding back onlookers. Only shooters were allowed inside the park. Around the perimeter people were lined up, several deep, as though watching a parade. Instead of floats, majorettes and clowns, the star performers were sleek starlings tumbling from the sky. Their lifeless bodies dropped, carpeting the grass, shrubs, benches, and walkways.

When a wounded bird fell to the pavement, landing beside a shooter's polished boot, Alastair was choked with pity for the creature. Suppressing the desire to run through the barrier and rescue the bird, he watched as it struggled to right itself. Moments later, the shooter finished his round. He looked down, considered the fractured bird for a split-second, then crushed it with his heavy boot, scuffed it away and reloaded.

The sanctioned brutality reminded him of Hitler's cull of Jews. Newsreel images of the innocents felled by Nazi firing squads flashed through his mind as the shooters reloaded, took aim and, on call, fired over and over again at the birds.

Throughout, Alastair's urge to run into the centre of the organized chaos and scream *STOP!* was almost overwhelming. He gripped the handle of his tool case until his knuckles ached and his fingernails left half-moons on his palm. Feeling desperate and alone, he scanned the crowd, searched the faces. Did anyone else feel this way? That's when he spotted David Mallory.

As the feathered torpedoes fell, Mallory's arms hung limp at his sides. His fedora was pushed back at a defeated angle as he regarded the slaughter, expressionless. There was a time when Alastair had envied Mallory. Not now. A swell of sympathy filled Alastair's throat. Only months ago, Mallory's young son had died. Alastair had read the obituary, but didn't tell Lily. To protect her from needless upset, he reasoned, for the poor boy had been their Jennie's age. Besides, they hadn't seen the Mallorys in years, and Alastair had no desire to resurrect their friendship.

Alastair decided to leave for his appointment. They'd be waiting, wondering where he was if he took much longer. Once more he looked at Mallory. The fedora was lower now, obscuring his eyes. A young lad stood in profile, slightly behind Mallory. *Impossible. The child is dead.* Without warning, The Boy stooped down and then popped up. He held something out, in his palm, towards Mallory. Alastair gasped, horrified. The child brought the lifeless starling to his chest, he petted it, appeared to talk to it. Throughout, Mallory stared forward, never acknowledging the child beside him with the shattered bird. With a final smile down at the starling, The Boy moved into the crowd and was gone.

Feeling lightheaded, Alastair left the park, the birds, Mallory, The Boy, and walked on towards his business call. Afterwards, he didn't stop at the King Eddie. Anxious to see his family, he went to the bus stop.

When he walked through the door and shouted, "I'm home," Jennifer came running from the kitchen, a smile on her face.

"Daddy!"

Lily followed. She was drying her hands on a tea towel. "You're early," she said, sounding happy.

How We Danced

He scooped up Jennifer into his arms and held her close. "I wanted to come home and see my girls."

Lily walked closer, tentative. "Are you okay?"

He thought about the culling, the chaos and carnage. He thought about The Boy with the starling. He thought about David Mallory, the sad tilt of his hat. He thought about Mallory's dead son and he held Jennifer closer. For a moment, he thought about telling Lily all of this.

Instead, he had said, "I love you," and held out his hand. When she had taken it, he pulled her to him and Jennifer. He had embraced his family, vowing to never let them go.

There was a plaintive, *woo-OO-oo-oo* and a flutter of wings as the dove's mate arrived and nestled onto the window ledge.

Lily came over, adjusted his pillows. "I love you, too." She took the hand he offered, careful to avoid the intravenous tubing. "Can I get you anything?"

Embarrassed by his confusion, he said the first thing he thought of, "Pass me the paper."

She handed him the newspaper and walked away. Settling back and, as was his habit, he picked out the classifieds first and scanned the obituaries. A name jumped out. Then a face. He stopped reading and watched Lily move around the room, righting something here, replacing something there, searching for evidence that she'd read the paper and, like him, discovered David Mallory's obituary.

❋ ❋ ❋

Lily looked around her garden and smiled. The earlier blooms were gone, but in their place others were coming; a few chrysanthemums and, of course, the roses were still thriving. It felt good to be outside in the sunshine, getting a bit of exercise, even if it wasn't as much as usual. Her injured ankle had healed well, but kneeling still hurt. She was using a green folding stool Jennifer had purchased. She was with her father now, doing his feet, "a mini pedicure," she had called it, as she drew a bowl of warm water. As Lily pulled out unruly shoots from the soil, she recalled the way Jennifer, head bent over Alastair's feet, had said to her, "Why don't you get out for a bit and do some gardening?"

Although Jennifer phrased this as a question, it sounded more like a statement.

Lily paused before answering, "If you don't mind—" When Jennifer hadn't responded, Lily had turned and left.

There was nothing wrong with her daughter's suggestion. On one hand, she was grateful for her consideration and the opportunity to get outside to be amongst her flowers. But in replaying the comment, Lily felt something wasn't right. The more she thought about it, she realised it wasn't just the formal edge to Jennifer's tone, it was the rigidity of her back, the protective stiffness that extended to her shoulders, and the tightness that pulled at the edges of her mouth.

When Lily turned her attention back to the garden, she noticed a large dandelion wedged between a cluster of lily leaves. It always amazed her how they shot up from nowhere, their sinewy roots deep and merciless; a nuisance. They flourished, while her beloved lilies suffered. Life wasn't always fair.

With some difficulty, she got down on her knees, and with a trowel, dug deep and pulled out as much of the root as she could. No matter how hard she tried, she could never get it all. Tossing the bothersome weed aside, she decided that when she went back into the house she would ask Jennifer what was troubling her.

Lily played the scenario out in her mind, how she'd hold Jennifer's hand, how she'd phrase her question. But Lily knew Jennifer's response would be silence or a dismissive shrug.

Easing back onto the stool, Lily thought it might be best to let things be, allow Jennifer some space, and then perhaps she'd come to her without prompting. Besides, it was likely her father's worsening condition was the reason behind Jennifer's changed attitude.

But another voice inside Lily disagreed. Until the day the two of them had driven down David's street, Jennifer hadn't been short of words.

The trowel slipped from Lily's hand as an image of David's house bloomed in her mind. *A mistake.* She admonished herself, and pushed the image away. *We should never have gone there.*

How We Danced

But they had gone there. She sat back as a sick feeling settled in her stomach. What if Jennifer suspected something? Or worse, had discovered their connection to David Mallory? *Ridiculous.* Lily shook her head, drew a deep breath and exhaled. She reached over and picked up her trowel, looking for more weeds. She returned to her original conclusion: Alastair's deterioration was a more logical explanation for Jennifer's strange demeanour.

There was another reason Lily regretted having returned to that boulevard. For now, in the hour of Alastair's greatest need, she was distracted. Even as she busied herself with his care, fragmented memories of David intruded. Round and round she went without relief. When old memories eased, new questions presented themselves. *Had he moved? Gone to a retirement home? What of Catherine? Their son?* Perhaps, she hoped, finding answers would bring a measure of satisfaction and her obsession would abate. She'd be set free to return her focus where it belonged, on Alastair. Convinced this was true, she went into the house to look up David's telephone number.

As she pulled the phone book from the kitchen drawer, she heard Jennifer and Alastair talking in the bedroom. Fumbling, she opened the thick book, fanned the pages to 'M'. Wetting her fingertip, she flipped the next few pages until she found David's name, his address and phone number. Lily whispered the number aloud. After glancing into the empty hall, she picked up the phone and dialled. Several rings later, a message came on: *This number is no longer in service.* Heart thrumming, mouth dry, she replaced the receiver.

She remained near the phone for a moment, confused. The house must have sold; he had already moved on.

Lily returned to the back garden. Weeding didn't appeal to her anymore. She gathered her tools and returned them to the shed. The air inside was humid and heavy. Flies buzzed; one landed on her foot, another on her arm. She shook them off. Pots, half-empty bags of soil, baskets and unused waste bags cluttered the counter. She thought about tidying up but made no effort to do so. Instead, she tried to puzzle out why the Mallorys had moved.

If David or Catherine had passed away, it would have been in the newspaper. She glanced at the blue recycle bins: one for glass and plastic, the other for paper. As the years progressed, checking the obituaries had become a normal part of her routine. Since Alastair's illness they frightened her, knowing in the not-too-distant future his name would be there. For this reason she often skipped them. This meant if David's or Catherine's name had appeared lately, she could have missed it. Even if she wanted to check now, the bins were empty. No answers there. She left the shed and wandered back to the house, thinking that if David had passed, she would know; she would sense it.

Jennifer was in the kitchen, sitting at the table drinking orange juice and reading the morning paper. "Finished already?" She turned away for a moment and rubbed her eyes.

"I don't have the heart for it right now." Lily paused and searched her daughter's face. Her complexion was blotchy, and Lily wondered if she'd been crying. "Is Daddy all right?"

"He's fine. I left him to rest." Jennifer tossed the section of paper she'd been reading over to Lily. "Here, have a look. I'll get you some orange juice." She got up and went to the fridge.

The fine hairs on Lily's arms stood on end as she sat down. Something was wrong. "Did your father enjoy his pedicure?" She tried to sound lighthearted.

As Jennifer placed the orange juice on the table, Lily felt her daughter's anger radiate like heat. Why? She could think of nothing that she had done to displease Jennifer.

Unnerved, Lily picked up the section of the paper in front of her. As she tried to think of what could be troubling Jennifer, she turned the pages, scanned the headlines without reading.

There it was—a tribute article about the recently deceased David Mallory, past President of Elliott Steel and local philanthropist. Lily felt the blood drain from her face, her heart racing while her arms and hands tingled. Feeling Jennifer's eyes on her, she did her best to appear calm as she searched the article for key points.

He'd passed away several weeks ago. Her breath caught. She covered her mouth, pretended to cough. So she had missed his obituary.

How We Danced

The beginning of the article highlighted David's career accomplishments. She was pleased at his success and proud, although she knew she had no right. How sad. They'd loved each other once and created a child. Here she was, sitting with a glass of orange juice reading about his life and death in the paper. The distance was heartbreaking and surreal. She set aside what might have been and read on. She learned Catherine had passed away several years ago. Certain she was mistaken, she read it again. She felt ill when she saw that his son, Michael, had died at the age of four.

Somehow she managed to turn the page and pretend to keep reading. She did this for a few more minutes. Finally she closed the section and placed it on top of the others. Without a word, Jennifer got up and went to the counter. Arms wide, she braced the ledge and stared into the empty sink.

Lily stood. "I'm going to rest on the front porch." Her body felt heavy, weighted. Her injured ankle throbbed and she stumbled.

Jennifer didn't answer or comment as Lily limped to the front door.

Outside, she made her way to the settee. She thought of David's little Michael, dead at four. Losing a child was the worst thing that could happen to a parent. Now she felt sorry for Catherine and for all the times she'd envied her. How fortunate she was to have Jennifer, and her grandchildren. She tried to conjure Michael's little-boy face. A bowl cut, bright smile and David's eyes. It was the most she had ever thought about the child. She had dismissed him. A nuisance. No doubt David had loved him. He was the boy's father.

Tears filled her eyes. The maple tree with the swing blurred. *That's why he came.* Again, David was there, crouched down talking to Jennifer. She remembered her anger and fear, the way she chased him off. *Don't come back. Ever.* Now in her memory details emerged that she'd overlooked or ignored. The pain etched on his face as he backed away; when he turned, the stoop of his shoulders. Hurt and betrayed, she'd never considered what his choice had cost him.

It occurred to her that he may have come that day to claim more than Jennifer. She circled this idea around in her mind, and wondered whether it would have made a difference. Before she could decide, voices from the open bedroom window intruded.

"Daddy, you're up." Jennifer said something else but Lily couldn't make it out.

Alastair called out, "Where's your mother?" He sounded disoriented, fearful.

Lily placed her grief for David aside. "Don't worry," she called back, wiping her eyes. "I'm right here."

CHAPTER 15

Most of the dishes were stacked in the drying rack. There were only a couple of pots left to wash. Jennifer had allowed them to soak. Now she was rummaging under the sink for a scouring pad.

Her mother had walked into the kitchen. "What are you looking for?" She sounded distracted.

"Something to get the stubborn stains off these pots." Jennifer backed out of the cupboard and held up a scouring pad. "Maybe this'll work."

Lily didn't respond; she stared at the stack of letters she held, filing one behind the other. Confusion crossed her face. "This is for you." She held out an envelope. "It's addressed to Jennifer MacAulay."

"That's weird." Jennifer dried her hands and took the envelope.

"It's from Ross & Rose, they're lawyers," Lily said.

"Yes, I see." Jennifer stared at the line of type bearing her maiden name. It seemed odd, living in this house again, sleeping in her childhood bedroom, being without her husband, children, and now receiving mail in her old name. Closing her eyes for a second, she brought Cam's image forward, tried to remember what his touch felt like. She imagined the weight and warmth of his big hands on her shoulders, his breath in her ear as he whispered, *"Let's go upstairs."*

"Well, aren't you going to open it?" her mother asked.

The image of Cameron vanished. "Of course." Jennifer ripped open the envelope, unfolded the single page and scanned it.

"You are named as beneficiary in the estate of David Michael Mallory."

Her stomach lurched as she re-examined the line, certain she had misread it. But no, she was named in Mallory's estate. Surprise turned to confusion. Why? But as she asked this question, his words, a confession, came back to her. "I have a daughter ... but sadly, we're *estranged* ..." He'd emphasized this word, trailed off. "... The fault is all mine."

"Please contact our offices to confirm that you have received this letter and that the information we have on file for you is current and correct."

There was a phone number and the name of a clerk.

"Well?" her mother asked.

Jennifer put the letter back into the envelope before looking at her mother's expectant face. "It doesn't make sense." She shrugged. "I'll sort it out later."

Her mother looked unconvinced. Before she could ask anything more, Jennifer stood. She needed time to think, process. "I'm going for a shower."

Inside her room, back pressed against the closed door, Jennifer's mind jumped from question to fact to question. David Mallory had been her mother's lover. Did that mean he was her father? But the word father, the concept and definition, all went back to the man in the bedroom down the hall—Daddy—the reason she was here, away from her family. Did Daddy know? Had there been some arrangement made, an adoption?

After putting the lawyer's envelope inside a t-shirt and tucking both at the back of her dresser drawer, she sat on the bed and removed her slippers and socks. Perhaps that was it. If she was legally adopted by her father, Alastair, she was still his daughter. But Mallory had said *estranged*. Not lost or given up or anything else that indicated he'd voluntarily relinquished his rights. Closing her eyes, she tried to imagine herself as someone other than Alastair's daughter, but couldn't. Biological facts didn't change how she felt.

She lifted her sweatshirt over her head, tossed it on the bed. How did her mother figure in all of this? For a moment she also questioned her maternity, wondered if she'd been abandoned. She pictured a younger Mallory, too busy to care for an infant after his wife or lover died or ran off. As she imagined Mallory placing her infant self in Mammy's arms, she saw the heart-shaped mole on the inside of her mother's right forearm. She looked down at the same mole on her own arm and placed a finger on it. Getting up, she pulled off her pants and underwear, slipped on her robe and walked the short distance down the hall to the shower.

The water ran warm and fast. Eyes closed, she tilted her head back, ran her palms over and through her wet hair. The only sound was the rush of water, the drone of old plumbing. She remained like that for a few minutes, smoothing water from her face as old images of her mother, wearing Jennifer's favourite dress and ready to go out with Daddy. The skirt is full, the fabric rustles.

Jennifer looks down at her flannel nightgown, twirls round and pretends it's a party dress. People arrive at the house, friends of her parents', the babysitter. Jennifer thinks her mother is the most beautiful woman in the room. A friend of Daddy's thinks Mammy is beautiful also. He says so and asks for a kiss. Mammy is blushing, laughing, telling him no, but Jennifer sees yes in her eyes. Angry, Jennifer tells Daddy, "Stop him."

She snatched the soap from the ledge and lathered the washcloth. She rubbed the soapy fabric on her arms, neck and chest until they tingled and her skin was red. Mammy's neck and her chest were mottled after the man had asked for a kiss. Daddy had looked at his watch and put his arm around her. "It's time we left," was all he'd said. Why had he allowed that man to blatantly flirt with her? Cameron would never stand for it. Or would he?

She warmed the cloth with running water and lathered it again. Why was she thinking about this now, anyway? She drew the cloth across her breasts, held it there. Had Mammy been lonely, neglected?

The memory of Mallory on their front yard surfaced; the same, but different. The angle was new, the picture sharper, the voices louder. She's inside the house, behind the screen door, watching him hold her mother, he's pleading, *I mean no harm.* But this time he doesn't leave, her mother doesn't rush back up the steps and into the house. At least not right away. This time they're both crying. They embrace, kiss. Mallory runs his hands down Mammy's back and presses her to him. It takes several moments for her mother to step back from him. Then she is pushing him, *go, just go, never come back.*

Alarmed by this new conjecture, Jennifer dropped the washcloth. It landed with a soft thump at her feet. She stood stock-still as the water cascaded down her shoulders, back and legs. She thought of the lawyer's letter in her dresser drawer. She closed her eyes, and with a shake of her head, turned and faced the shower. It was too much to believe, too much to bear. She covered her face with her hands. "Leave me alone." Her words spilled out unheard, unheeded, as Mallory returned. He is crouched down beside her little-girl self, she holds out her plum and smiles at him. For the first time she saw his eyes as they were, full of love and longing and how he'd knelt on the ground beside the swing, asking questions, how carefully he'd listened to her answers. Their affair had ended. It wasn't Mammy he'd been after. He'd come to see his daughter.

Jennifer made a decision. Before she lost her courage, she rinsed off and stepped out of the shower. She wrapped her long hair in a towel, threw on her terry robe and headed straight for her bedroom, stopping only to make sure the door was closed behind her. Pulling open her drawer, she retrieved the lawyer's letter, found the phone number, sat on her bed and dialled.

As the phone rang, she shook out her damp hair and walked over to the closet. There was a neat row of hangers, all empty. Everything she'd brought to wear was in the dresser or still in her bag on the floor. She was living like a teenager. Hand on hip, she peered into the closet. It was shallow, but ran deep along the wall. She hid things back there when she was a teenager, she pushed the hangers to one side. Was she imagining it, or could she still smell the Tabu Eau de Cologne that had made her feel alluring? Her throat constricted. She swallowed hard and sniffed. How simple life had been in those days, when an inexpensive bottle of fragrance was all it took to make her happy.

"Ross and Rose," a woman's voice.

As soon as Jennifer stated her name and the purpose of her call, she was put on hold. Listening to Barry Manilow croon, '... *when will our eyes meet? When can I touch you?*' She yearned for Cameron. She closed her eyes, *I miss you.* It was ages since they'd touched or even talked about anything other than the practical issues. He knew nothing of David Mallory or her connection to him. The music stopped and Jennifer tensed.

"Harrison Ross here." A man's voice this time. Breathless and urgent. "Ms. MacAulay?"

"Yes." The single word softly echoed around the closet walls as her heart banged in her chest and her mouth went dry. There was no turning back now. She was tempted to hang up. Instead, she cleared her throat, excused herself. "I received a letter, but I think there's been some mistake."

"Perhaps. That's something we can discuss. Are you free today?" He spoke in a rush as though something more important beckoned in the background.

"Well, yes ... but—"

"I'm retired for the most part. As usual, I'm cramming five days into one, so I must excuse myself. I promise you'll have my full attention when we meet. Does 1:30 work? At my office?"

"I suppose." She squeezed her eyes shut, prayed for strength. Dear God, she didn't want to hear what this man was going to tell her. "But if you're too busy—"

"1:30. See you then."

The line went dead.

Lily tensed as she watched Jennifer read the lawyer's letter, stuff it in the pocket of her sweatshirt and leave the kitchen. Lily had to force herself to stay put, not chase her daughter and hound her for details about the contents. There was more to it than Jennifer had let on. She told herself that Jennifer had every right to keep her personal business private. But it wasn't simple curiosity; Lily was troubled. It was her fault, after all, that Jennifer was here.

She filled the kettle and set it on the stove, as she thought of how much she had asked of Jennifer. Lily worried that taking Jennifer away from her husband and kids had created problems. A man left alone for as long as Cameron had been was vulnerable. She hoped he hadn't fallen prey to someone else's charms.

As soon as the thought entered her head she berated herself for selling her son-in-law short. He was a good man and an excellent provider. He and Jennifer had a solid marriage. And there were the girls. Cameron adored them. That letter could mean many things. As Jennifer had said, it could be an error; misguided junk mail.

Lily sat at the table and drummed her fingers on the plastic table cloth. Who was she kidding? Ross & Rose was one of the most well-established and reputable law offices in the city. Even if the "Ross" half of the equation was a little odd.

Lily had met Harrison Ross only once, years ago, but there wasn't much she didn't remember about that evening at David and Catherine's home. A small, older man and, at first glance, nondescript, Mr. Ross had nonetheless made an everlasting impression. Believing she would never be in David's home again, during the course of the party she had moved away from the clutches of boring martini and Manhattan drinkers and wandered to a quiet corner lined with tall shelves and filled, floor-to-ceiling, with leather-bound books.

She ran her fingers along the row of spines without consideration of the pages within. As her fingertips bumped along, she imagined David's hand landing on top of hers, bringing her exploration to a halt. *He pulls her forward and then wraps her in his arms. She closes her eyes and waits for his lips to meet hers …*

"Quite the collection, isn't it?"

Lily spun around, almost colliding with a little man in a tweed suit.

He stepped back, raising his martini glass so as not to spill a drop. "I'm sorry, my dear. I didn't mean to startle you."

She swallowed and tried to catch her breath. The little man stuck his hand out. "Harrison Ross. I'm David's solicitor."

"Lily MacAulay." She took his hand.

His grip was firm but tender, and for that moment, while they stood bound together, he gazed the depths of her eyes as though searching for something. Unnerved, she pulled away. "Nice to have met you."

Bowing his head with deference, Harrison Ross had moved aside. She had wandered over to a group and accepted a martini —or was it a Manhattan?—offered from a fresh tray making its way round the room. As she had pretended to sip the vile concoction, she had felt Mr. Ross' eyes on her.

That was the last she had heard of Harrison Ross. Until today.

Now that she considered it, a firm like Ross and Rose didn't solicit business. Jennifer's letter couldn't be a mistake. But why had they used her maiden name? Could she have been the one to contact them first, using her former name and address as a cover?

How could that be? As far as she knew, Jennifer was content and happy with Cameron and the girls.

As far as she knew. How much does anyone know what goes on in someone else's marriage?

She thought of her old friend, Jean. Lily recalled how she'd always envied her and the relationship she had with her husband, Bill. Until one day Jean had arrived for an afternoon visit and ended up sharing how unhappy she was.

"He comes home from work, grabs a beer and plops in front of the TV. He barely says two words all evening. When we go to bed, rather than snuggle in—you know what I mean—he rolls over and is snoring before my head hits the pillow," she said.

Lily had reached out and placed a sympathetic hand on Jean's arm.

In a small voice Jean confessed, "I'm seriously considering taking a lover."

"Oh no, don't!" Lily blurted.

Jean pulled her arm away. "It's easy for you to say. You and Alastair have a great marriage."

For a moment Lily was stunned into silence. She had always thought their friends had known, or were at least suspicious, that things weren't quite right between her and Alastair. She felt relieved, a little like learning she'd arrived somewhere early, rather than late. Yet she wanted to help her friend.

"That's not it," Lily said.

Jean made a dismissive sound, lifted an eyebrow.

"It's not," Lily insisted.

Jean's back was rigid and she had angled her body away from Lily. She wrestled with how to warn Jean without revealing anything about her own situation. Spying the tartan tin of biscuits next to the stove, she had an idea.

She reached out for Jean's hand. "I have another good friend, she lives in Scotland. Her situation was similar to yours, and she did take a lover."

"Oh?" Jean relaxed. She turned, head tilted, eyes alert.

Lily nodded, confident that Jean was listening. "It didn't end well."

"Did he find out?" Jean leaned in, her expression eager.

"No," Lily hesitated, "worse."

"Worse? What could be worse than her husband finding out?"

Lily shrugged and waited. Seconds later Jean gasped, "Pregnant? She got pregnant with her lover's baby?"

Lily had nodded, adding, "She and her husband had been having trouble conceiving."

Jean had paled but managed to regain her composure. "Why didn't she just leave her husband and marry the other man?"

Lily had paused for effect. "He already had a wife."

The kettle whistled and the past vanished as swiftly as it had appeared. Lily got up and turned off the burner, but remained standing at the stove. Could she risk a conversation like that with Jennifer?

Again she thought of Jean. Lily recalled how, afterwards, they had sat wordless and staring at each other until she could no longer bear Jean's scrutiny. "More tea?" she'd said and filled their cups without waiting for an answer.

Her daughter would never be put off so easily.

❀ ❀ ❀

How We Danced

Alastair's bed was in the middle of the room. The nurse was on one side, Lily on the other. They were arguing about his medication. Lily wanted to increase it, the nurse said it wasn't necessary. He wanted to settle the argument by telling them he was fine, but when he tried to speak, his voice had no volume. He could form the words, utter them, but there was no sound. Panicked and screaming, he looking from his wife to the nurse. He thumped the bed with his fists, tore at the blankets. But they paid no attention to him as their debate continued.

Alastair woke, glanced about and was relieved to find his bed was against the wall.

Soon after, Lily walked into the room and proceeded to repeat the precise conversation with the nurse she'd had in his dream. The only difference being they were farther away, over by the desk. The fine hairs on his arms stood on end as he listened, feeling both mesmerized and terrified. He cleared his throat and was relieved to hear a gravelly grunt. He tried it again, this time hoping they'd look his way and he might interject. They didn't. In truth he hadn't expected them to. As in the dream, he was mute.

Ever since he'd been confined to bed, he'd had these premonitions. One time he had watched the door, knowing Lily would walk through it and that she'd be carrying a vase of flowers. Another time, Jennifer sat down to tell him a funny story about Emma at school that day, of how the class was asked if they knew any songs that represented their varied cultures. As Jennifer talked, Alastair had seen the whole thing play out in his mind. Emma stands at her desk. She's singing a song about a murder in the fish shop. It was a ditty Alastair had taught her from his own childhood. Before Jennifer finished the story, he already knew how it would end. He saw the teacher's amused expression as Emma sang, heard the other children's titters. He felt proud of Emma as she gazed around undaunted. When the teacher suggested the song wasn't a fair representation of her heritage, Emma stood firm.

"My granddad is from Scotland, he taught it to me. He should know."

Jennifer had related the incident, but he had experienced it. As his body was withering, something else, some other part of him was blossoming. He thought of the voice within that he perpetually talked to, the one that often berated him, that he bounced ideas off of, the voice that said no or yes to a plan, that helped him decide if something was worthwhile or not. It was as if that voice was the part of him that wouldn't die, and that's why it was getting stronger while he was getting weaker. His body had betrayed him. Perhaps his spirit had not.

When he was a lad he'd gone to church. He recalled the minister talking about a person's soul, how it never died but lived on long after your bones had turned to dust. At the time the idea had frightened him. Even as a grown man the thought of dusty bones filled him with dread. But now, the suggestion of his soul surviving appealed to him.

His mind drifted back to that church, the rough-cut stone walls, the hard wooden pews, watery sunlight filtering through lead glass and the musty smell of the open hymnal. The minister is at the front standing at the pulpit, the organ music fills the space, and fills Alastair. The minister sings and, raising his arms, commands everyone to join in. The old man beside Alastair bellows, *I was blind but now I see*. Alastair is confused and frightened by the lyrics, and by the fervent plea in the man's voice. Seventy years later and feeling wretched, Alastair thought he finally understood.

Soul or spirit, that part of him was on high alert today. Someone was coming. Alastair couldn't say who, or when, but soon the doorbell would ring.

It was late afternoon, and as the sun began to set, Alastair wondered if this time he'd been mistaken. No one was coming. As the clock in the hallway chimed the hour, Alastair decided he had no soul, no spirit. It wasn't intuition, only his imagination; the ravings of a desperate man, sick of mind as well as of body. There was nothing divine within him.

Then he heard voices outside, footsteps on the porch stairs. The doorbell rang.

Alastair pulled himself up higher onto his pillows.

The nurse was sorting through his tray of swabs, tubes and bags. "Sounds like you have visitors. It'll do you good."

He recognized Duffy's voice. "We'd finished our game … talking about Alastair … thought we'd stop by."

Alastair's heart sped up. Gord and Steve were there, too. He heard Lily say, "I'll see if he's up to visitors." He knew from her tone she wasn't pleased. She hated it when people showed up unannounced; she thought it was rude.

Lily came into the bedroom, closed the door behind her and addressed the nurse. "The men Alastair used to play billiards with are here," she whispered, her nose screwed up with distaste. "Do you think it's a good idea?"

Alastair realised he wasn't surprised that Lily had directed her question to the nurse and not him. He had become a spectre, not worthy of an opinion; someone to be taken care of, a burden.

The nurse stopped her sorting. "No reason why not." She covered the tray with a white towel.

Alastair let out the breath he hadn't realised he was holding. "Go on then," he said to Lily, "show them in."

Alastair smiled when Duffy's beefy face peeked around the partially open door. He looked uncharacteristically nervous.

"Come on," Alastair waved him in.

Duffy smiled then and pushed the door open. All three men walked into the room.

"Take a load off."

There was only one chair by the bed. Alastair pointed to another by the desk, one across the way. "Set them down over here."

"Excuse me," Duffy spoke to the nurse. "Is it okay if we move the chairs in?"

"Of course," she said.

The men gathered the chairs and settled in.

Gord spoke first. "How's it going?"

"I'm all right."

Alastair's pool cue is in the palm of his hand, he's bent over the table, he slides the cue back and forth, the weight is just right, he takes a breath, holds it. He shoots, the balls scatter.

"How are things at the Legion?" Alastair asked.

The three men exchanged glances. Duffy cleared his throat. "Same old."

"Still billiards on our regular afternoons?" Alastair asked.

Duffy nodded.

Three was an odd number. Another guy must have joined them. Strange that he'd never thought of this before. He wondered who had taken his place. He was just about to ask when Gord spoke up.

"Bill Proctor started playing with us," he paused, his face flushing, "just while you're laid up. You know, so Duff has a partner."

Duffy stared out the window.

"That's good," Alastair said, trying to sound happy. "He's a pretty good shot, as I recall."

Steve looked crosswise at Duffy who was grinning. "I'll say. Me and Gord haven't won a round in, when was the last time, Gordo?"

"We won last week," Gord said.

"No, you didn't," Duffy was adamant.

"Duff's right," Steve said. "We come close though."

"No wait." Gord's brow furrowed. "Don't you remember ..."

Alastair sunk deeper into his pillows as his three friends volleyed details of their latest game, over and around him. Even if they had wanted to include him, he had been gone so long he had nothing to contribute.

His mind drifted back to the Legion. He wished he could climb the narrow stairs up to the hall, the stairs he'd always cursed as a nuisance. What if there was some kind of miracle and he did get better? He could get up and go back to his old life. Would they want him?

Alastair tuned in to the conversation again as Gord's voice rose a notch.

"You know what, Proctor's a sandbagger. I never saw him play like that until there was money on the table."

"You're just a sore loser, Gord," Duffy chuckled. "We won fair and square."

Alastair leaned forward. "Remember the time those hot shots from down east showed up, Duff? Thought they could take us no problem?"

Duffy rubbed his chin. "Hmm."

"Come on, you remember," Alastair encouraged, "they were on their way to Toronto."

"Oh, I think I remember," said Steve.

Alastair looked at Steve. "Young guys."

Duffy nodded and said, "I think I remember now."

There was a pause. Alastair didn't know what else to say. He could see Duffy didn't remember the men or the fact that together they'd won the game.

Alastair was thankful when Lily came in the room. The men stood up. Gord mumbled what a good nurse she was. They were on their best behaviour. Perhaps they had picked up on her displeasure at their surprise appearance. He hoped not. Maybe they were just being extra polite, on account of his illness.

"Would you like some tea?" he spoke to his friends and then looked hopefully at Lily. When she said nothing, he continued, "We were just talking about the time some guys from another branch turned up and thought they could beat us and how we showed them."

Lily's smile looked forced. "Did any of you *want* tea?"

What a way to ask. Now who was being rude, Alastair thought. Irritated, he avoided eye contact with her.

The men were still standing. Gord spoke up, "We don't want to be a bother."

Duffy looked at his watch.

"The Missus will shoot me if I'm late for dinner. We just wanted to stop in and say hello. Let you know we were thinking of you, Alastair."

Steve sat down. "Come on, Duff. We got time for a cup of tea. Give Cathy a call, if you're worried."

Duffy pulled a cell phone from his pocket and stared at it. "Cathy got me this damn thing, but I haven't a clue how to use it. And I can't see the numbers." He held the phone out as evidence, gave his head a shake and then returned it to his pocket. "We shouldn't be that long."

"I'll put the kettle on." Lily turned and left.

Duffy and Gord settled in again.

After a moment Gord said, "You heard they caught the guys that killed Peter."

Alastair rubbed the old scar on his leg. He didn't want to think about Peter, much less talk about him.

"Yeah, that was awhile ago now," he said, hoping to end the discussion.

"As it turned out he did have AIDS," Duffy said. "Remember, I called it the day he was killed. The police suspected that's why he was beaten to a pulp. Somebody was pissed."

"He didn't have AIDS," Gord said. "The paper said he was HIV positive. There's a difference."

"Not much," Duffy said.

"Well now," Steve started in, "Gord's right. HIV is the virus. You can have that without it turning into AIDS."

"Are you freaking serious, Steve?" Duffy laughed. "What makes you an expert? I'm afraid to ask."

Alastair gripped the bed sheet, twisting the fabric in place of Duffy's neck. "What does it matter, eh? The man's dead. Let him rest in peace." All three visitors nodded.

Alastair hadn't meant to reprimand them so loudly. He wanted their company. Now, he was worried they'd leave. He decided to take the conversation in a new direction.

"Do you know what I was thinking about the other day? The time we went to Kitchener-Waterloo for Oktoberfest. Remember the beer? And those sausages!"

"I can't eat that stuff anymore," Duffy said, making a face. "Gives me heartburn."

"Me neither," Gord agreed. "Lately we've been eating fish and vegetables. I feel a lot better."

"Us too," Steve said. "I saw this documentary on TV that said too much meat can cause cancer … oh … I … shi …"

Duffy cleared his throat and looked away as Gord nudged Steve. The movement was subtle and quick, but Alastair saw it. Weary, he slid down on his pillows. "No worries, Steve."

They sat, no one speaking for a few moments. Then Jennifer walked into the room.

Alastair smiled. "You remember my daughter, Jennifer."

This time the men rose only halfway up from the chairs before settling back.

"It's been a long time," Gord said.

Jennifer smiled. "It has," she responded, then addressed her father. "I just popped in to say hello."

"Stay." Alastair hated the pleading he heard in his voice. But he was so happy to have his best friends and family together. And this was probably the last time. "Mammy's bringing tea. Here she is now."

Jennifer had agreed to stay, but Alastair thought she looked awkward and uncomfortable, perched at the side of the desk as she was. When Lily began serving the tea and biscuits, Jennifer made no move to help. As for the rest, they were all so quiet Alastair wondered if something had happened, something he'd missed. Maybe he'd dozed off between the time the guys arrived and before they'd come into his room. That happened now, because of the drugs. He'd fall asleep without even realizing it. Knowing only when he woke up.

When Lily passed the biscuit plate to Duffy, she glanced sideways at their daughter. It was fleeting, but for Alastair, the look confirmed something was wrong. He wondered if, like her mother, Jennifer was put out with his friends stopping by. Perhaps the burden of caring for him was weighing so heavily on his wife and daughter that the addition of visitors was too much.

"Alastair?" Lily sounded alarmed.

Confused, he looked up. They were all staring at him.

"You're white as a ghost." Lily rushed to his side. "Lie down."

Duffy set his tea cup on the tray. "We should be going."

CHAPTER 16

Jennifer and Lily escorted her father's visitors down the hall. Her mother said her good-byes and took the tea tray into the kitchen. The three old men stood with their backs to the open door, staring at Jennifer. The only sound was the ticking clock.

What did they want? She had been angry that it had taken them so long to come. Now she just wanted them gone. Her parents needed her. So did her husband and kids. These guys who had let her father down? She didn't owe them anything. Still, the dejected look on their faces made her uncomfortable.

A sudden rush of running water from the kitchen drowned out the clock, her cue to speak. "Well," she said, "thanks for stopping by. I could see that your visit meant a lot to Daddy."

Duffy twirled the cap he held in his hands. "It's so sad, seeing him this way."

Perhaps fear had held them back. Regardless, Jennifer thought it was a poor excuse for their absence, but she said nothing.

Head down, Steve examined his nails, pushed at the cuticles. "It's awful," he said.

The other man—Gord, Gus?—nodded in agreement. "Are you sure there's nothing that can be done? My wife's cousin had cancer and his family put him on a special diet. All raw, natural.

Anyway, he recovered. They think the vegetables are what did the trick. Apparently romaine lettuce has something in it."

"Might be worth a try," Steve said, his voice pleading.

The idea was absurd, but Jennifer didn't have the energy to challenge it. Instead, she nodded. "I'll mention it to his doctor."

With each second that passed she was becoming more and more depleted. Hoping they'd take the hint, she moved a little closer to them and the door.

"Did the doctors say how long he's got?" Duffy asked.

"They weren't specific," Jennifer said. It was a common question, not entirely unfair. Still, it rankled. She hated the thought of her father's death being set, and then having him fall short or exceeding someone else's prediction. Surely a life, his life, meant more.

"I've known your dad a long time," Duffy's eyes glistened. "Since before you were born." He shook his head. "I just can't imagine him never coming back to the Legion, us never shooting another game or sharing a few beers."

Gord sniffed.

"We should have visited before this," Steve added.

That was something. At least they realised their mistake. Still, it seemed to be about how *they* were feeling. What did they want or expect her to do?

Duffy said, "It's just not the same without Alastair. I don't know what I'll do without my best friend."

Jennifer dashed in behind the men and opened the door to its full extent. "And I don't know what I'll do without my father, gentlemen. Now, if you don't mind …"

Duffy opened his mouth to speak but seemed to think better of it. He looked to his friends but they wouldn't meet his gaze. Head down, he stopped twirling his cap, stuffed it onto his bald pate and walked past Jennifer. The others followed.

She closed the door and stood there, hand pressed against the cool, smooth wood, taking slow, measured breaths to calm her racing heart. She'd said it to push back, put them in their place. But it was true. *I really don't know what I'll do without my Daddy.*

❁ ❁ ❁

"You need to keep up your strength," Jennifer said to Lily. "If not for your sake, do it for Daddy's."

To tempt her, Jennifer rhymed off several options: soup, sandwich, an omelette. At the mention of eggs, Lily suppressed a gag. Seeing the fearful appeal in Jennifer's eyes, Lily agreed to a turkey sandwich.

The sandwich plate was on her lap, the smell of roasted meat and mayonnaise wafted up every now and then, and made her retch. Jennifer was right, Lily knew she should eat, but the reality was she couldn't. Grief and regret clogged her throat, making it impossible to swallow.

After reading David's tribute article, she had forced herself to focus on Alastair. He needed and deserved her full attention. But as much as she'd tried, there were small reminders of David everywhere she turned. Before she was even aware, her mind had wandered back in time: the first glimpse into his eyes, the tilt of his head when he smiled, the feel of his lips, soft and searching. She continued to care for Alastair, but her efforts and touch were distracted.

Lily feigned taking a bite of the sandwich.

Jennifer pulled a chair over and sat facing her. "You've barely touched it. What's going on? Are you ill?"

The truth, Lily decided. "I just don't have an appetite."

"I can see that," Jennifer sounded exasperated. She brushed her hair back from her brow and looked down at the floor. "The nurse is worried about you," she hesitated, "so am I."

"Daddy's nurse?"

"Right. She says you look unwell, that you need a break."

"It's not me who should concern her." Lily put the sandwich plate onto a small table that was within reach. She sat back, crossed her arms.

Jennifer heaved a long sigh, rubbed her eyes. "Let's go for a short drive. I could use a coffee."

Lily snuck a glimpse at the nurse and could see that, although the woman was fiddling with Alastair's intravenous tubing, she was also paying close attention to the conversation Jennifer was having with her. Lily didn't want to go, but neither did she have the energy to protest.

How We Danced

Jennifer stood and held out a hand. Lily took hold.

Looking up at her daughter smiling down on her, something pleasant stirred in Lily. Jennifer hadn't met her eyes in some time. Lily was glad she'd agreed to go.

Jennifer helped her into the car. And Lily needed it; not just because of her injured ankle, either. Every single joint and muscle in her body ached. She wasn't certain whether it was from longing or grief. Perhaps both. Now that it was impossible, she yearned to see David, to talk to him, to explain. She strapped herself in as Jennifer ran around to the driver's side.

"Tim Horton's, okay?" Jennifer asked as she backed out of the driveway.

"Sure." Lily didn't care where they went. She was only going to please Jennifer, to keep her talking to her, looking at her. That was the one thing she did still desire.

Lily wasn't sure why Jennifer's attitude towards her had changed. Only that it had changed. Although Lily kept telling herself it was grief over Alastair, she wasn't convinced. Her mind kept returning to the day Jennifer had received the letter from Ross & Rose, the one she readily dismissed as an error. Perhaps Jennifer was hiding the truth, if not about her and Cameron, about something else. Harry had been David's solicitor. Could it be the letter related to David?

Lily looked at her daughter, now focussed on turning into the coffee shop's parking lot. In her profile, Lily recognized the man who had fathered her. Guilt rushed in with such force, that Lily marvelled that she'd never realised it before, that she'd lived all these years in such denial. Not only had she deceived Alastair, she'd deceived David. In so doing, she'd deprived him of his daughter. As it turned out, his only child.

She tried to comfort herself that David had been the one to abandon her, not the other way around, but it was no use.

"Mammy? What's wrong?"

Jennifer had parked and turned off the engine. She laid a hand on Lily's arm.

"Nothing, why?" Lily swallowed. Saliva had gathered in her mouth, she felt queasy.

"Never mind," Jennifer said. "We could both use some sugar and caffeine." She got out of the car and came around to the passenger side and helped Lily out.

Lily sat at a table adjoining a young couple while Jennifer entered the queue leading up to the counter. As Lily settled in, the hubbub of the coffee shop faded. The couple next to her were about the age she and David had been when they met. Under the table, the couple held hands. Their whole lives lay before them. Hers was fast reaching its conclusion. Alastair was dying. David was dead. Too few memories were all she had now.

One Saturday afternoon, she and David had risked a visit to a little downtown diner, a place she figured Alastair didn't frequent. They'd sat in a booth, ankles touching, and talked about their future together.

"Where would you like to live?" David asked.

"You mean after," Lily looked around to make sure no one she knew had come into the diner. She lowered her voice, "when we're together?"

David smiled and a rush of joy swept her body.

"We can go anywhere," he said. Although he still smiled, a shadow crossed his face.

"Because of your job, right? You'll have to leave?"

Lily knew her question was rhetorical. She'd raised the issue before. It was clear to both of them he couldn't stay at the helm of Catherine's father's company. Not when he planned to divorce her.

"Never mind that," his smile widened, "let's plan our future. The bright one we're going to have once all the trouble is behind us."

They discussed returning to Brockville, where David was raised. He described the beautiful Thousand Islands and the town of Gananoque where he was born. He told her about his brothers and sisters and the many aunts, uncles and cousins he'd grown up with. Lily longed to live there, raise their children near his family. In the end they decided on Toronto, where it would be easier for him to find work.

"I have an idea." He reached across the table and took her hands in his. "It's a beautiful day and we've got the afternoon ahead of us. Let's go for a drive. We'll head towards Toronto, do a little house hunting. What do you say?" He was already reaching into his pocket to pay for their coffee.

"Oh, I don't know," her stomach fluttered. She wanted to go with David but feared bumping into someone she or Alastair knew and getting caught. Alastair would eventually find out, but when the time was right. She wanted to be the one to tell him.

"Don't worry. No one will see us." He got up and pulled her out of the booth. "Come on."

They headed out of the city, meandered through the back roads, and south, along the shore of Lake Ontario. She sat close to him, their hands entwined, her thigh pressed against his. They'd been driving for a while, not saying much but content in being together. She wished this moment, this day, would last a lifetime.

"Look," he said, pointing to the building with an extension that jutted out over the water. "Do you know where you are now?"

"I do. We're in Burlington." She turned to the shore. "That's the Brant Inn." She had been disoriented, but at the sight of the Inn, she knew where she was. They'd gone to several dances there and, at Catherine's suggestion, attended the Inn's extravagant New Year's Eve celebration. Fred Purser and the Washingtons had played, and she and David had managed a few dances together. On her dresser at home was the group photograph, she and David together in plain sight.

"Maybe we wouldn't need to go as far as Toronto," David said. "Let's look at the houses here or in Oakville."

She laughed. "You're insane."

He reached out and tickled her rib cage. "Is that any way to talk to your future husband?"

She giggled and pushed his hand away. "Keep your eyes on the road."

They turned off the main road and drove up, down and around the residential tree-lined streets that fanned out from Lakeshore Drive. On one, he pulled the car over to the curb.

"What do you think of that house?" he asked, pointing to a clapboard bungalow with a large front yard. "I like the slope of the lawn. We could plant a rock garden."

She looked at the modest house and recalled the mansion where he lived with Catherine.

"Are you sure you wouldn't mind?" she asked.

"Maybe," he said and paused.

Her high spirit plunged. She knew it had all been too good to be true.

"I tend to prefer brick. What about you?" He twisted in his seat so that he fully faced her, a cheeky grin on his face.

"Oh you!" She gave him a shove. "You know what I mean. I think this house is nice, but it's nothing compared to where you live now. You'll be giving up so much. Are you sure you want to do this?"

David lifted her chin, looked into her eyes. "Marrying Catherine was a mistake. Nothing I have belongs to me, not my job, not that house and certainly not Catherine." His voice softened. "You belong to me, you're all I want." He pulled her close and kissed her.

As they continued their drive, every so often, Lily would ask him to slow down or stop when she saw a house she liked. As they dreamed and planned their new life together, Lily had started to believe it would really happen.

"So it's true," Lily had said on the drive back. "You love me and we're going to do this?"

David had squeezed her hand. "We are. I promise."

❀ ❀ ❀

Jennifer sat a coffee in front of her. "Double cream, double sugar, just the way you like it."

"Thanks." Tears blurred Lily's vision as she removed the lid from the cup.

Jennifer opened a paper bag, put a doughnut on a napkin and shoved it forward. "Your favourite, a honey cruller."

Lily tried to hold back the tears, but it was impossible.

"Mammy?"

Lily heard the surprise and panic in Jennifer's voice. She kept her head down, embarrassed at her public display of emotion. Her shoulders shook, and it was all she could do to stifle the sound of her sobs.

"Never mind," Jennifer's said, her voice tender. She got up and came round to her, rubbed her back. "Let's get you home."

How We Danced

Later that night, lying in bed, Lily prayed for peace. As she stared at the ceiling, begging for God's mercy, none came. But she did sleep. She awoke in the morning, heard her stomach growl and realised she was hungry.

❀ ❀ ❀

Alastair was uncomfortable. He licked his parched lips, wishing the nurse would come over and swab his mouth. The pain was escalating as well. His next round of morphine must be overdue. Or was it? Nothing could be trusted. Time had lost its rhythm and meaning. The clock chimed the hour one moment, the half hour the next. Even the people he loved most—Lily, Jennifer—seemed to come and go without warning. Often their words were scrambled, and try as he may, he couldn't comprehend what they said.

The nurse was nearby. He could hear her moving about. Opening his mouth, he called for her, but the sound that emerged from him wasn't right. He tried again, carefully forming the words in his mind, pushing them out across his tongue and over his lips. A weak moan was all that emerged. He closed his eyes. He wanted to scream, but all he could manage was a pitiful whimper.

On one level, he experienced these sensations, on another, he was a witness. He marvelled at his newfound ability to both participate and watch his life and wondered if this was a taste of what was to come in the afterlife—if, like a voyeur, he would be able to witness his family's activities but not participate. Eternal frustration.

An hour later, or was it a minute, the nurse was there, and little by little the crushing vise eased, his body relaxed. Soon he was pain free. He felt light, airy. The mattress below him vanished.

He turned to see her, but she was gone. In her place was an 18th century ship's captain wearing a red tricorn hat and blazing blue cape. Intent on steering his ship, his back was to Alastair.

With eyes wide open, Alastair looked around. The walls were changing shape. Slowly at first, and then with increased speed, they curved out as though they bore great weight. Windows were opened; their curtains billowed as the salty breeze of the sea rushed in, the roar deafening. The captain, struggling at the helm, twisted around. There was no mistaking him; the arrogant tilt of his head, the cocky smirk. He was older than Alastair recalled and a lot thinner. A blistery rash butterflied across his nose, cheeks and ran down his neck. It appeared that what the guys said was true: Peter had been HIV positive.

"Peter?" Alastair whispered.

Peter nodded and abandoned ship, landing beside Alastair's bed. He pointed to his face. "This could have been you," he said.

Although Peter's insight was baffling, it was also true. In the late eighties, the AIDS scare had left him terrified and impotent, literally and figuratively. Through sheer luck he'd been spared. And so had Lily.

The wind died down, the windows closed of their own accord. And the ship vanished. Alastair couldn't believe his eyes. It was there one second and gone the next. Once again the nurse was ensconced in her swivel chair, carrying on a phone conversation as if nothing out of the ordinary had occurred. Peter moved closer to Alastair. He noticed some of the red blisters on Peter's face were leaking fluid.

Sickened, Alastair looked down at his hands. "How can you be here, Peter? You were murdered in the back alley of the Legion. The guys went to your funeral."

Alastair was sorry he hadn't gone. It was petty of him not to attend.

Peter cocked his head, but offered no explanation for his presence.

Alastair persisted. "It's not as though we were friends."

"No, we weren't friends."

Peter stretched his arms open. As he did, the floor beneath Alastair's bed gave way. There was the sensation of falling and then Alastair was on his feet, outside his home on the sidewalk. It was a moonless night. Air, cold and fresh, streamed in his nose, out his mouth with effortless ease.

He heard men talking on the path between his place and the neighbour's. His stomach lurched when someone said, "You've made a mistake." He recognised his own voice, remembered his futile plea for reason before the beating.

Sensing movement, he looked towards the house. Jennifer was on the porch. The clothes she wore, her hair; something was off. She looked no more than fourteen. This young version of his daughter stood motionless, her head angled, listening.

When Jennifer had called out that night and the men had run off, Alastair had assumed she'd heard the loud clang of the pipe after they'd beaten him and tossed it aside. He had no idea she'd heard the exchange.

Jennifer was moving with her back pressed against the bricks, and she eased closer to the corner of the house.

"You're the queer who hit on my kid brother. I had him point you out to me."

Feeling even more impotent than he had that night, Alastair watched as Jennifer flinched at the insult.

Again his shadow voice rang out, "Look buddy, whatever your brother told you, it's not true."

"Don't call my brother a liar, you filthy pervert!"

Alastair squeezed his eyes shut and turned away. Oh my God, Jennifer heard.

There was a dull thud and a loud groan. A few seconds later the peal of metal on concrete.

Alastair opened his eyes in time to see, panicked and terrified, his teenage daughter running down the stairs over to the pathway.

"Daddy!"

Blinded by his own pain all those years ago, he'd missed hers. Alastair covered his face and sobbed. Jennifer had known, yet she'd never let on, never told. And never judged.

Alastair opened his hands and wiped his tears. The horrible scene had vanished.

He was in Aaron's office at the back of his shop. Alastair was on the sofa, facing the desk by the window overlooking the garden. Sun poured in and he surmised it was just before noon. Judging from the blooms it was springtime, although how time had moved forwards—or backwards—was a mystery. Alastair closed his eyes and took a deep breath, still marvelling at his ability to do so. This scene was familiar. Aaron was here, just behind him, and any moment now he would touch him, and speak.

A second later, large hands straddled his shoulders. "I assume the tears are because you're pleased with my gift." Aaron's breath was warm against his cheek.

Alastair glanced down at the coffee table, where an expensive watch lay nestled in a velvet case. "It's beautiful," he said, "but I don't deserve it."

"Nonsense." Aaron walked around the sofa and sat in front of him on the coffee table. "Why would you say such a thing? Love is to be celebrated."

Aaron took the watch out of the case, thick fingers nimbly undoing the buckle. For such a large man, he was surprisingly tender and sentimental. And never more so as he strapped the timepiece onto Alastair's wrist.

"Today isn't special," Alastair said.

Aaron smiled. "It could be." He folded the strap into the safety band and sat back. "Come here, stay with me. Set Lily free. You can't love her," Aaron said.

Heart thumping, Alastair stared at the second hand on the watch. He couldn't love Lily the way she deserved. That was true. And yet ...

"Alastair?" Aaron said. "Look at me."

Alastair met Aaron's gaze. "I can't just leave her."

"Why not?" Aaron asked. "It can't be much of a life for her, married to you."

Alastair scowled and turned away.

"Oh come now. You know what I mean." Aaron leaned forward, laid a hand on Alastair's arm.

Alastair pulled away. "I convinced her to leave her family, to come here with me. She has no one else. What kind of a life would she have if I left her high and dry? For that matter, what kind of a life would I have?"

"One that's authentic, I should have thought." Aaron's expression was blank, but the colour drained from his cheeks. He got up from the sofa, walked to the window.

Poor Aaron. Not his fault. It was all so confusing. Alastair stood; he wanted to reach out, to comfort him. But when he stepped forward, Aaron vanished and Alastair was back in bed, struggling for breath.

CHAPTER 17

The clock in the hallway struck the quarter hour. There wasn't much time between now and her appointment with the lawyer. If she was going, she'd best get dressed. She wanted to look nice, and respectable. No doubt Harrison Ross would be courteous, but she guessed that behind his professional façade he'd have an opinion on the situation.

Jennifer moved to her bag on the floor. There wasn't much. She pulled out black slacks and sweater and placed them on the bed. Both pieces looked tired and old. Using her hands, she tried to press out the wrinkles. Perhaps a scarf or necklace would help?

Remembering her little-girl jewellery box, she crossed the room to the mirrored dresser. Curious and hopeful there might be something left of value, she lifted the lid. Nothing. Only the tiny ballerina that had stopped spinning years ago.

Ross & Rose was a short drive from her parents' home and easy to find. It was situated on a major artery that dissected the city, west from east. Century homes now functioned as law and doctors' offices, upscale cafes, or trendy boutiques. The office of Ross & Rose was on a corner in what had once been a private Victorian mansion. Jennifer stood on the sidewalk and tried to gauge whether the massive house had been artfully restored or perfectly maintained. Either way, the past had left its mark. Buildings were like people, they bruised.

Her mind wandered the way it always did when she was nervous. *Focus.* She wasn't here to observe architecture; she had come for a meeting. Eyes on the front door, she followed the pathway to the pillared porch. Despite the internal pep talk, a chill of fear ran the length of her arms. Mallory had shared a little of himself with her when they encountered each other at his home. What she knew of his relationship *to her*, she'd surmised. Nothing had been confirmed. She had a powerful sense that once she entered Ross & Rose, all that would change.

What of David Mallory's relatives? Would they be waiting inside? She regretted not asking Mr. Ross if their meeting was private, but had lacked the courage to call back. The thought of meeting Mallory's family filled her with dread. What would they think of her? Of her mother? The idea of strangers judging her family seemed unfair. She told herself to focus on the immediate and moved forward. She shuddered as her steps reverberated across the planks. Still unwilling to enter, she placed a hand on the warm bricks by the door.

Just another minute, she'd allow herself that.

The door opened and Jennifer stepped back.

A young woman smiled and motioned for Jennifer to come in.

Ready or not, there was nothing to do but enter. "Thank you," Jennifer nodded.

There was a rush of air as the woman left and the door closed behind her.

Alone, she glanced around the wide hallway. There was a carved staircase in the centre, doors lined the walls on either side. One of the doors opened, and an elderly man stood beneath the frame. She assumed it was Harrison Ross. Where was his staff, she wondered.

"Ms. MacAulay?"

There it was again, her maiden name. The one her father had given her. The father who had loved her, raised her, who now lay dying only a few kilometres away. She must correct Mr. Ross.

"Yes—" she drew the word out as she struggled with whether this was the right time or not.

"Excellent." He smiled and motioned her forward.

She stopped as soon as she crossed the threshold. Although the house was large, his private office was small. Perhaps it was an illusion owing that it was covered, wall-to-wall and floor-to-ceiling, with deep shelves lined with books. Mesmerized, she turned around. Books up, down and across. Leather-bound works rested against pocket paperbacks. Some shelves appeared to be filled two books deep. Volumes were stacked on a work table and piled in the corners.

"A bad habit, I'm afraid. I can't seem to throw any away." He smiled and stuck his hand out. "Harrison Ross. It's nice to finally meet you."

She smiled, "Finally?"

He paused, a tilt of head, flicker of smile.

His hand was warm and dry but calloused for one who spent his time behind a desk. She wondered what he did in his spare time. Perhaps he shared David Mallory's love of gardening.

"Please, sit down." He motioned to an old leather wingback positioned in front of his desk.

Jennifer did as he asked, undecided as to whether he had ignored her question or not heard it. He had to be eighty, maybe older.

"Well now, let's see." He lifted a file from one of several stacks on his desk.

"Will it just be the two of us, Mr. Ross?"

"Please, call me Harry." He put a thick manila file on the desk between them and folded his hands atop, school-boy style. "Yes, it will just be the two of us."

She couldn't wait a moment longer. Unhappy she'd let things go this far, she drew a long breath and launched in. "Mr. Ross, Harry, there's been some mistake. I am not Jennifer MacAulay." When his eyebrows shot up, she put a hand out to stifle his concern. "Or at least I'm not any longer. My married name is Roberts."

He appeared to relax.

"Of course." He opened the file, grabbed a pen and scribbled a note. "I'll need documentation. Your marriage certificate will do."

"But wait ..."

He put his pen down and looked at her.

She struggled for words. "Are you sure I'm the one you're looking for? That there hasn't been some error?" She looked down. The question, she knew, was an absurd attempt to stave the truth.

"There's no error, Mrs. Roberts." He stopped and smiled. "May I call you Jennifer?" When she nodded he continued. "Jennifer," his voice softened, "I knew David Mallory for many years. He wasn't just my client, he was my friend."

"I see," she said, but she wasn't sure she did. Did that mean he was privy to Mallory's secrets? That he knew about her, about Mammy? Of course, he must. She cleared her throat to ease the thick, tight sensation. "Your letter said I was named in David Mallory's estate."

He sat back in his chair. "That's correct."

"Are there others?"

"Well, none that you need concern yourself."

She stood up. "Oh my God!"

He came around the desk, grabbing a small, wooden chair for himself on route. "Please sit down. I'll explain the estate; the various properties, holdings and investments, and answer any of your questions."

"Properties? He had several?"

"David was a wealthy man."

"But why?" She hung her head and let the question fade away. She knew the answer, and obviously Harrison Ross did, too. Whatever she'd expected, it wasn't this. What would Cameron say? Certainly he'd be shocked. He wasn't materialistic, but he was practical. For him the money would be a positive. She'd have to tell Mammy. Considering that conversation, Jennifer felt queasy.

He removed a white envelope from the file. "This is for you. It's from David. I don't know what it says, but I have an idea." He placed the envelope on the desk, softened his voice again. "You're upset. You've had a shock. I understand." He sighed, sat back and gripped the arms of the chair. "Take the envelope with you. Read it in your own time. Come back. We'll talk more then."

With trembling hands she picked up the envelope. "There must be someone else, brothers, sisters, cousins? His wife's family? Wait! His niece, I ..." She thought better of mentioning their encounter. "The point is, there must be *someone* more entitled than me?"

"Jennifer, all those who stood to benefit from David's death have been taken care of. His will is iron-clad. I made certain."

"But is it fair?" Jennifer asked.

"Fair?"

"To the others, I mean? Those who knew him. Loved him."

"As I said before, I knew David for years. We were friends. Best friends, actually. And confidants. The only thing that I feel is unfair, and I cautioned David about this, is the information contained in the letter you're holding."

Jennifer glanced down at the envelope in her hand, then back at Ross. "You know what's in here?"

"If you mean have I read it? No. But I knew David and I assume ..." he trailed off.

"You think it was wrong of him to write it?" She wondered if Ross also disapproved of her. The idea made her uncomfortable.

"No, my dear," he sighed and paused. When he spoke next, he stared off, with unseeing eyes, in the direction of the bookshelf. "I simply find its necessity sad."

Her pulsed raced and her cheeks burned. She had to get away, to read this letter, to think. She faltered when she stood. "Excuse me, please, but I've got to go," she said, unable to disguise the quake in her voice. With a trembling hand she stuffed the letter into her handbag.

He nodded and slowly rose from his chair. "Of course."

She rushed out of the office, down the hall and into the fresh air. She stood for a moment drawing deep breaths until the rubbery feeling in her knees subsided.

Rather than go to her car, she headed down the street, crossing over when she spotted a café. After buying a coffee, she headed for a back booth without stopping to add cream and sugar. She took a seat and put the steaming black coffee in the centre of the table. She didn't want it after all.

How We Danced

Taking the letter out, she set it down. For a few moments she stared at it, knowing the truth of her life was likely inside. Jennifer MacAulay was handwritten in blue ink, the penmanship neat and tight, but not without flair. Taking a deep breath she opened it, mindful not to tear into the contents. She pulled out a single sheet, unfolded it and spread it on the table.

Dear Jennifer,
Many years ago I met your mother, Lily. I fell in love. But I was married and could not claim her—or you, as my own. So you became Alastair's daughter. To protect you, Lily held me at arms' length and as much as it hurt, I came to realise she was right and I kept my distance. Other than you, I have no heir, my son died as a child, my wife passed away recently.

Jennifer drew a sharp breath and stopped reading. Mallory had said his wife had died a few years back, which meant he must have reorganized his affairs after her death. This letter had been sitting there for some time, waiting for her. She checked the top of the page, searched for a date, but there was none. Swallowing hard, she read on.

My wife's niece is the only other claimant. I've ensured she's looked after, so you won't be harassed. The bulk of my estate, however, goes to you.
I understand money cannot make up for what I was unable to offer you or your mother. Let her know that I did love her, that I never stopped.
Harry will fill you in on the details.

Your father,
David Mallory

Tracing a fingertip over his signature, she closed her eyes. She remembered David Mallory seated opposite her the day she'd fallen in front of his home, not realizing who she was, or that soon she'd be reading this letter, his final statement. Again she heard the sorrow in his voice.

I have a daughter, but sadly we're estranged …

Jennifer pictured her father, Alastair, lying in the hospital bed at home, oblivious to their deceit. Soon he'd be gone, too. In a way he already was; stolen from her. And she from him. She snatched the letter and crumpled it. As the sharp edges of the paper dug into her palm, the seat beneath her seemed to disappear, she felt weightless, insubstantial. All the sights and sounds around her were muffled as though she was somehow separate.

Unclenching her fist, she looked down at the balled paper in her hand. The weightless sensation ended, the café resumed its normal appearance. She put the wadded letter on the table top, smoothed out the creases and folded it back into her handbag.

She stood and adjusted the handbag onto her shoulder, a man and a little girl slid by her and into the booth she'd vacated.

❀ ❀ ❀

Lily dug her fork into a piece of roasted potato and shoved it beside the steamed green beans next to her untouched chicken cutlet. She knew she should eat, but she didn't feel hungry. To make matters worse, her throat constricted, as though she'd choke if she tried to swallow. She felt guilty about her lack of appetite. Jennifer had prepared such a nice meal.

Lily had told her not to bother cooking, but when the evening nurse arrived, she'd said they needed to stay strong and eat well. When Lily had balked about taking more time away from Alastair to eat, the nurse suggested they take their plates into the bedroom. At first Lily felt odd, eating in a sick room. The nurse insisted that Alastair would enjoy their little dinner party even if he couldn't fully participate.

Lily looked at Alastair. The nurse had turned him onto his right side and placed another pillow under him. These simple changes had eased the gurgling sound emanating from his throat which had alarmed her and Jennifer. Lily had tried to rouse him, but he remained unconscious, pale, and even though swaddled in blankets, cool, as she had discovered when she'd stroked his face.

Despite the nurse's encouragement, she couldn't see evidence of his enjoying their company. He took a stilted breath, and she waited for him to draw the next. Compared to earlier, there was more and more time between each. She chewed her lower lip and stifled the desire to call out a warning. Didn't he realise where he was headed if he insisted on going down this path? Lily longed to grab him by the scruff of the neck and pull him back, but she couldn't. Nor could she travel with him. She'd keep him company as far as she was able. Just breathe, she silently urged. For encouragement, she filled and emptied her own lungs. With a low moan, Alastair drew a breath and then lapsed into shallow panting.

"Mammy. Did you hear me?"

Startled, Lily looked up to find both Jennifer and the nurse staring at her. "Sorry, no. I was thinking. What were you saying?"

Jennifer pushed her TV tray off to the side. "You're not eating. Please, try and have a few bites, for Daddy's sake."

Lily folded her napkin. "Isn't it a shame that your father can't enjoy this with us? He would've loved this meal. He always was a meat and potatoes man."

Jennifer smiled. "I remember his hissy fits when you made spaghetti and meatballs! He called it foreign."

"I know," Lily laughed. "You're the only reason I got away with serving it every once in a while. You loved pasta."

"Still do." Jennifer sighed and then fell silent.

Lily yawned and checked Alastair again. The shallow puffing had stopped and the persistent crease between his brows had eased. "That's odd. Your father's breathing has changed." She asked the nurse, "Is everything okay?"

"He's enjoying listening to the two of you," the nurse said. She looked over at the bed and lifted her chin. "Isn't that right, Alastair?"

Lily turned back to Jennifer who shrugged.

How had their life come to this? Lily wondered. It didn't seem that long ago that she and Alastair were young, going out every chance they could—to the cinema or dancing. She looked where Alastair's thin legs appeared as a small mound beneath the heavy covers. It's too bad he'd damaged the one; he'd been such a good dancer. Somewhere she still had the first place ribbon they'd won at a contest they'd entered, on a whim, at The Palais, back in Glasgow. Lily closed her eyes. In her mind, she could still hear the orchestra, feel the floor beneath her feet, Alastair's guiding hand on her back.

"What's that tune you're humming?" Jennifer asked. "It's familiar."

Lily smiled. A memory flash: dancing with four-year-old Jennifer. "Begin the Beguine," she said. "It was your favourite when you were little. Don't you remember how I'd put the old records on and we'd dance?"

Jennifer shook her head. "It was Daddy and me who used to dance."

"No, sweetheart, it was us." Lily waited for a moment before continuing. She could see Jennifer was struggling to remember. "Oh, you were so cute! All dolled up in my old dresses and jewellery."

"I do remember," Jennifer said. "But I thought for sure it was Daddy. I loved putting on those necklaces and clip earrings."

"What's wrong?" Lily asked. "You look worried."

"Nothing. I was just trying to remember." Jennifer's frown deepened.

Jennifer looked flustered. Perhaps Lily shouldn't have corrected her. Maybe Alastair *had* danced with her as well, although she doubted it. Around that time Alastair had been distracted, not the family man he later became. Lily put her fork down. None of that mattered now. They'd done better than most; put their differences aside, raised Jennifer and lived their lives. She looked at Alastair. A whisper of what he once was. It wouldn't be long.

❀ ❀ ❀

Alastair heard Lily and Jennifer talking and sensed the nurse's presence nearby. He felt a touch, Lily's or Jennifer's; their caresses a welcome reprieve from the isolation of the island where he was stranded. But there was another presence in the room, one he couldn't quite grasp. It, or they, for he sensed there were several, hovered out of reach, like a thought you cannot claim.

Curious, Alastair turned from the security of his family and drifted toward the mystery. A shimmering black curtain appeared and parted; an invitation. Alastair accepted.

How We Danced

On the other side, a formless cloud swirled, taller and wider, fashioning a blurred but distinctly human shape with smoky tendrils for arms and legs.

"Alastair," a woman called.

He knew the voice.

"Mammy?" he asked, incredulous.

At the sound of her name, the ghost-like shape transformed into his mother. She appeared as she'd been, before her illness had whittled her away.

Tears of joy stung Alastair's eyes.

He turned back to Lily, Jennifer, and the nurse. He could hear them, but barely. The curtain had closed; it was now an incandescent film separating him from them. Alastair reached out and touched it. His hand went through as though it were a bubble of soap, the sort Jennifer played with as a child. He pulled his hand back and looked to his mother. She was still there, waiting, smiling. Behind her, in the unknown, were other ghostly forms. Alastair sensed they were also ready to reveal themselves if summoned by name.

He took a step forward and then realised he was on his feet, pain free, breathing, moving, not stretched out on his sick bed.

His mother held out her hand, but said nothing.

"Am I dead?" Alastair asked.

His mother smiled. With a subtle wave, she beckoned him forward.

Alastair was tempted to go. He turned to the glistening barrier. As he did, it began to vibrate. From the other side, Lily hummed. The film responded like a drum skin to the rhythm of her voice. He recognized the tune but couldn't name it. He longed to remember.

His mother took a few steps back, then a few more. Alastair hesitated. In that pause, his mother was drawn into the void and disappeared. There was a deafening rush of wind and all the oxygen was funnelled from the air. If he wasn't dead, Alastair was certain this maelstrom would finish him off. Choking and gasping for breath, he was sucked back through the dark, shimmering skin. Moments later, he was flat in bed, wracked with pain. But the fear of dying was gone.

Lily continued to hum. As Alastair drifted towards sleep, the title of the tune flashed in his mind: "Begin the Beguine."

CHAPTER 18

Jennifer shivered as she set her fork down. Beside her, Mammy, still humming, stared pathetically at Daddy. Why would her mother claim the memory she had of dancing with him? She turned her back to Mammy and glanced at the nurse, tending to what remained of her poor father. When so much of him was already gone, she couldn't bear for more to be taken. Mammy must be mistaken. Yet, the music, the certainty in her voice, made Jennifer wonder. She needed a detail, something in her memory that would prove her recollection was the correct one.

Jennifer picked up her fork and looked at the round plate in front of her; she imagined the old record player, the black disc with the red label in the middle spinning, around and around.

She is wearing her dress-up clothes, costume jewellery and a wide-brimmed hat that keeps slipping down over her eyes. The music starts and stops, starts and stops. Daddy goes over to the machine, lifts the arm and places it down again. The jumpy sound is gone, only the music is left.

Ready to start again, she bounces up and down. The too-big hat slips, covers her eyes. Laughing, she pushes the brim above her forehead and looks up. Daddy smiles down at her. He takes her in his arms. They both laugh when Mammy's high heels fall off her feet. He hugs her close. They move slowly at first, but soon they are spinning around the room. She tilts her head back. The pictures on the walls, the furniture, whirl by. She feels Daddy's heart beating beneath his shirt; he's warm and soft. Dizzy, she closes her eyes and burrows her face in the crook of his neck. She loves the way he smells—like the scent that comes out of a bottle with a ship on it. She likes to watch him splash it on after he shaves. Sometimes he teases her and dabs a bit behind her ears. Now she takes a deep breath and readies herself for the familiar scent. But instead he smells like Mammy's Nivea cream. Confused, Jennifer leans back and looks up. Mammy, still breathless from their dance, is smiling at her.

"Impossible ..." Jennifer said.

"What?" Lily asked.

"Nothing," Jennifer said. "I was just trying to remember ..." She had an idea. "Never mind." Jennifer got up and rushed out.

As the clock marked the quarter hour, she entered her room, sat on the bed, and using her phone, searched for the tune, "Begin the Beguine." As she typed and scrolled, she thought of her confusion, wondered how she could have been so wrong regarding the dance. Now she questioned if there were other scrambled memories. With a sigh, she continued her search for the song. Finding it, she clicked on the Artie Shaw version. As the big band played, she tried to think of another childhood memory she could run by Mammy, to confirm or deny.

Her parents had taken her on many outings when she was little—ice skating, parades—and the annual Shriners' Circus, which had been her favourite. Most of it was a blur now; pretty girls in sparkly suits hanging from trapezes, silly clowns and pink performing poodles. Every year Daddy would buy her a toy, or at least she thought it had been Daddy. One year he'd bought her a gypsy doll. It was still on the dresser, propped against the mirror.

Then they'd stopped going to the circus.

Why? Had it been her parents' decision? No, it had been hers. She'd told them she didn't want to go anymore. Something had put her off. What was it? Odd that she could remember pink poodles jumping through hoops, but she couldn't remember what had brought her favourite annual outing to a halt.

She walked to the dresser and picked up the doll, stroked the red satin dress.

She was at the circus. Daddy bought her candy floss. He stood her against the wall and told her to wait, not to move, he'll be right back. She watched him go to the men's bathroom door. He stops to let another man go in first, and then he follows.

The candy floss is sticky and sweet. Before tearing off a piece, she burrows her nose into the fluff, loving the sweet-strawberry smell. Daddy is taking a long time. She checks every man that walks out to see if it's him, but each time it's not.

She's finished her floss. Her hands are gooey and she's thirsty. A trumpet blares inside the arena. It's starting! Why is Daddy taking so long? She walks over to bathroom door and calls in, "Daddy?" When he doesn't answer, she steps forward and peeks in. Sinks line one wall. Across from them are the funny toilets men use for peelng, but no one is there. Now she is frightened. Maybe he left and forgot about her. Panicked, she calls out, "Daddy!" her voice bounces off the open metal stalls. The one door that's closed flies open and Daddy rushes out doing up his belt.

"I told you to wait outside, at the wall."

He sounds angry.

Frightened, she starts to cry.

"Go on, I'll wash my hands and be right out." His voice is kinder now.

She goes back to her spot by the wall. Now she is worried he'll say something to Mammy.

Moments later, Daddy comes out of the bathroom. He crouches down, takes the empty candy floss cone from her and smiles. "Would you like to buy a toy?"

She nods enthusiastically and looks around. Vendors line the hall with balloons, stuffed monkeys on sticks, paper kites and colourful flags. Over Daddy's shoulder, she sees a man rush out of the bathroom. All at once her stomach hurts and she doesn't care about the toy.

"Let's get back to your mother." Daddy touches her chin, turns her face back to his. "Afterwards, you can choose whatever you like."

When they return to their seats Mammy laughs. "Look at your face! I see Daddy bought you candy floss. Let me clean you up."

As Mammy wipes her mouth with a dampened napkin, Jennifer looks down at the circus floor. The lights are already dimmed and a woman is dancing. She's wearing a red dress with a full, heavy skirt. A kerchief is tied around her head and her ears are pierced with big, gold hoops. Daddy tells her the woman is a gypsy. The woman whirls round and round, the skirt of her dress flares like fire, revealing her orange, yellow and blue crinoline. Jennifer wants to enjoy the dance, but Daddy's angry face and voice from the bathroom keep jumping into her head. Rubbing her grubby fingers together, she balls up bits of melted candy floss and licks it from her fingers. It doesn't taste good any more. She's had enough of the too-sweet smell. Maybe she's going to be sick. She tries to think about buying a toy. The man who was hiding in the bathroom jumps into her head, too. If she hadn't gone in, would he have hurt Daddy? Sniffling, she puts her face down to hide her tears. When Mammy asks what's wrong, Jennifer says she doesn't feel well. It isn't a lie. In big sobs, she tells Mammy her stomach hurts. Mammy pulls her close and says to Daddy, "Should we take her home?"

They leave the arena. On the way out Daddy buys her the gypsy doll. When he gives it to her he says, "I'm sorry, sweetie."

Jennifer set the old doll back onto the dresser. Daddy was the one who'd bought it for her. At least she'd been right about that. She tried to focus on the memory of her father's face, his expression as he'd apologized, but it wasn't clear. What was he sorry for? That he'd kept her waiting? That she'd taken ill?

Thinking on it now, she was upset, not actually sick. These days no one would park a little kid outside of a men's bathroom unsupervised. Although they hadn't been gone long enough to worry Mammy, there had been time to finish the candy floss. Maybe this explained why the sickly-sweet smell of the spun sugar triggered her gag reflex. And why she'd chosen not to go back to the circus. She had been frightened—perhaps due to the wait. No wonder she recalled the man who exited the bathroom as a villain, of sorts.

An imagined scenario: Her father is in a bathroom stall, his back is to her. His pants are puddled around his ankles. Through his white legs, she sees a man sitting on the toilet. Big hands, the fingernails rounded, grip the back of her father's thighs, heavy black shoes bracket his feet.

Jennifer gasped. Disgusted with herself, she banished the vile fantasy and went back to her reasoning.

The man's exit was easy enough to explain. In her fear and confusion, she'd missed the other closed door when she'd gone into the bathroom. She thought of her own daughter, Emma, just a little older than she would have been then, and how traumatized Emma would be if Cameron left her to wait, alone in a busy arena's foyer. How could her father have been so thoughtless? Her thoughts drifted to him now, lying in the next room, barely breathing. Being angry was pointless. It was many years ago. Times were different. The world was more innocent, the rules more lax.

While she'd been thinking, "Begin the Beguine" had finished. Picking up her mobile, she headed back to her parents' bedroom.

❊ ❊ ❊

In a moment of cruel clarity Alastair realised all that lay ahead was an unbroken chain of agony. Lifting his eyelids was a Herculean feat. All he could focus on was breathing. This simple act took all his strength.

He must breathe or die. Lily was telling him this now, over and over again. Her face was next to his; a whiff of tea with milk. Not wishing to disappoint, he drew in air. It was ragged, but enough. Not that long ago breathing was something he took for granted.

As he had with many things.

Of all his sins, this was the worst: his inclination to take for granted the basics. His wife, his daughter, Jennifer's kids—his girls—and his home. Yet, now they were all that mattered.

Lily slid her hand down his arm, took his hand. He wanted to squeeze back, let her know how much he appreciated her touch.

But his fingers wouldn't cooperate. He felt her slip away, heard her speaking to Jennifer.

"I'll be right back," Jennifer said.

Alastair sensed the energy in the room shift. This ability to size up who was nearby and how they were interacting with one another was new, and interesting. As though his failings had rent open an undiscovered part of him. Perhaps it was the sixth sense he'd heard about but assumed was nonsense.

✻ ✻ ✻

Lily spoke to the nurse, "I hope our talking and running about hasn't upset him." She set her tray aside and started to get up.

The nurse waved her back. "It's okay, honestly. Sit and eat. He knows you're here, and I'm keeping an eye on him."

The tightness in Lily's throat eased, and she managed a few bites of food. Then Jennifer returned, phone in hand.

"What are you doing?" Lily asked.

"Just give me a minute." Jennifer thumbed a few keys on her phone. "There we are!" The music started and Jennifer came over to Lily and held out her hand. She was smiling, but there were tears in her eyes. "Let's dance."

"What?" Lily looked past Jennifer to the nurse. "I can't, it doesn't seem right."

Her own meal finished, the nurse was at Alastair's bedside. "Go on, it'll do you and Alastair good."

"I don't know if I remember how." Lily took Jennifer's outstretched hand and stood. "What about my ankle?" She looked down at her foot.

"Just do what you can. I won't go fast." Jennifer pulled her close and led them around the room, just as Lily had done with her years ago.

As the walls, the windows, the furniture glided by, the angry undercurrent she'd sensed from Jennifer was cast off. Feeling loved and safe in her daughter's arms, Lily relaxed and closed her eyes. "Begin the Beguine" played in her mind and heart.

"Do you remember how you used to burl me?" Jennifer broke free from Lily's arms and twirled around. "And how I loved it when my skirt billowed out."

"How could I forget? You always insisted on a crinoline as well. You loved them."

"I remember," Jennifer laughed. "I can't imagine why I was fixated."

"I know why," Lily said. "You saw a dancing gypsy at the circus and fell in love with her crinoline. Don't you remember? I bought you the doll. It's on your dresser."

Jennifer stopped dancing and stared at her.

"What's wrong?" Lily asked.

Jennifer shook her head and pulled her close. Happier than she'd felt in some time, Lily didn't resist. As they continued their dance, she smiled over at the nurse who was taking Alastair's pulse.

The music from the phone continued.

❋ ❋ ❋

Alastair had no memory of falling asleep, yet he woke to music. The tune was an old one, "Begin the Beguine."

There was movement, airy and rhythmical. He sensed that Jennifer and Lily were dancing. This, and the gentle melody, breathed life Into the room, into him. He longed to get up and join them.

All at once he saw Lily embraced in their daughter's arms, he witnessed them circle the room, smiling at one another. He marvelled at his ability, but let it be. No need to question. He wanted to remain grateful, engaged.

He drew a long breath and his lungs filled with sweet air. The old lyrics were tempting and, as Lily and Jennifer spun past, he was on his feet simply because he willed it. He looked back at the bed, expecting to see only the imprint of his body on the sheets. Instead, the nurse was beside him taking his pulse.

Impossible.

Alastair looked down at his hands, wiggled his fingers. He didn't understand, but refused to miss this chance with his wife and daughter. As they floated by, he opened his arms, pulled them to him and took over the lead. He could see the sheen of Nivea cream on Lily's throat; feel the pump of Jennifer's heart beat as they circled the room. Laughing, laughing he was lifted above them, but not away. Their strange, wonderful connection remained. Delighted, he closed his eyes. It was only a moment, a reflex to his intense pleasure, but when he reopened them, his perspective had shifted.

Deborah Serravalle

From the ceiling's height, he looked down at his own, still form on the bed. The illusive Boy who had shadowed him for years was there at his bedside, holding his hand. His wife and daughter were out of reach. Yet, the music played on and they continued their dance. As long as he could hear their song, Alastair knew he was still leading their steps.

He drifted farther and farther from the room. He couldn't stop; didn't want to. He felt so light, so free. The Boy smiled and waved him on. Lily and Jennifer gradually disappeared from sight. Soon the house, his street and the city below receded. Still, he clung to the music, determined to see their dance to completion.

When the music ended, Alastair released them and faced the star-filled sky.

❀ ❀ ❀

"That's enough." Lily pressed a hand to her chest.

Jennifer's arm lingered on Lily's waist. "Are you okay?"

"Yes." Touched by the look of concern on Jennifer's face, Lily reached out and stroked her daughter's cheek. "I'm just winded. And my ankle is starting to speak to me."

Smiling, Lily glanced over at the bed. The nurse's hand covered Alastair's which lay atop the blankets. She motioned for Lily and Jennifer to come closer. "He's gone." Eyes glistening, she smiled. "Drifted off while you were dancing."

CHAPTER 19

Jennifer lifted the suitcase from the floor and set it on the single mattress. The funeral was over, and she'd helped her mother with the initial paperwork that had followed. Still, she had worried about leaving her mother alone. Last night Jennifer had tossed and turned, eventually falling asleep sometime before sunrise. Just before waking, she'd had a fleeting vision of Mammy, the tail-end of a dream, and in it, she appeared resigned; at peace. Jennifer had risen from bed knowing it was time to pack up, to go home to Cam and the girls.

Jennifer looked around the room and then back at the suitcase on the bed. Other than some underwear in the dresser drawer, her clothes had remained in the case. Odd that she'd unpacked her panties and bras, yet left her outerwear in the suitcase. She looked quizzically at her reflection in the dresser's mirror. What did that say about her? The woman looking back offered nothing. Frowning, she lifted a jar of face cream, tightened the lid and set it back. Beside it was her make-up pouch, a brush and a hair clip. That was it. Not much. Everything she'd needed for the past few months had been compressed in one small suitcase.

It wasn't as though she couldn't have gone to her own house for more of her belongings. There, her walk-in closet was lined with row upon row of tops, blouses and sweaters; below them hung umpteen pairs of jeans, slacks, skirts. But the rushed exit to her parents had forced her to pack only the basics. The rest she had left behind. What surprised her was that she'd managed the absence of her "things" with ease. Perhaps her needs had changed. Or was it the other way around?

Either way, what she needed now was her husband and her children. And they, her. In their last conversation, Cam told her Emma had asked him to promise he wouldn't die and leave her. Daddy's passing had affected the girls, too.

Passing. The term applied to ease the harsh reality of death. It even sounded softer. Puffed from the mouth; a breath, an exhalation. Whereas uttering "death" caused the tongue to hit the teeth with firm finality. In her father's case, though, "passed" did seem more appropriate.

Another vision of Mammy appeared. Not a dream.

Mammy's face is registering what the nurse is saying: *He's gone. Drifted off while you were dancing.* Mammy is beside him, smiling, silent tears streaming down her cheeks, telling him it's okay, saying she loves him.

The memory collapses.

Jennifer turned from the mirror and walked to the bed. Unzipping her suitcase, she threw back the lid. As she refolded and organized the contents, she hummed "Begin the Beguine."

Mammy had been surprisingly light on her feet when they'd danced together, following her around the room without stumbling or hesitation. Obviously, Mammy's damaged ankle had healed. So had Jennifer. At some point during that dance she had stopped feeling angry with her mother. With that thought, another shard of the early morning's splintered dream materialized. Jennifer sat on the bed and stared into the middle distance as one piece after another appeared, finally merging to form a picture.

Mammy and Daddy are dancing. Artie Shaw and his band are playing "Begin the Beguine." Jennifer is at a table, full of love, watching them. She turns to look at the band, and marvels at their full sound. When she turns back to the dance floor, she is startled to see her mother has been replaced by a man. He looks at Jennifer and waves. It's David Mallory. For a moment she stares at her father and Mallory, mesmerized by the absurdity of the scene, curious about what they'll do, wondering if it's a joke. When the charade continues, she calls out to them, wants to tell them to stop, that their gag isn't funny. Her mouth opens, but no sound comes. She rushes onto the dance floor, one arm thrust out, palm forward. The closer she gets, the farther they recede. Neither notices her efforts; they're focussed on their dance, and each other.

Frustrated and breathless, she stops and wonders if there's another way to reach them. Someone takes her hand. She turns; it's Mammy. She's returned. Or did she ever leave? Even in this anxious state, Jennifer marvels at Mammy's youthful complexion and dark hair that curls at the nape of her neck. Jennifer notices the frothy pink dress Mammy is wearing, how it stirs as though ruffled by a summer's breeze. Mammy looks at the men, back at Jennifer, and lifts a shoulder. Irritated by her mother's complacence, Jennifer tries to rush at the men. Mammy smiles and comes alongside, rubs a soothing hand on her back.

Surfacing from the dream-memory, Jennifer blinked.

She released her hold on the suitcase beside her and rubbed her palm. She must have gripped the edge tightly during her recollection, hadn't realised she was clinging to it. Just as she hadn't realised the dream had been so detailed and focussed on her parents. Or that Mallory had appeared.

She stood up, ready to finish packing. Remembering the dream had further affirmed her mother would be fine. Opening a dresser drawer, she grabbed her few undergarments and put them in the suitcase.

As she gathered her toiletries and packed them, she thought again of Mammy and their dance together as Daddy was passing. While they held each other and the old familiar music played, something between them had shifted. Unlike the old days, Jennifer had assumed the lead. Mammy had acquiesced with grace.

Jennifer glanced around the room. Confident she hadn't left anything behind, she snapped the suitcase shut. Time to go home.

When Jennifer opened her front door, Cameron stood in the foyer. Isla was there, too, clutching a stack of letters, her long, manicured nails chipped. She smiled; Cameron looked uneasy.

"Cam was just saying you were coming home today. Welcome back," Isla said.

Jennifer set her suitcase off to the side. "Thanks."

Isla held up the letters. "I just got home myself—a short gig in Chicago. Your hubby was kind enough to collect my mail." She started to the door and stopped beside Jennifer. Placing a hand on her arm Isla spoke softly, "I'm sorry about your father. I hope you know I would have gone to the funeral, had I been in town."

Jennifer saw the sensitivity in Isla's eyes. "Not to worry. Cam gave me your card." She patted the delicate, flawed hand perched on her arm. It was like stroking a sparrow. She looked at Isla. She seemed less sophisticated than she remembered. This close, the fine lines around Isla's mouth and eyes were more deeply etched than Jennifer recalled. The porcelain skin, too pale; the blue eyes, dull.

Isla dropped her hand as she turned back to Cam. "Thanks again," she said and flew out the door.

Jennifer frowned at Cam. "Is she okay? She seemed stressed."

"Maybe. I'm sure she'll bring you up to date." Cameron stepped forward. "Come here, you."

She met him halfway and was in his arms. Eyes closed, she relaxed in his firm embrace. Right Guard deodorant mingled with his cologne. When he lifted her chin and tentatively kissed her, she parted her lips.

She broke free. "Where are the girls?"

"At the Bennett's pool." His voice was husky, his need obvious. "We have a little time to ourselves. Walt said he'd drop them off later."

She took his hand and without a word, led him upstairs to their room. Still silent, she removed his shirt, unbuckled his belt and pants. "I've missed you," she said, her voice thick with emotion. He gathered her in his arms and took her to bed.

Cam was asleep on his stomach, bare shoulders above the comforter, gently snoring. Jennifer pulled herself up against the headboard and looked about the bedroom they shared. Until this moment, she hadn't realised how much she'd missed being here. Most of all she'd missed her husband and their girls. She stroked Cameron's hair; the corners of his mouth lifted, but he slept on. Their marriage wasn't perfect, but it was far from broken. She thought of her parents, David Mallory and his wife, solitary Isla. By comparison, any problems she and Cameron shared seemed trivial. But still ...

The front door opened and closed. Seconds later, she heard the girls bounding up the stairs. "Mom?" Lindsay called out.

Cam groaned and rolled onto his back. "The party's over."

Laughing, Jennifer gave him a shove. "Up here, girls." Jennifer secured the covers under her arms. Lindsay appeared first. She hovered at the entrance. Emma tried to barge through; Lindsay grabbed her by the arm. Emma wrenched herself free. "I want to see Mommy."

"Come on, squirt." Lindsay took Emma's hand. "Mom will meet us downstairs. Let's get you a freezie."

"We'll be right there, Lindz," Cam said.

"I want a blue one," Emma demanded.

"Whatever." Lindsay grinned at her and Cam over her sister's head.

Jennifer felt her face redden. Through the closed door Jennifer heard Emma ask Lindsay why Mommy and Daddy were sleeping in the afternoon. "Because parents do that," was Lindsay's response.

And there it was. Jennifer realised with sudden, sad clarity that her own parents hadn't belonged together. At least not like she and Cam did. They had made the best of their situation, there had been love, but they lived parallel lives, all of them.

"You okay?" Cameron asked.

As Jennifer watched him pull on his shorts, his brow wrinkled with concern, she knew with certainty that their marriage was nothing like her parents', that her fears had nothing to do with him, or their relationship.

"Fine." She stood up, scooped her clothes off the floor and went over and kissed him. "I'm going to grab a quick shower. I'll meet you downstairs."

Later that evening, after the girls had gone to bed, Jennifer opened a bottle of wine and asked Cam to sit on the patio with her. Between sips, she explained how she'd always felt there was something amiss with her parents, how she'd witnessed her mother hiding things in the clock and what she'd learned. She brought out the letter David had written and handed it to Cam.

She watched as his eyes widened and mouth fell open. He folded the letter. "Does your mother know?"

"She will."

He pulled his chair closer to hers, took her hand. "I can't believe you've been dealing with all of this *and* Alastair's death. Why didn't you come to me?"

"I suppose I needed to work it out on my own."

"This is a lot to take in. Are you okay?"

"I wasn't at first. But I am now. It explains a great deal about my parents. And, as strange as it may sound, the understanding of it has given me some peace." She turned her body to face Cameron. When she spoke, her voice cracked with emotion. "It also makes me appreciate us, how much we have together."

Cameron lifted her hand, pressed his lips against it.

Jennifer nodded to the letter still lying in Cam's lap. "You haven't asked how much David left me."

Cameron shook his head. "No. I'm trying to take all of this in. I assume he had a home, maybe some modest investments?"

Jennifer leaned over and pulled out the file from under her chair. She removed the financial statement Harry had sent her and handed it to Cameron.

He scanned the pages and then looked at her in disbelief. "This is a life-changer; you realise that, don't you?"

Jennifer nodded. "If you want, you could leave the company. I know you've been worried that a buy-out would leave you without a job. I will certainly quit the board and focus on the girls more. Maybe we could invest in our own business, like we've always dreamed of. What do you think?"

He didn't answer. Instead, he set the file on his lap. The muscles of his jaw were tensed.

"Cam? We don't have to do any of that. It was only a suggestion."

"No, it's all good. I guess I'm just stunned, and I feel a little weird."

"Because of the money?"

"Yeah. On one hand it's like winning the lottery, on the other ..."

"I know."

"What will we tell the girls?" Cam asked.

"The truth," she said. "I received an inheritance. In time, we'll tell them the whole story. Everything with my parents was hidden. It left me always wondering and wary. I realise that now. I don't want that for our girls. It's their story as much as mine."

CHAPTER 20

Lily walked out to the garden with her morning tea. Rather than sit in her chair, she remained standing and took a sip. It soured at the back of her tongue. Making a face, she set it down. A waste. She shouldn't have bothered to make it, hadn't really felt like it, but gave in out of habit. Perhaps she'd go for a walk later, stop by a coffee shop and try one of those lattes Jennifer raved about. She smiled at the thought of telling Jennifer, who'd no doubt think she'd taken leave of her senses.

Wandering into the middle of the flower beds, she looked around. Summer waned, but her planning had paid off and plenty of plants still bloomed. A butterfly lighted upon her favourite English tea rose, its golden wings almost indiscernible from the blossom. A sanctuary to countless creatures, her handiwork was something to be proud of. But most of the effort now involved maintenance. That had been her goal, but now done, she felt hollow. She'd wanted to make changes, uproot and start again. She had allowed Alastair to talk her out of it. "A waste," he'd said, "it's fine as it is." She glanced back at the tea.

It was still difficult to believe Alastair was gone. She half-expected him to call out through the kitchen screen and ask where something was in the fridge, even though it was right before his eyes. *That was something she wouldn't miss.* The angry thought had formed before she'd had time to censor it.

How We Danced

Startled, she surveyed the garden again, focussed on a spray of ornamental grass, the long, slender variegated blade. The butterfly whiffled past, so close she felt the air stir near her cheek. Then the wings lifted, and it flew over the fence and out of sight.

Perhaps she also needed a change of scenery. Rather than fly off, she'd dig in. Why not? There was no one to stop her from redesigning the entire yard. She tried to picture it as a blank canvas. Her heart fluttered at the thought. What would she paint? Images, combinations and configurations of lilies, grasses and a host of new flowering perennials rushed at her. Inspired, she wanted to tear over to her workbench, grab her garden gloves and a shovel and get to work. Could she manage it alone? Alastair used to help with the more strenuous tasks.

Alastair, shirtless and sweating, is turning over the soon-to-be-planted flower bed in the back corner. Young Jennifer stands beside him. He calls out smiling, "You're working me to death!"

A fierce wave of grief threatened to bowl her over. The pain often came like that, sudden and savage, but no longer unexpected. She drew a deep breath and moved through it. Alastair's shirtless image receded, along with little Jennifer; the blooming, mature back corner garden returned. Taking a deep breath and then releasing it, Lily resumed her train of thought and decided that, yes, if she was careful not to put too much stress on her healed ankle, she could do this by herself. Jennie was coming for a visit, something about legal paperwork; likely final things that needed addressing. She glanced at her wristwatch. If she began now she could at least make a start.

After retrieving her gloves, garden shears, a pointed spade and several large waste bags, she considered where to begin. At the back, the smallest bed, off to the right. Marching through the garden, dragging her tools, she dug into a patch of forget-me-nots that filled the corner. Some time ago, Alastair had brought a single plant home as a gift. She'd hesitated about planting it. She knew it spread like a weed and had strategically placed it in the back corner where she'd still had a devil of a time containing it. Now it was time to yank it all out.

Deborah Serravalle

Soon she was bathed in sweat. Two tall yard waste bags were filled with discarded flora, a sizeable portion of topsoil cleared and turned. Still gripping the shovel, she stopped to wipe her brow and looked back at the house. The grass pathway leading to the deck needed to be cut and trimmed. She'd get to that tomorrow. Maybe in the fall, she'd replace it with a cobblestone walk, veined with moss, like she'd always dreamed of. She returned to her chore and pushed the shovel into the soft soil with renewed vigour.

"Mammy?"

Lily spun around and almost bumped into Jennifer who steadied her with a firm hand to the shoulder.

"I didn't mean to startle you," Jennifer said. "I did call out several times."

"My fault. I was too caught up to hear anything." Lily fanned her face. "Goodness gracious," she said. "I had no idea it was so late."

Jennifer surveyed the garden. "What are you doing?"

"Just making a few changes."

Jennifer nodded in approval. "Nice work, Mammy."

Her daughter's immediate enthusiasm pleased her. She cleared her throat. "Come inside. I'll get us a cold drink."

She poured them both a glass of minted lemonade as Jennifer prattled on about Cam, the girls and a recent trip they had all taken to a friend's cottage for some much-needed family time. When Lily joined Jennifer at the table, she grew silent. Lily took a sip and waited. She saw Jennifer was struggling; she'd taken Alastair's death hard, and dealing with lawyers was never easy. Lily glanced at the big handbag Jennifer had set on the table. Doubtless, she was worried about upsetting her with whatever paperwork she'd brought.

After a moment, Lily stretched out a hand, "It's okay, sweetheart."

Jennifer looked confused. "What do you mean?"

Lily drew her hand back.

"I don't want you worrying I'll fall apart because you've brought some papers that need tending. These things have to be done."

"I haven't come about Daddy's estate," she said.

The pleading look in Jennifer's eyes made Lily sit up straighter. "All right, what then?"

Jennifer reached into her handbag and removed a thick file. She slipped out a letter which she opened and set in front of Lily.

Lily's eyes swept the page, registering the key points.

... fell in love ... married, could not claim her – or you ... Alastair's daughter ... my son, my wife passed away ... estate goes to you ... money cannot make up for what I was unable to offer you or your mother ... I did love her, never stopped.

Lily shut her eyes.

Once again they are toe to toe and face to face. David supports his weight on elbows as he smoothes hair from her damp brow. "I love you," he whispers, "I'll never stop."

Lily opened her eyes and, with a finger, traced the echo of that oath in the final sentence. She recalled the day Jennifer had received the envelope from Ross & Rose, and how she'd dismissed it.

Lily looked at Jennifer. "This is what the lawyer's letter was about," she said, voice calm and even.

"Yes—"

"And this," Lily held up David's letter. "Harry Ross passed on this note from David."

"That's right," Jennifer said. "But there's more."

Lily listened as her daughter recounted how she had uncovered the hidden box in the clock, the way her sleuthing had led her to David Mallory and how she'd gone to his home and met him.

The idea thrilled Lily, but she said nothing.

Jennifer went on to describe her visit to David's street, their strange encounter and conversation. She reached across the table and took Lily's hand. "I know this is a shock."

Lily shrugged, patted Jennifer's hand, then released it. "And a relief."

Jennifer's lips parted, but she said nothing.

"You're surprised?" Lily asked.

"Well, yes. But then, no. A secret like this ..." Jennifer's words trailed off.

Deborah Serravalle

Lily finished the sentence, "Festers."

"It hasn't been easy for you," Jennifer said.

Lily shook her head. There was no point trying to explain how difficult her life had been, how sad, and how she wouldn't change a thing because it had meant having a child, her.

"I always knew something wasn't right between you and Daddy."

Lily raked a hand through her hair. That much she'd figured. Jennifer was intelligent and watchful, even if she didn't always say what was on her mind.

Jennifer continued, "What was wrong? Help me understand."

Lily sighed as she drew a finger down the lemonade glass, leaving a clear streak through the beads of condensation. "I had such high hopes when I married your father. I loved him. And he loved me." She faced Jennifer. "He adored you."

Jennifer released Lily's hand and sat back. "Yet something led you to take up with David Mallory."

Lily looked away. "Your father was never interested in me."

"You mean sexually," Jennifer offered.

Lily nodded. "We tried, but it didn't go well. Times were different then, people didn't talk the way they do now. I was young, naive. I thought that something was wrong with me."

"How awful," Jennifer said. "Did you talk to Daddy?"

"Many times," Lily met Jennifer's concerned gaze. "But it always ended badly. He drank too much. It never did any good. Eventually I stopped asking."

"I'm so sorry," Jennifer said.

"Then I met David. It wasn't something I planned." Lily hesitated. "He and his wife went to the same dances as your father and me," she said, her tone serious. "He approached me."

"What I don't understand is why you didn't leave?"

Lily explained how David had let her down when she'd telephoned to tell him she was pregnant.

"Oh." Jennifer put a hand to her mouth.

"It was difficult." Lily heard the words as though they were coming from someone else. Three words to summarize the most heart-wrenching thing that had happened to her seemed almost laughable. Yet it was far from funny. She could fill a book with the pain she'd felt, the sense of loss for her, for Jennifer.

"Wait a moment. What about Daddy? Did he never suspect?" Jennifer's eyes widened. "Or did you both keep this secret?"

"No, it wasn't like that," Lily trailed off. Through the years she'd often questioned if Alastair knew, but she'd pushed the concern down and away. It was too painful, too scary.

"He never said anything at all?"

Lily nodded. "He was a good man, your father."

This was true. But since he and David had died, Lily's mind had started to wander and wonder. What she had accepted, when her need for herself, for Jennifer had been so great, now seemed questionable.

"Maybe Daddy liked having a family." Jennifer stretched out a hand towards Lily.

Lily blinked but otherwise gave no indication of how startled she was by Jennifer's intuition. "I hope so," she said and took hold of Jennifer's hand.

Lily closed her eyes. As she did, memories of a youthful Alastair appeared, just out of reach, his back to her, shoulders curled inward, walking out the door to work or down to his basement workshop. Near the end, his skeletal backbone shrouded by light cotton pyjamas, calling out for Erin.

❋ ❋ ❋

Lily stared into the open drawer of Alastair's bureau. She had known a time would come when she'd have to go through his belongings, but the idea was still painful, even though more than half a year had come and gone. She lifted up a pair of his balled work socks, unwound them. They hung lifeless in her hand.

It was their family's tradition to use socks just like these at Christmas, rather than the pre-fab, embossed and sequined variety now popular. It had been Alastair's socks they'd used when Jennifer was young, and now the roomiest socks Cameron owned hung over the hearth. Lily smiled, picturing the ragtag assortment of men's hosiery that always drooped beneath the garland of Jennifer's pristine mantel. That was something Lily loved about her daughter: she put family first.

Since the girls were born, they'd celebrated Christmas at Jennifer's home, she and Alastair staying overnight in the guest room. On Christmas Eve they'd have dinner, go to church and then, afterwards, open their stockings. Santa brought the other gifts that would be unwrapped come morning. This year, their first Christmas without Alastair, they had followed tradition.

Upon returning from church they'd headed into the family room. As usual, Jennifer had set out hot chocolate and shortbread. For Lily, the attempt at normalcy had accentuated Alastair's absence and her sense of loss. Feeling melancholy, she looked at the fireplace, expecting to see one less stocking, but when she counted, there were six. Thinking she'd made a mistake, she counted again. With a question in her eyes, she looked at Jennifer who, judging by her impish expression was waiting for Lily to come to this realization.

"I'm confused," Lily said, "the stockings ..."

"When I filled them, I felt so sad leaving Daddy out, that I thought, why not?" Jennifer went to the mantel and took down Alastair's stocking. From it, she removed five slips of paper, five pencils. "Each of us," she said handing them round, "is going to write down a special Christmas memory of Granddad. Just a few key words. Then we're going to share our memory with one another."

Lily looked down at the scrap of paper in her hand. Grateful tears filled her eyes, she sniffed them back, and took her pencil. Years of wonderful Christmases flashed through her mind. Which one would she choose?

Hand raised, Emma bounced in place. "Mommy, can I go first?"

"Yes, we'll go youngest to oldest, the way we've always opened our stockings," Jennifer said. "Okay, let's take five minutes." She looked at her watch, "Go!"

Lily wrote three words and looked at her family, all thinking or scribbling. This Christmas, this moment, pivotal, despite Alastair's absence or perhaps because of it, would also long be remembered.

In due course, Jennifer said, "Time's up! You ready, Emma?"

Emma shared about a Christmas when Alastair had put the head back on her doll. Lindsay remembered Granddad taking her hand in church one Christmas Eve while they sang "O Holy

Night." Jennifer shared a special walk home in the snow from a church Christmas party when she was about Emma's age. Cameron recalled the Christmas Eve he had asked Alastair for his permission to marry Jennifer and the words Alastair had said. Then they all turned to Lily.

"Our first Christmas with you, Jennifer." Lily faced her daughter. "You were about ten months, just old enough to enjoy the excitement, but young enough that you went to bed early without bother. Daddy lit a fire, poured us a wee dram," she smiled, recalling the sweet scent of Drambuie. "We sat there with the fire's glow and the tree lights shining, not saying much." She swallowed the lump in her throat. "Nothing special. But we were happy. That I know."

Jennifer reached out for her hand. "That's lovely, Mammy."

Emma broke the silence. "What now?"

Jennifer laughed, "Now we're each going to put our paper into the fire and send it out to Granddad with a prayer. "Here, Emma, I'll help you."

After they had all sent their Christmas memories and prayers to Alastair, Jennifer announced they'd open their own stockings. "But this time," she said, "we're going to do it oldest to youngest."

Lily braced, thinking there would be a protest from Emma, but instead she giggled and squirmed closer to her sister.

"What's going on?" Lily asked. Even Lindsay looked jittery.

"Nothing," Jennifer said as she handed Lily her stocking.

Lily accepted the stocking along with Jennifer's explanation about the girls. Maybe they'd drunk too much hot chocolate, eaten too many biscuits.

"So, what do we have here?" she peered into the sock. It weighed next to nothing, and for a moment she wondered if they'd forgotten to fill it. But no, something was lodged in the toe. Lily pulled out a small paper-wrapped box.

Emma started to bounce and clap her hands in glee. Lindsay was sitting forward.

Lily put the tiny box on the table. Earrings or a necklace, she wondered? "Maybe I'll wait to open it," she teased.

"No, Gran, that's not fair!" Emma said.

Lily laughed, "All right." In truth, she was curious.

The paper peeled away to reveal a small jeweller's box, longer than it was wide. Figuring she guessed well, Lily lifted the lid. Pressed into a wad of batting lay a key. She took it out, held it up. "A key? To what?" she asked.

The girls scurried to one side of her, Jennifer the other. Cameron pulled his chair in.

"It's the key, not the real one of course, to the home we're having built." Jennifer smiled at Cameron, who nodded. "We've included a Granny Suite in the design. We want you to come with us. And the property, Mammy, wait until you see how beautiful it is. You can have full reign over the garden, design it any way you please, hire as much help as you think you'll need." She took out an envelope from the drawer of the coffee table, pulled out a photo, design plans. "Here, have a look."

Too stunned to speak, Lily accepted the pages, glanced at them with one hand, still holding the empty sock in the other. Grateful but confused, she had agreed to think about it and give them her decision at New Year's, which meant she had only this week to make up her mind.

Lily rolled Alastair's socks back into a ball and returned them to his bureau. She still couldn't sort through his belongings, wasn't ready yet. Perhaps she'd ease into the task in less personal territory. With that, she headed to the basement, just for a look.

In her gut, she knew she'd agree to the move, yet something had prevented her from saying so at the time. Even now she didn't feel peaceful about the decision, yet she couldn't say why. Her relationship with her daughter wasn't the issue. Jennifer now called or stopped by every day. Lily thought back to their phone call this evening. Jennifer had asked for her Scotch Eggs recipe which she planned to serve New Year's Eve. It was a simple thing. But Lily knew Jennifer could have just searched a recipe online. Instead, she had turned to her, something she was doing more and more since Alastair's death, and David's. It was an outcome Lily had never anticipated and was grateful for. So why couldn't she just say yes, sell the house and be done with it?

How We Danced

Having reached the basement, Lily now stood facing Alastair's workbench. This small room had been Alastair's workshop for as long as they'd lived here. A radio sat on the bench top, a tiny TV was perched on a raised shelf to the right. Through the years he'd spent many an hour down here. Lily smiled, remembering that Lindsay had referred to it as Granddad's "Man Cave." Like Jennifer, Lindsay had often followed Alastair downstairs. How they spent their time was a mystery; saws and such were of no interest to Lily.

Wondering where to start, she glanced at the photos and prints of all the old sailing ships scattered on the walls. They brought to mind a time, not that long ago, when a fleet of tall ships had sailed into the bay. Alastair had gone down to see them and raved for weeks. Lily ran her finger around one of the framed prints. Lindsay was right, there was more to this space than screwdrivers and drills. Why hadn't she noticed before? What else did this room say about Alastair? There was only one way to find out. Lily went out to the storage room to get the unopened packing boxes she'd purchased for the job.

Alastair had been more organized than she realised. Everything had a home. There were no stray tools or bits lying about. The majority of items hung on the peg boards that lined the room; others were placed in one of the many labelled drawers. Nails and screws lay in sealed containers; all she had to do was stack them in a box. The packing went quickly and wasn't as difficult as she'd first imagined it might be.

Taking a breather, she stretched her back and looked at the shelving unit. On the top shelf was a black typewriter case. Lily found the step stool, pulled the typewriter down and put it on the workbench. She recognized the casing, an old Underwood, Alastair's favourite. This she'd keep. Pressing the nibs of the clasps, she lifted off the lid and set it aside. A faint whiff of ink and ammonia tickled her nose, and her memory.

She walks into Alastair's shop with Jennifer swaddled in her arms. She is accosted by the tang of chemicals, as powerful as Alastair's pride as he whisks the child from her, stalks across the room and introduces his newborn to the boss. "She's perfect," says Alastair.

Lily winces, knowing the man has a brain-damaged son who ingested house paint as a toddler.

Lily laid her fingers atop the keys of the Underwood before her and stilled the sounds of the past, careful not to press too hard, in case they jammed. No one to repair it now, with both the trade and Alastair gone. Lily replaced the lid on the typewriter, set it aside. She'd deal with it later.

What's this? On the same high shelf stood a cardboard box. Again Lily climbed the step stool. She pulled the box into her arms, surprised at its heavy weight and made her way to the bench. With an old towel she wiped away the grimy past. Then she lifted the lid.

Under layers of crumpled, yellowed newspaper, there was another typewriter. A Smith Corona, often found in offices. Nothing special. She wondered why he had stored it away with such care. Holding onto the machine, she pulled the box it was in forward and let it fall to the floor. Pushing the typewriter farther back onto the workbench, she examined the keyboard, estimated it was from the fifties, or sixties at best. It must have meant something to him, but what? She reached down into the box on the floor and pulled out some of the dry, crinkled newsprint to check the date. It was a long time ago, the year Jennifer was born. Maybe that was the significance? When she pulled out more of the paper, two cards tumbled onto the floor. One was the business variety, *Designs by Aaron*; name, address and phone number printed in cursive, black script. Lily froze. She knew the shop; it used to be on Main Street, at the bus stop near Dr. Henry's. She'd been there, once.

The jangle of the bell, a rain-soaked umbrella and high spirits, the back room phone call, David's crushing news.

Her chest tightened. Even after all these years, the memory of David's betrayal was breathtaking. Forcing herself to calmly inhale, exhale, she examined the card.

Why would Alastair have it, kept it? She put it down and picked up the next one, a gift card. On it, a handwritten message in tight scrawl, *Congratulations. Enjoy the Macallan. Have a drink for me.* It was signed *Aaron*, but wasn't addressed to anyone. Perhaps it, and the business card, belonged to someone else and were left in the box by mistake. Lily glanced down at the handwriting and recalled the big, friendly fellow who'd shown her the office that day. There had been a *Hamilton Spectator* article, a few years ago, a feature on how Aaron had sold his well-known shop and retired. There was a photo spread of his home, a beautiful Victorian mansion with an extensive, flowering garden, which was part of the reason she recalled the article so well. Most photos were of the house and the property, but there was one of Aaron and his male partner. Having met Aaron, however briefly, she wasn't surprised.

Lily put the box on the bench beside the machine. Why would Alastair keep this typewriter? Frustrated, she read the few words on the gift card again, searching for clues. When she got to Aaron's signature she whispered it aloud, an invocation. Her accent softened the "a" to "e." Startled, she let the card slip from her fingers onto the scarred surface of the workbench. Not Erin, a woman, as she'd thought. Alastair had cried out for Aaron.

The wedge of denial that both she and Alastair had supported, slipped into place. Alastair preferred men. Was it that simple, yet that complicated? Lily grabbed a nearby stool and sat down. She scanned the partially dismantled workshop. Poor Alastair. His burden had been tremendous. His sacrifice as big as hers.

A comment Jennifer had made about him, the day she shared her knowledge of David, came to mind, maybe Daddy liked having a family. Something tightly wound within Lily for many years uncoiled. Relief. It wasn't her fault. She had provided Alastair with a family; he had given her the same.

❀ ❀ ❀

After lighting a log in the fireplace of the darkened living room, Lily went in search of some sherry and found, tucked at the back, a bottle of the Macallan Scotch, and with it, a cigarette and matches. She smiled, shrugged, put them in her pocket. That rascal. She took out the Scotch bottle, ran her fingertips around the label. The eighteen-year-old version, pricey for Alastair, not like him. There was only a small amount gone. Surely it couldn't be the same bottle mentioned in the note? Outside, the wind rattled the windows. She shivered and, bottle in hand, took a few steps forward, looked outside. It was a clear night; through the naked boughs of the maple tree, a rash of stars covered the sky. Again the wind cried, the boughs bent and the glass windows rattled. Turning her back on the cold, she returned to the liquor cabinet, poured a finger of Scotch and sat down.

On the floor, beside the chair pulled close to the hearth, was the dismantled box in which she'd found the typewriter, the gift card and note. On her opposite side, on a small wine table, lay the items associated with David she'd saved and cherished: the blue Birks' jewellery box, the pearl earrings he'd given her, a note, a matchbook.

She reached for the poker and adjusted the log, now burning brightly. Satisfied, she picked up a piece of cardboard and hurled it onto the raging log. Remembering the cigarette and matches in her pocket, she cast them in, watched as the matchbook flared then shrivelled. Next she tossed in the jewellery box ... *on the Wondergrove's dance floor, earring in hand, she hops around, stumbles into David's arms, Catherine's wrath* ... another bit of cardboard flies in, the edges blacken and smoke ... the earrings are swallowed by a burst of orange flame ... *tiny Jennifer, safe, asleep; Alastair absent* ... more cardboard ... *Alastair, giving little Lindsay and tiny Emma horsy-rides* ... the gift and business cards are thrown into the flames together ... *Games night with Jennifer, Cameron, the girls, their family, arguing, laughing, together, always.*

The table was empty, the dismantled box and cards, gone. The wind gave a final howl and then was still. The reliable Westminster chimes filled the silence and marked the hour, midnight. Lily sat back, closed her eyes. When the chimes finished, she sniffed the Scotch, a hint of wood and sherry, took a sip, then another. It trickled down her throat, liquid heat. She'd take the bottle with her New Year's Eve, and come midnight, she'd share it with Jennifer and Cameron, honour Alastair's memory with them. Lily cleared her throat and softly sang,

> "For auld lang syne, my dear,
> For auld lang syne ..."

How We Danced

The fire blazed, filling the room with an ethereal, golden light. Its warmth ran up her shins, onto her lap. She held the tumbler up to the fire's glow, watched as the final remnants of their bound secrets, now beautifully distorted by crystal and whisky, burned to ashes.

❀ ❀ ❀

www.ingramcontent.com/pod-product-compliance
Lightning Source LLC
Chambersburg PA
CBHW070449260626
47161CB00004B/1250